THE THINGS WE CARRY

The Town Series

Book 1

KATE ANSLINGER

Lighthouse Pen, LLC

After

APRIL 2021

Lauren

My eyes tear open with a start. *Buzz, buzz, buzz.*

I slap a hand on the nightstand, my palm landing on the dancing phone with impressive aim. *Twelve-thirty a.m.* The time glows on the screen, teasing my thoughts.

Like any mother of two teenage daughters, I'm thrown into the worst-case scenarios and a parade of tragic moments march through my head like soldiers in formation. *Rape, drugs, alcohol, accident.*

Thirty minutes past Lily's curfew. Maybe she's stranded somewhere and needs a ride? She is the only one of her friends who doesn't sample sips of alcohol at the high school parties, or so she says. The truth is, I believe her. She's always been so disciplined, so self-aware and organized. The strait-laced kid who sifts through the popular circles, thanks to her good looks and outgoing personality.

With one press of the green circle, a crackle comes through the receiver, followed by the stern vocal cords of a man. The voice of an authority. "Mrs. Rivers?"

The title before my name catapults me upright, the quick movement sending a thousand bubbles to my brain, followed by a wave of nausea.

"Yes, that's me." I push the words into the phone. Ryan, with lips parted, snores peacefully beside me, a sleeping trait that I'd grown used to in nearly twenty years of marriage.

Tap tap tap. The wind outside pushes the branches against the glass in rapid succession. I focus on the sound; its soothing repetition easing the fear that's swelling inside me, as the next words hit my ear with blunt force. "This is Officer Wright from the Flagport Police Department. There's been an accident."

2

Before
APRIL 2009

Evie

"We're here boys." I turn around toward the back seat, resting a hand on a sleeping Liam's sneakered foot, sealing the Velcro with my palm. He reaches for one eye, while opening the other, and I watch as his memory falls back into place and a crooked smile spreads across his spaced-out teeth. He remembers where we are.

"I gotta pee." The voice of Jack rises on the other side of the back seat. Never one to cookie-coat his words, the six-year-old has said what he means since the day he latched onto my nipple. He wants what he wants, and his dictionary only extends so far. Both hands rush toward his penis, one on top of the other in a cupping motion. "I get the bathroom first!" He sends a competitive look in Liam's direction.

"There are three of them dude, so you're good," Matt says, gliding one hand over the other across the steering wheel in an effortless turn onto our new street. Eight-eight Sutton Lane. He navigates his way down the freshly paved road slowly, as if we are approaching a castle. Which, for us it is. It only took one medium-sized moving truck to carry our furniture, clothes and supplies from our Ohio apartment to Flagport, the quaint seaside town we are uprooting to. The rest of the stuff is jammed into our old Jeep Cherokee and the eight-by-four-foot U-Haul cargo trailer that we're pulling. The trailer lets out a creaky squeal as it settles into position alongside the house, the combination of vehicles too lengthy to fit in the singular driveway that greets the dead-end street. Henry, our aging golden retriever, pulls himself to a sitting position, ears erect, head tilted to the side and two curious gems for eyes.

"It's better than I remember," I say, taking in the lilac trees that frame the front staircase of the house, the white mailbox that matches the white window boxes and shutters. Even though the beach is a half a mile down the road, the weathered gray shingles make me feel as if the house is perched on a cliff overlooking the ocean. While this is probably the smallest, most modest-looking home in Flagport, it is a mansion compared to where we were before.

Matt rests a palm on my thigh, agreeing to my statement. As soon as the SUV stops, the four of us, along with random belongings and our golden retriever, fall out as if we are clowns emerging from a tiny car. It takes less than thirty seconds for a parade of trucks and Teenage Mutant Ninja Turtles to line the walkway that greets the side door that we've already decided will be our main entrance. The front door, in my opinion, isn't an option, as it faces Sutton Lane, and the side entrance is technically on the private way that is home to only a handful of houses. *Who uses front doors anyway?* Jack races to the entryway, as Liam toddles behind. They stop at a pile of rocks and go to work lifting the rocks and moving them into a separate pile like two mini construction workers managing a project. Jack, having forgotten that he had to pee just seconds ago, leads the excavation and Liam follows only half-listening to his brother's directions. I never imagined myself as a boy mom. As an only child, I was raised alongside the girlfriends I collected at every military base my father's career moved us to, as if we had to stick together amid the overly male populated military culture. Our entertainment was reliant on Barbie dolls, Cabbage Patch Kids and the color pink. I don't think I had ever touched a truck until Jack was two, when he pulled a bright yellow toy excavator off a shelf at Target. Now at six, he's accumulated dozens of these plastic vehicles, and at three, Liam is just starting to feel the satisfaction of pushing the trucks along every surface, connecting the dots that wheels make things move.

"Looks like you have your work cut out for you." Matt stands beside me, pulling me into his side.

"Darn straight I do." I look around the yard. The first signs of spring have brought with them the reality that the landscaping needs a lot of work. The uneven yard is made up of sections, some that contain clusters of brown and yellowed grass clinging to life, others that are layered with dirt and seeds, and a few random chunks of plush green that sprout from the dirt haphazardly. "I'll have a lot of time to tend to our lawn now that I'm jobless." I hear the pity seep from my lips. I feel sorry for myself that I had to forego the regular landscaping clients I had in Ohio.

"You will fill up with clients in no time, honey. Stop doubting yourself." Matt pivots his foot on the muddied earth and looks around at the neighboring houses. He's trying to make me feel better but I'm well aware that the residents in this neighborhood have thick ties with the landscapers they've been using for generations. Flagport, Massachusetts is the type of town that is built on connections. The townies are diehard about committing to *their own*, staying true to the past generations that paved the way before them. I know this because I immersed myself in the town Facebook pages. I researched landscapers and gardeners in the area, and they've all been established for decades. Several of these residences are mansions lined up in a section of town that reaches outward like a stem, spilling out into the Atlantic Ocean. With ocean views and posh lawns, my guess is that landscapers are a dime a dozen, all fighting for the chance to work on the high-paying properties. Nobody is going to want to hire an out-of-towner with "mom hours."

Just as I'm about to respond to Matt, I race to Liam and clutch his arm, stopping him as he winds up to hurl a rock at his older brother. "Liam! No throwing!" I take the rock and toss it across the lawn.

"But, Mommy, you just threw it!"

I look at Matt, exasperated, and my laughter gets the best of me. He raises his eyebrows, waiting for my next steps. And then he jumps in to save me. "Mommy meant no throwing at *people*."

"Or things," I retort, finishing up the life lesson. At the age of three, Liam needs very specific directions, otherwise he will test the waters until told otherwise.

"Yes, or *things*," Matt says, as he rumples Jack's hair and dangles the keys in his hand. "Now, who is ready to see our new home?" His face lights up the same way it does when he's just made a big sale. A wide grin spreads out reaching his almond-shaped green eyes. It was the same smile he made when he approached me six years ago at Boxby's, a dive bar I went to regularly. At the time I was only twenty-two and attending horticulture classes at the community college. I had gone for a drink with my friend Sam, who had on more than one occasion tried to move the needle on our friendship and get in my pants. Matt walked in the bar looking as foreign as he possibly could, with a button-down shirt and loosened tie, mussed hair and a briefcase, of all things. Even back then, briefcases were outdated. His physical appearance opposed mine completely, and his image was a one-eighty from any other guy I had dated. Back then I had a firm rule about men with muscles. Maybe it was something I'd grown accustomed to from all those years of hopping bases and being surrounded by muscly men in fatigues.

Matt was not that, and I could tell it when he offered me an ear-to-ear smile from across the bar. His cartoonish grin was and still is Cheshire-Cat-like, greeting his almond-shaped eyes that peel downward when that smile hits his lips. A friendly grin but one that says, *I'm trouble* at the same time. As they say, he had me at hello. He wasn't anyone I expected myself to date, but change was good. I'd grown out of the meat heads and was ready for something new, so when he had the bartender slide me an apple martini to replace the can of Coors Light I was drinking, alongside a note that said, "you're too good for him," I naturally accepted. Sam got the hint and left, opening up the seat beside me, allowing Matt to slide into my space effortlessly.

Matt was on business in the Midwest, scoping out new potential branches for a company he was helping expand through his sales prowess. At the start of his career at the time, but already making his name stand out. I still think his selling success is all in his smile, but his bosses over the years have assured me that it's in his incredible people skills, and his strong work ethic. That work ethic was instilled in him by the two parents that he rarely saw when he was growing up in California, because they too, were working nonstop, leaving him home with a new nanny every month. That's what we had in common when we first met. Our ability to adapt when we met new people, changing our colors like chameleons. Since then, he's been telling me I'm better than I tell myself I am, boosting up my confidence on a regular basis as if he is my human daily affirmation. His trusting smile gained him the approval of my father, and we were married two years later, a young marriage, but that was the norm in small towns and on military bases. His trip to Ohio to scout locations for the company he was working for turned into a permanent move when he convinced his boss to let him take the lead in opening the offices, a strategy he used to be closer to me. I had been dead set on not moving again, having made a promise to myself. I was now an adult and no longer had to follow my father's career around, I would stay in one state for at least five years. I wasn't budging, but Matt did and much to his chagrin, Ohio became his next residence.

He looks down at me, waiting for my approval. "You ready to do this?"

"Yep." I slap my hands on my thighs, emitting a smacking sound. "All right, who wants to do the official unlocking, boys?"

"Me, I'm the oldest," Jack says, reaching for the keys that Matt is dangling in front of him. Liam doesn't pushback with any competition. He knows his role of younger brother well. And he's still consumed by the newness of everything. He holds himself in a squat the way only three-year-old's can. With bent knees that keep him effortlessly tethered to the ground, his hands clutch the patch of dirt at the base of the staircase. He scratches at the earth with chubby fingers, pulling it up in clumps.

"All right, Jack, it's all yours."

Jack wiggles the key into the cylinder on the knob, the sleek red metal circle with Matt's company logo, the O hugging the H, for Onyx Health, clinks against the door. When Jack finally manages to get the right blend of wiggling and twisting of the key, the knob gives way and the white door opens up wide, hitting the wall with one loud whack.

Liam toddles into the house, his dirty palms gliding along the wall as he makes his way into the kitchen, pulling open every cabinet along the way. The house will need some updates, but thankfully they're mostly cosmetic. "It seems bigger in here now." I rest my palm on the dark granite island anchored at the center of the large kitchen. This room is the reason why we bought the house. Unlike my own childhood, I wanted to make sure my family was sitting at the same dinner table every night. It was mostly my mom and I, while dad was deployed or working late.

"It probably helps that the gaudy furniture is all moved out." Matt lets the backpack he's carrying slide off his shoulder and onto the tiled floor. In two strides he's embracing me, pulling me into his chest. "Welcome home, Mrs. Sullivan."

━━━

BY THE TIME we wrap up unpacking for the day, it's early evening and the temperature has dipped, but Matt is still sweating from the repetitive hefting of boxes. "Is that it?" I ask, looking into the empty trailer.

"Is that *it*?" Matt holds his arms up, showing off two circles of sweat beneath his armpits.

"Okay, so maybe you had the heavy lifting, but my job was no cake walk." I cross my arms and sit on the bumper of the trailer, giving myself a minute to take in our new surroundings while the boys make a fort out of empty boxes on the grass. On the opposite side of the street, the trees serve as a privacy fence for the neighbor's yard. The only thing I can see is a string of lights that hang from a pergola, which I'm assuming is a patio area. A little girl's voice pierces the air, words strung together and softened like a song. And as if on cue, Jack catapults off the grass and darts across the street.

"Jack!" I march across the street after him, continuing my rant as I go. "You can't just run across the street! What have we said about looking both ways?" I place my hands on his shoulders and spin him toward me like a puppet. This isn't the first time I've had to physically move him to teach him how to do something. His body is limp as I go through the motions. I can tell his mind is elsewhere; the little girl's voice is getting closer, and I watch as his eyes move, left to right, up and down, his thoughts following closely behind. Gripping his bony shoulders, I start to direct him back across the street, when the little girl appears like an apparition between two arborvitaes.

"Hi, I'm Lily."

Jack turns back, detaching himself from my grip. As his mother, I know every detail of his life, including the fact that he has known what he wanted since the day he was born. When he was learning to walk, I would watch him persist, pulling himself up off the floor like it was a sport. The boy is naturally determined, dead set on what he wants and at this moment, he wants to meet this little girl, a new friend for him to add to the collection that he left behind in Ohio.

He takes two more steps, the lace of one untied shoe trails behind him and for a second I pray that he doesn't trip, the side of me that is still scarred from my own self-conscious childhood. I was never the cool kid, but I'm certain that Jack will be. I'm even certain that he'll have no problems recovering even if he did fall. Like Matt, he'd probably have some charming quip that would bounce him back from any embarrassment he did feel. Living with these two is like being a wallflower watching the popular kids dance effortlessly on the dance floor.

"Hi, I'm Jack."

They stand inches apart, assessing one another, until the sound of a screen door slams shut. "Lily, what are you doing?"

Lily rocks back and forth, pushing aside a curtain of dirty-blonde hair that conceals one cat-shaped blue eye. "I'm over here, Mama, with Jack," she says the words as if the two have been best friends for a lifetime.

Jack kicks at the dirt beneath the tree, loosening a chunk of earth. He bends down and holds up a shiny piece of rock in front of Lily. "This is mica. It's good luck."

"It is? Is it magic?"

Jack holds the piece of earth out to her. I wonder if he'll be this smooth with the ladies when he's in college.

"Lily, it's almost time for dinner!" A woman with a chubby tot on her hip steps forward, standing behind Lily. She looks around, startled by our presence. "Oh, oh my goodness, I'm so sorry. I didn't know you were really talking to someone." She rests a careful hand on the back of Lily's head. She pushes herself up onto the tips of her toes, craning her neck behind us. "Oh, you must be the new neighbors! Welcome, I'm so sorry." She cups a hand around her mouth and whispers. "Sorry, it's just Lily has been having some chats with imaginary friends and I didn't realize she was actually talking to real life humans this time." She winks a blue eye that is as feline-looking as her daughter's. "I'm Lauren Rivers, it's so nice to meet you. We've certainly been looking forward to having some other kiddos in the neighborhood, haven't we, Lil?"

Before I can respond, Jack follows Lily into the trees and the two of them wander off before I can stop him. "I'm Evie. It's nice to meet you." I watch over her shoulder as Jack slips easily into the role of a puppy dog on all fours while Lily pretends to lead him around. If this is any premonition of his future relationships, I'm going to have to look out for him.

"Sorry, she has a tendency to take over. I guess that's part of being the oldest sibling. She adjusts the toddler on her hip and pushes a sweep of pale blonde hair out of the child's face. "This is her little sister, Piper."

Right away I'm drawn to the little girl. She stares at me with round blue eyes accented by eyebrows that are several shades darker than her hair color. I decide that her blonde hair will be left behind and she'll be a brunette in just a few years. Her smile grows across her face, showing imperfect, spaced-out teeth, heightening my adoration for her. She lays her head against Lauren's chest and pops a thumb in her mouth while she clutches to a blue blanket dotted with rainbows and unicorns. I conclude in that moment that if I had a daughter, I'd want her to be like Piper. And I do, desperately want a daughter. Matt and I have been trying since Liam was nine months old to no avail.

"Well, Piper, I have a little boy who might want to play with you sometime," I say.

"Wait, you have another one?" Lauren asks, looking around, as if I'm hiding candy.

"Yes, and he's just about your age, Piper. Liam turned three last month."

"Did you hear that baby girl?" Lauren rests her nose on her daughter's temple. "How would you like a little friend to play with?" Right away, Piper grins. "She's never really had a friend to play with. I guess Lily is always the one with the social life and poor little Piper just tags along. So this will be good for her."

Lauren looks around, as if searching for someone else. "I'm sure you are exhausted from all the unpacking. Want to come over for a bit?" She adjusts Piper on her hip. I'm surprised by the invitation. Maybe people are nice here.

I look around, feeling the pull across the street. I should be helping Matt unpack or at least keeping Liam in line while boxes get shuffled around, but I decide in that moment that, this move is his doing, so he can bear the brunt of it for a few minutes. Their house is on the other side of the small dead-end terrace that we share, an extension of Sutton Lane. "Sure, I could use a break."

Lauren turns and I follow, the sound of Lily and Jack's voices getting closer. We pass through a wide cobblestone driveway, the neutral color rocks rising and falling in a way that makes it feel as if we're walking across a Parisian street. The driveway is greeted by a pergola that is viewable from our driveway, the lights strung in a way that looks perfectly haphazard, dipping in one giant crisscross in the center, the chords miraculously all hidden from view unlike the tangles and knots of the wires that held our modest light setup in the miniature garden area of our apartment. It had to be a top-notch electrician involved. The pergola is greeted by matching cobblestone steps that wind down and give way to a plush green lawn, where Jack and Lily are currently kicking their shoes off and climbing into a bounce house. A zip-line chord runs the length of the posh yard, cutting through the center and ending at a landing pad made of an assortment of mats. The entire yard is marked by entertainment. A smaller bounce house sits in another corner of the yard, and a rectangular sandbox, framed by low colorful wooden benches, is in another corner. Four cobblestone pathways lead up to the sandbox from each corner of the yard. Along the pathways are child-sized benches and chairs.

"This yard is a child's paradise," I say as I follow Lauren to a patio that overlooks it all, complete with an outdoor kitchen, a bar that backs up to the rear of the house, and no shortage of sections to sit and socialize. The theme is gray and white. Four white Adirondack chairs circle a silver gas fire pit on the lawn, the perfect setting for a gathering in the cooler months. Outside the kitchen, a patio sectional that is bigger than the one in my living room, circles a stone table, two outdoor heaters standing erect on each end. It's hard not to gawk. The place is beautiful, straight out of a Home and Garden magazine. "And I take it this is the adult's paradise."

Lauren lets out a laugh that I notice doesn't meet her eyes when she looks back at me. "This is all my husband's doing, I can't take the credit for this one."

"Did he design and build it?"

She laughs again, as she slips down into a patio chair and places Piper on a seashell-patterned outdoor carpet that sits beneath the coffee table and expands beyond the set. Shades of blue, green and gray swirl together, punched with white seashells that enhance the other white furniture and decor.

"Oh God, no. He has friends in the building business and put them to work. It was a huge pain in the rear though. I mean our yard was hardly usable for months."

I look around the expansive chunk of land, and then upward

toward the house which towers over us. My gaze takes in another set of lights seemingly strung from nowhere, creating the perfect party atmosphere. I force myself to lift my chin, closing my jaw. Surely, she hears just how gorgeous this yard is all the time. "I'm guessing you spend a lot of time back here."

"The kids do. And when we have parties, of course, we always spill out of the house and back here."

"I can imagine. I don't think I'd ever be inside if I lived here."

Lauren leans forward and gently tucks one of Piper's loose blonde strands behind her tiny ear. "So, where are you guys from anyways?"

"Ohio. Well, that's where we lived before here anyways. Matt is from California originally. I'm from…well… everywhere. Military brat."

She nods but I'm not sure she understands the meaning behind the term. "Are your parents in Ohio still?"

"Yep." And then I do what I'm best at. I transfer the spotlight back on her.

"What about your parents…where are they?"

"Oh, still in town. Die-hard Flaggers." She rolls her eyes, but I'm guessing that's the term she's adopted for herself as well because she's still here. It's then that I pick up on her perfectly aligned white teeth, the lips a tad too plump for the structure of her face. She's had work done, but not in a way that is overly done and laughable. Instead, it's classy like her laugh, carefully managed like the skinny jeans that mold to her body and land just above her ankle bone in a way that would make me argue that they were made just for her. I wonder if she has her jeans tailored. Her pale-green cotton shirt falls effortlessly off a tan shoulder, revealing a collar bone that is decorated with a shiny silver chain, a collection of birth stones lined up on her bronzed skin. Based on her daughters' pale skin tone, it's unlikely that her tan is natural, but again, it's done in a way that looks unflawed. Her wrists aren't marked by excess sunless tanner, there are no questionable unblended areas, nor are there any shades of orange peeking through, like the over-the-counter tanners my pale friends have used in the past. Thank God my skin maintains a

13

creamy bronze sheen in the summer months and holds on to the sun exposure I get from landscaping.

"Evie?" Matt's voice marks the air between me and Lauren, calling out to me like I'm a lost puppy dog.

"Shit! He caught me taking a break." I cover my mouth immediately, reminded by Piper's innocence. "I'm so sorry. I've got a thing with swearing. I never realized how bad I was until I had children." I'm immediately ashamed. I jump to the assumption that Lauren doesn't swear. Rich people don't swear, they carry themselves with poise and spin etiquette in the conversation any chance they get.

"Don't apologize on my behalf. Her daddy's got a trucker's mouth, so she's heard worse." Again, Lauren lets out a delicate giggle and leans her forehead into Piper's, inciting a release of giggles before she turns toward the edge of the yard, alerted by the swishing sound of the seagrass that outlines her property. Matt emerges between two hearty plants, still in pots, like a lion in the wilderness.

"There you are." He swats at a twig that landed on his shoulder as Liam releases his hand and runs to me, nearly knocking me backwards onto the patio. I heft him up on a hip, with his back to Lauren and Piper.

"Mommy, where are you?" Liam looks around, bewildered.

"Honey, I'm at the same place you're at right now. This is our neighbor's yard, and guess what?"

His eyes expand into two saucers. "What!?"

"They have a daughter your age. This is Piper." I angle my body so he is facing the strangers standing behind him. He burrows into my chest, but keeps one eye peeking out toward them, curious but cautious.

"Wow, this yard is beautiful," Matt announces, stepping forward. He keeps his hands low on his hips and takes in the view, accompanying it with a low whistle of approval. I'm never embarrassed by my husband, but at this moment, I feel my face growing hot. Based on the casual way Lauren has spoken of her model yard, I imagine this was just considered a minor upgrade. Yet Matt is whistling like a brand-new car just pulled up in front of him, making a big deal out of it. And some warped side of me is silently scolding him, as if his whistles will peel down a layer of our own family's finances.

"I'm Lauren." She steps forward and extends a hand, releasing her grip from Piper's bum. Again, I feel like an idiot for failing to introduce them.

"Oh, hey, sorry." He accepts her hand and shakes it firmly while making sure to acknowledge how adorable Piper is.

"Thank you, it's nice meeting you. I was just telling Evie how nice it will be to have neighbors with little ones. Did you move here for work?"

"Yes, it's my fault." Matt shrugs his shoulders and displays a guilty expression on his face.

"What is it you do, Matt?"

"I work for Onyx Health…it's a startup that designed an app used for fitness facilities and personal use, so I'll be tackling the sales in the northeast region."

"Wow." Lauren's blue eyes grow wide, the first signs of excitement arriving on her face since I'd met her moments before. "Well, I'd love to hear more, and I'm sure my husband Ryan would as well. We're always interested in learning about new products and investment opportunities."

Matt's face lights up at the sound of investment opportunities. Having been in the startup world for the past few years, he's seen the good and bad in funding and it was always a good sign when someone with money wanted to take a chance on a product. I can see the potential churning in his thoughts. "Absolutely! I'm pretty sure our CEO has some future prototypes up his sleeve too. I'd love to talk to you about them and gauge your interest—"

"Daddy!" Jack comes barreling up the lawn with Lily in his wake. Without slowing down he crashes into Matt. "Did you see this yard, Dad? They have a zip line!"

"I did, dude, it's awesome." Matt transitions into boy-dad mode, acting as if he is one of them and slipping back to his own youth with ease.

"We should probably get back to unpacking though." I turn

toward Lauren. "I'm sorry for completely crashing your yard here. It was so nice meeting you."

"Oh, gosh, our house is like a revolving door so never worry about crashing anything over here. Lily's playdate schedule is busier than my social calendar, so we're pretty used to having kids here nonstop." With a lift of her voice, she addresses Jack and Liam. "And, boys, I gotta say we have a pretty darn good snack cabinet inside. I'm sure my girls would love to have you boys over for a play-date and picnic sometime."

Jack bounces up and down like a jumping bean, as Liam follows his lead. "Can we, Mommy, please?" Both boys' voices dance together in begs and pleads.

"I'm sure we can schedule something, guys," I start to herd them toward the seagrass path Matt came through.

"How about tonight?" Lauren stops me in my tracks.

"For a playdate?"

"For a cocktail hour slash playdate, slash get-to-know-your-neighbors gathering." Lauren says matter-of-factly, with raised eyebrows as she sets Piper down on the patio.

Before I can respond, Matt says, "Sure!" I'm certain he still has the idea of *potential investors* swirling through his mind.

"Yes!" Jack pulls his elbow into his side in a satisfactory win.

"Say..." Lauren looks down at her watch. "...six-thirty? Ryan will be home by then and I'll have these two fed."

I look around at my three agreeing boys. "Sounds great!"

The trek from the patio to the edge of the property makes me realize just how colossal their yard really is. Blades of grass reach up and tickle the bare skin that peeks out from my casual sneakers, my footprint cushioned by the hearty lawn. As the four of us push ourselves through the small path between the seagrass plants, Lauren's voice reaches us. "Sorry about those plants, we have a landscaper who is supposed to put them in for us." At the word landscaper, Matt introduces me all over again.

"You've got a great landscaper right here." He motions to me. "Evie makes her livelihood talking to plants and placing them perfectly."

"You're a landscaper?" Lauren's eyes light up. "Oh my, did you move in at the right time. We've got some good ones in town, but they're mostly on their way out if you know what I mean. Let's talk more about this tonight. I could potentially have an entire client list for you in no time."

3

Before

APRIL 2009

Lauren

I watch as our new neighbors cut through the seagrass and make their way back to the other side of the private terrace. They look like the perfect little family of four. I liked Evie immediately. She isn't like my other friends. She seems unbothered by materialistic things. I could tell by her Target top that she either isn't interested or can't afford the pricey boutiques that line the main streets of Flagport. I don't think Evie will be purchasing a one-hundred-dollar cotton tee from Flare anytime in the near future.

Evie Sullivan and her family aren't the norm here and I knew it the second her house sign flipped from on sale to sold. I knew it when I learned that it wasn't an investor who scooped up the property for a flip, and instead it was a couple who put a minimal down payment on the home. Having decades of life experience in this town and a family history that dates back over a century, I'm privy to things a newcomer will never have access to. My cousin Brynn was the real estate agent who sold the home and kept me in the know on every step of the Sullivan's move. I hate to admit that I took advantage of her newness to the real estate industry, and I pushed for more details about the family who would be sharing a street with us. From Matt's career trajectory to the fact that their youngest son saw a behavior therapist briefly at the age of two, I have grips on the little details it would take a normal person years to pull together. Matt grew up in California, skipped college, and Evie spent her childhood traveling the United States, living in Army base housing for two-year stints. Fort Rucker, Alabama, Fort Benning, Georgia, Fort Leonard Wood, Missouri, Fort Hamilton, New York, Fort Sill, Oklahoma, Fort Irwin, California. And then there was Ohio, but I couldn't seem to find an Army base there. At the age of twenty-eight, this girl's residential resume makes mine look incredibly boring. Movement, even when it's forced upon a person, makes them seem mysterious, as if they can pack up and leave a life behind at the drop of a dime. It's a quality I lack, a quality I'll likely never have.

I gathered all the details and put them in my control crockpot, letting them marinate for a while before they pulled up on their move-in date, April 12th, circled in bold red on my calendar.

Compared to their home, our house is posh, but that's only because we had enough money to completely renovate it when my parents purchased it for us as a wedding gift. We had the old cape bones enhanced, expanding outward and upward to create a body that is equivalent to the beautiful waterfront homes in town.

By the time six-thirty rolls around, I have a full spread laid out on the kitchen island, complete with kid-friendly options. I adjust the charcuterie board, making sure the cheeses and meats are angled evenly, and wipe off the sweat that is dripping down the pitcher of margaritas. "Ryan, they'll be here like any second!" I say. Like everything in my life, each detail has to be perfect.

"I'm here!" He slides across the living room floor in stocking feet, after he steps off the staircase that winds upward toward the second level. Our house is open concept and I'd have it no other way. I like to have my eyes on everyone and everything at all times.

I assess him from head to toe. He wears a pale-blue Vineyard Vines shirt that reaches just above his wrists. I lean forward and tug at the zipper, so it lands where it's supposed to, level with the small navy-blue whale logo that sits just above the left breast. "They're from Ohio…let's not scare them away with too much Flagport style." Vineyard Vines is on display in all the storefronts of the town and it's near impossible to go anywhere here without seeing one of those navy-blue whales emblazoned on the pockets, backs and fronts of shirts.

"Is this better?" Ryan unbuckles his belt and lets his jeans drop low, displaying the edge of his boxer shorts so he looks like a thug.

"Nice try," I say. Ryan couldn't look like a bad boy if he tried. His big, round blue eyes alone are always a solid option on a man, but the fact that they are paired with a full head of dark hair makes him smoldering. Unlike half the men his age, his hair has yet to show any signs of thinning and he takes advantage of that with the various pomades and gels that are lined up in his bathroom cabinet. This evening, after a full day of work pushing homes for McCue Real Estate, his hair is still held impeccably in place, molded into a wave-like shape. Although he's from western Massachusetts, he fits in perfectly in Flagport and has adapted quite well to my family's lifestyle.

"When are they getting here?" Lily demands as she too slides across the freshly polished living room floor.

I look down at the pale blue face of my Tiffany watch and shudder when I see it reads six-thirty-eight. I don't like when people are late. It cuts into my time, and I have a lot to do tonight to get ready for the annual Easter egg hunt at the Flagport Yacht Club tomorrow.

The front doorbell rings and Lily and Piper race to the entry-way. I stay back to glance over the appetizers and drinks one more time. "Get some ice for the margaritas," I hiss the demand at Ryan, and monitor him as he goes to work, scooping ice out of the deep freezer and into our white monogrammed ice bucket. He grabs each of the rope handles and sets it on the island. As I hear the blend of my daughters' voices and the Sullivans' getting closer, I twist the bucket so the capital R for Rivers is facing the guests as they walk into our kitchen.

"Hello, thank you guys so much for coming over." I step across the kitchen and embrace Evie with a gentle hug. She offers a loose hug back, as if she's not quite comfortable enough with me to share a full-blown embrace.

As always, it takes the kids less time to warm up to one another than it does the adults and Lily is pulling Jack toward the first-floor playroom, while Piper and Liam stand in front of each other staring the way toddlers do.

"Wow, this house is beautiful." Matt strolls around the kitchen as if he's touring a museum, holding a platter of cheeses that look like it was purchased at Market Basket, not one of the fine wine and cheese shops in town.

"Matt." That's all Evie has to say for him to step out of his reverie.

It's not lost on me how Evie immediately changes the subject. She's embarrassed at how her husband is gawking. It's cute. I'm not used to having friends who aren't as well-off as us. I know you're not supposed to judge a book by its cover, but I can tell the way they hold themselves that they had humble upbringings. I know this because Ryan was the same way when I met him, until I molded him to fit in with our lifestyle. It didn't take him long to get comfortable with my family's money. And while he's never used it, he's privy to the power that my family holds in this town.

I step into my hostess-with-the-mostess role and pour two margaritas in pre-salted glasses, handing one to Evie and one to Matt.

"Lauren, did you ever think that maybe they don't like margaritas and would want something else?" Ryan steals my show.

"Who doesn't like margaritas?" I come back with a snappy response as I watch Evie and Matt take a generous sip.

"Me," Ryan says as he pops the top of a PBR beer can and takes a gulp as if he's a frat boy. As much as I've changed him over the years in other areas of his life, I haven't been able to get him to shift his alcohol preferences. He claims he sticks with the classic beer, because it's low in alcohol content, compared to the scotch and bourbons my family has been imbibing in for decades.

"No judgments here." Matt raises his glass to Ryan's PBR. I can tell they are going to be fast friends. "Ahhh, brings me back to my roots."

"Speaking of your roots. Where are you from?" I pour my own margarita and gesture for them to sit at the massive island surrounded by white bar stools. I lean in, resting my chin on a fist doing my best to act like I don't know their life story.

"I was born and raised in California and landed in Ohio of all places when I locked eyes with this beauty." He leans toward Evie, who rolls her eyes.

I ask more questions and pick up more tidbits that I didn't have access to on my internet searches and real estate connections. Like the way Matt still seems smitten by Evie, after six years of marriage. How he bolsters her up every chance he gets with compliments and displays of affection as if it's his job to boost her confidence. Like the way she seems to feel uncomfortable and out of place, as if she's a fish out of water. I assumed she made fast friends since she traveled a lot, but there are a lot of layers that seem to shield her, like she has something to hide.

4

After

APRIL 2021

Lauren

Ryan pushes through the emergency room doors with so much force that the accumulated snow flurries lift off the pavement and dance in the air like a newly shaken snow globe.

"Piper, move!" For the third time since we got the phone call, I've had to yell at my younger daughter. Like always, Piper is taking this urgent situation and moving at a snail's pace, showing no sense of purpose. It's been the way she has moved through life since the day she was born, never with determination, but instead with a turtle-like gait, her free-spirited head tipped back looking up at the sky, unaware of anything going on around her. She's a dreamer to a fault. Over the years, my impatience has run thin with the young girl's wandering ways, but luckily, Ryan has found a way to stay in stride with her offbeat outlook on life.

He slows his stride and falls back. "You go, I'll catch up." Her brooding expression loosens up, freeing up a crooked smile as he grabs her hand, tugging her forward. *Daddy can do no wrong.* It was as if he single-handedly raised Piper and I singlehandedly raised Lily, the differences between the girls split in half like a river cutting through two towns. The rapid waters are me and Ryan, somehow molding ourselves to fit our daughters' opposing personalities.

I had only been in the hospital at this hour one other time in my life. The waiting room is unexpectedly busy. A child coughing into his mother's chest, a weary twenty-something man, and a family of four in quiet deliberation, an aura of worry wrapped around their tight circle. The woman behind the desk bites down on a granola bar, holding it in place between her teeth as she straightens out a handful of files on her desk. How can she be so calm while there is a young girl, somewhere in this hospital who has been in a car accident? I want to scream at the woman, shake her until she tells me what happened to Lily. "Hello?" I pull my shoulders back, put on a presentable face like my parents taught me so many years ago. *Always look confident no matter how you feel inside.* The woman looks up, the granola bar still held tightly between her teeth. No apologetic smile, no nerves fluttering around causing her to drop the folders. She raises her eyebrows, questioning my presence. *She obviously doesn't know who I am.* "My daughter, Lily Rivers, is in the emergency room. I just got a call. Can you please tell me what's going on?"

"Catherine." The woman says the name as she takes the granola bar out of her mouth, allowing a bite to break off the end. She looks at me as she chews, her face hard like a correctional officer. "Catherine!" she says louder.

My hands are shaking. I have a sudden urge to put them around the woman's neck. But I do what I've always done and remain calm.

A shockingly tall woman emerges from a small closet off the reception area. Frizzy tendrils fall from a ponytail and dark circles beneath her eyes enhance her pale blue irises. "Catherine, you gotta brief me. What happened tonight? Is there a Lily Rivers in the ER?"

"Sorry, shift changeover." The tall woman smiles apologetically. My fear gives way to paranoia, and I assume the woman is offering her pity. She knows what happened to Lily, she had a front row seat to her condition when she arrived in the most dreaded place someone could be at this hour. She knows if Lily is alive or dead, or bordering both. This woman, a sheer stranger, holds the answers to my emotional state. I pull in a breath of the antiseptic air, the tones of perfume that waft off one of the women, assuming it's the grumpy one new to the shift, the one who is about to receive Lily's diagnosis at the same time as I am. I conclude that Catherine is a mother, based on the way her head tilts sideways as she assesses me, the way her hands shake ever so slightly as she unfolds the file that is now being passed to the grumpy woman. Yes, Catherine has at least one massively tall child at home, and she knows the vulnerability that is involved in being a mother. She's well aware of the guilt that congeals all rational thoughts after you have a child.

"Miss Rivers, the doctor will be out shortly to give you an update on Lily." She uses my name and title. *It's always bad when they use a name and title.* They know me as the mother of the patient now, a real patient, not just as someone who was passing through for a mundane set of stitches. I start to protest her silence and beg for more information when the grumpy nurse gets the job done for me.

"Catherine, I need to know her status so I can proceed." Her raspy voice punches the air with a hiss.

Catherine sidesteps as if she's trying to avoid an IED. Her eyes shift to me, then toward the grumpy nurse, and back again. She wants to tell the grumpy nurse the latest on my daughter in private, without breaking the rules that demand nurses keep secrets and only doctors are authorized to share the latest updates on their patients. I adjust my bag, asserting my stance, unmoving until someone tells me what condition my daughter is in. At this point the news could come from the janitor, as long as there is confirmation that Lily is alive.

Catherine gets it. She walks on eggshells as she speaks. "Lily was brought in just after twelve. All I know at this point is that she was immediately taken into surgery."

My mind surpasses Catherine's next words and rejoices that she is in surgery. You have to be alive to go into surgery. Dead patients don't make it to surgery. As the information starts to line up in my head, I formulate a thousand questions that smash into one another in one massive mosh pit of words.

"Thump! Swoosh!" The sound of bodies hitting the entrance door to the ER erupts in the waiting room. Ryan and Piper charge into the space, matching expressions on their faces.

"Where is she? What's going on?" Ryan surpasses the niceties and gets to Catherine before she has a chance to slink out of the room and go home to her Amazon children.

"Sir, as I was telling your wife…I'm assuming this is your wife?" Her two eyebrows shoot up to the ceiling, and she proceeds after I nod.

I finish the response for her, "They can't tell us what's going on yet, so let's just sit down." I turn my back to the reception desk and usher Ryan and Piper to a section of empty chairs, between the coughing child and the twenty-something man, with a direct line of vision of the wary family.

"Why the hell are the nurses manning the reception desk anyways?" Ryan hisses as he sinks into the chair on the other side of Piper.

I know exactly why. It's the same reason why there were no receptionists the last time I was in the emergency room at this hour. "They are understaffed. They are always understaffed in this department." I share my insight and reach for Piper's hand. It's sweating despite the cold temperature in the waiting area caused by the drafts that have been sneaking in every time the doors open. Another burst of air thrusts into the room, surrounding the three of us like a cloak. A wave of frustration passes over me. The cold air feels good, and I'm annoyed with myself for thinking about my own comfort in a moment like this. And then, just like that, my frustration is replaced with surprise. Standing in front of me is our neighbor, Matt Sullivan, and his two sons, Jack and Liam. The neighbors who have become our closest friends over the years.

"Matt!" I stand and start toward him, readying myself to fall into a consoling hug, grateful that they showed up for what might be the most tragic moment of our lives. He wipes at a red-rimmed eye and darts toward the reception desk. "Matt, we already talked to them, they don't have any information yet," I say, as I look around the room for his wife, my best friend Evie. Ryan stands behind me now, his breath producing a hot blast of air on the back of my neck, counteracting the cold gust that is still circulating in the room.

Matt ignores me and proceeds to question the grumpy nurse. "I just got a call that my wife, Evie Sullivan, has been in an accident."

5

Before

MARCH 2010

Evie

We've only been living in Flagport just over a year, but we've already been to a dozen gatherings at the Rivers' house. Sometimes I think that our home mortgage came with a built-in social life. Lauren and Ryan have welcomed us to every event they've hosted and so far, we've only declined one invite. That was when Liam wasn't feeling well, and I was too worried about spreading germs to their guests. Sometimes their invites came in passing, while Matt and Ryan were conversing at the mailboxes, and other times they came tucked in nicely embellished envelopes, annotating the official start and end time of the party, along with a preferred dress code. These were usually the ones that the kids weren't invited to. At first my insecurity saw past these invitations, and I assumed they were only asking us because we lived across the street. After all, how could they not invite us when they had a five-person band and a dance floor that had to be delivered by a truck that was parked in front of our house. "Of course, they invited us...it would be incredibly rude not to." I would rattle off the various scenarios that forced them to share their party with us to Matt, allowing my self-doubt to sneak in. Surely, it wasn't because they actually liked us.

But they really did like us. I could see it in the way they opened their circle of friends, sharing phone numbers of the boy moms and dads so we could set up playdates. Bringing over extras on the occasions when they had a chef muster up meals in their cutting-edge kitchen. And then there was the time when they offered to feed Liam's new goldfish while we went to Ohio for a quick weekend to visit my mom. I never once saw them emit the signs of *uninterested neighbor*. I never caught them racing to their silver Land Rover SUV ducking heads to avoid us. Even in their most rushed family outings, they took the time to engage in small talk if we happened to be in the driveway, which was perpendicular to theirs on the opposite side of the street. Over the months, our individual driveways have turned into meeting spots for our children. The four kids gathered together, concocting plans for sunny afternoons, Liam and Piper always trailing behind Lily and Jack like minions during long play-dates that would inevitably end with the four of us clinking glasses at an impromptu backyard happy hour. Our weekdays, weekends, and social highlights had included them more times than not.

Their event attendees consisted of parents who had the same aged children as ours and a few single stragglers from Lauren's childhood. *Flaggers* is what they called them. If you were born and raised in the town you were considered a Flagger, if not, there was no hope of you becoming a Flagger. The title would only hit your family if a future generation was actually born into the town. If Jack and Liam decided to stay here, their kids would officially be Flaggers. Until then, we would be known as outsiders, although I've never felt more like an insider in my entire life. Lauren's group of friends welcomed our family with open arms, and while many of them had a house that made ours look like a shack, they never treated us differently. Sure, I saw the roaming eyes that assessed my Target tops and non-boutique-shop jeans, but it stopped there. Lauren had become my biggest fan and inserted my landscaping expertise into every conversation she had with both townies and new families. She was a well-known Flagger. Her great-grandfather was born in town and carved out a name for his future generations after his arrival from Ireland. It didn't take me long to learn that the name McCue was famous in town, but Lauren didn't reveal that it was her family's name until two months after we lived here, as if she was keeping the name hidden. If I was a McCue, I would share that with the world.

"Liam! Let's go!" Jack is already in the driveway, weighed down by the tall gift bag that houses a toy rocket launcher, covered in pink sparkly tissue paper. He claimed that Lily wanted it more than anything for her eighth birthday, and he would know, since he'd been with the girl nearly every day since we moved to 88 Sutton Lane.

Matt joins me at the small side porch that greets our driveway, echoing my beckoning for Liam. "Liam, get down here now!" With lips pinched together Matt shakes his head at me. "That kid is gonna be the death of me." Liam doesn't listen, but I always have to remind myself that he's still only four, a stage when boys have zero attention span and get distracted by moving bugs and roaring engines. It's hard for both of us since Jack came out of the womb with a fondness for sleep, a natural ability to take in his surroundings and assess before making a move. Liam was a walking tornado, spinning into every room with zero control, his emotions lifting up and outward with no warning. At only three he was getting a repu-tation for dropping word groupings that were off the wall and described as bizarre by his daycare teacher. "He certainly says what's on his mind," Miss Sophie had said, crediting his outbursts to a creative imagination. I held on to her assessment of his artistic wildness and pictured him being a famous innovator one day, but Matt's patience was thinning.

"Here." I turn to see Liam holding something wrapped in toilet paper and coloring book pages, and just like that, my frus-tration gives way to pure love, and I'm swept away by his big heart.

"Oh, buddy what is that?" I kneel down in front of him, analyzing the mystery package. He places it in my open palms, and

I feel a mishmash of shapes beneath the paper. The object is hard and rounded on the edges. "Can I take a peek?"

"Yes." Liam reaches over and starts to peel up one corner, a section that is covered in one of Spiderman's web shooters. I take over and hold the piece of furry tape up so I can see more. That is when I learn what my son has wrapped. I drop the package, the sound of bone hitting the decking, and press a palm to my mouth, looking over at Matt for help.

"What is it?" He crouches down beside Liam who is now lifting the package up to his chest like it's his most prized possession.

"It's some type of bone," I tell Matt, trying my best not to make a big deal out of it, hearing the pediatrician's voice in my head. *Try not to make a big deal when Liam does things that we don't consider normal. It will only shine a light on it, and make him insecure, or worse…drive him to seek more attention.*

Matt, now eye level with Liam, tries to grab the package out of his hands but he's stopped when Liam pulls it to his chest and turns, running down the steps and across the street toward the Rivers' house. "Get him!" I whisper-yell to Matt. If Liam shows up to their house with what could quite possibly be the bone of a dead dog, I'll be mortified.

Jack drops the gift bag in the driveway and stops Liam before he gets to the seagrass that borders their lawn. The seagrass that I placed and accented with banana plants and jewel-toned dahlias when Lauren hired me to take over her old landscaper's duties. Before Liam can cut through the plants, Jack tugs on his fleece jacket and pulls him into his chest. He falls on his back and rolls down the slight hill that greets the street. By the time Matt gets to them, the boys are a full-blown tumbleweed with arms and legs darting outward until they come to a complete stop. Liam, still clutching the package with clenched fists, escapes Jack and Matt with the prowess of a seasoned football player dodging his opponent.

It's me who ends up stopping him, pulling the package from his grip and parading a dozen different questions in his direction, after I reveal its contents and confirm that it is, in fact, a bone. One that is too big to come from last week's rotisserie chicken, but likely too small to be human. *Where did you find this? Why did you wrap it for Lily's birthday? What made you think she would want this?*

According to Liam the bone was a gift from Henry, who dug it up in the backyard. He pointed to the spot between our sagging deck and crumbling patio, and said matter-of-factly, "I want to give it to Lily for her birthday because she's always talking about the bones in the cemetery that she visits."

LILY'S eighth birthday party is everything I expected. Pink, sparkly, and each detail tended to with a fine-toothed comb. With a guest list that outshines my wedding headcount, the Rivers' yard is in full swing. The music selection consists of energetic beats of Lady Gaga and kids' popular lyrics sung by celebrities, an eclectic blend that ignites upbeat, happy smiles in all the guests. Kids are grouped together by ages, the babies placed inside decorated pack n' plays on the patio, tots stumble around the yard stealing toys from one another like mini drunks. Jack's age group is fully engaged in a game of tag, and the older kids have either taken on the roles of babysitters or congregate in clusters across the many gathering places on the property. A group of tweens dance to Just Dance on a mini stage centered on the patio, as if they are at a real outdoor concert. And it might as well be that, because this kid's party is better than any concert I've attended. But with Lauren having a part-time job planning events at the Flagport Yacht Club and her connections within the town, I'm not surprised.

Pink champagne is passed around to the adults, a non-alcoholic version is served in plastic water bottles labeled with "Lily's Birthday Bubbly." It didn't take me long to learn that I should always dress two notches higher than I would normally expect for an occasion at the Rivers' house. In my past life, I was safe wearing Walmart leggings and a basic T-shirt, emitting casual comfort in the same active wear that the other moms were donning. Today, I'm wearing a pair of capri jeans, jazzed up with nude wedge sandals and an emerald-green blouse that dips just low enough to share a sneak peek at my cleavage.

Unlike most children's birthday parties, Lily's has no end time. Starting at three in the afternoon, just in time for an early happy hour, the parents have all been informed that the kids can stay for the 7:00 viewing of *Up*. It's nearing six and I'm on my fourth glass of pink champagne. Compared to the other mother's I'm pacing myself, sipping slowly and breaking up my booze with gulps from the personalized mini water bottles. I look down at what is the fourth bottle of water I've slammed so far. *Drink Up! Lily's 8ʰ Birthday* is written in purple curly font, a bizarre message for a kid's birthday, but I get where they are going with it.

"Hey, babe, I have someone you need to meet." Matt appears from out of nowhere, followed by a woman in a pale-yellow maxi dress. I turn around, caught savoring some alone time on a side porch that is decorated with orange and red mums that I personally selected and placed.

"Hey." I lean in and accept the kiss that Matt drops on my cheek. He doesn't ask why I'm up here alone. He knows that I need brief reprieves from crowds, chunks of time where I can recharge and let my own thoughts float through my mind without interruption. He steps back and allows a willowy blonde to move forward. "Honey, this is Emily Nelson. She's the owner of Flagport Flowers."

I take in Emily's thin frame, the bony protrusions of her collarbone, the deep dip of her throat. Her arms dangle like two branches beside a body that is lost in her flowy dress. I watch as her eyes land on my cleavage, my only threatening feature doing its job. "It's so nice to meet you. Lauren cannot stop talking about how talented you are." She extends a branch and offers a surprisingly firm shake.

"Likewise." Lauren had raved about her oldest friend, promising me that we would mesh and get along well thanks to our love of nature, our natural green thumbs. "I heard we would make exceptional friends." I smile, showing her my second-best feature. My lips, particularly my upper one, full and smooth, with the rare ability to hold lipstick for hours.

Matt interjects, ready to move on and use his schmoozing abilities elsewhere. "Well, I'll leave you two to it. I'm out of booze." He looks down at the lonely drop of bourbon sitting at the bottom of his whiskey glass, and turns, heading back down to the party.

I wave off Matt and turn toward Emily. "So, Lauren tells me you've been in the garden biz since you were Lily's age."

"Even younger, actually, if you can believe that." Emily tucks a strand of golden hair behind an ear that is embellished with a rose-gold, feather-shaped earring that jingles every time she moves. "I used to visit the store often when I was a toddler. In fact, I think I took my first steps there."

"So, you were born a flower girl."

"No joke. Lauren always laughs about how I'm more interested in being with plants than people, but I'd be lying if I said I didn't feel some very surreal connection to my babies at the shop. They don't talk back and everything they need to survive is in nature." She laughs. "I'm sure you get it though. I mean, look at how you transformed this yard." She waves a hand around the property, showcasing the creative clusters of plants and flowers I've placed with perfection.

"Well, I had a pretty easy canvas. I mean, come on…look at this yard."

Emily crosses her arms, rubbing her palms over goose-bumped skin. "Yeah, Lauren has really come a long way. I'm happy for her. To think about what that woman has been through—"

"Well, there's my two favorite girls." Lauren appears from one of the many pathways that spill from the yard to the driveway and the patio. But I'm still stuck on Emily's last words. What exactly has Lauren been through?

6

Before

OCTOBER 2010

Lauren

Halfway through Lily's birthday party I start to feel the tugging on my emotions. I shouldn't be here celebrating my daughter's birthday, getting tipsy with friends as we launch into another year of life for the child who made me a mother. I don't deserve this. But I play the role I was born into. I'm a McCue and that is something that will never change, much like the emotions and regrets that swirl inside my head every morning I wake up and tickle my brain every night as I try to get to sleep.

I climb the stairs to the top deck where I can hear the low voices of Emily, my oldest friend, and Evie my newest friend. I need to get to them before too much slips from Emily's lips. She's never known the full story, but I can't let her spill even a morsel of that memory from so many years ago. Evie is too good of a person to allow it to slide if she finds out the truth. She's spent her life under the protective wing of patriotic parents who followed the rules. I know this, because I stared at her in awe when she recited some of the facts about her childhood. Her family lived in base housing which consisted of two bedrooms in a ranch-style home that was decorated with Walmart furniture because they were never any place long enough to warrant moving quality furniture. Her father's dedication to the country spilled into how she was raised and he and her mother steeped respect in Evie from a young age. You never lie, cheat or steal, and you always show integrity in who you are. Those were her exact words.

When I reach the middle of the steps, I hear Emily mentioning how I've come a long way, and I immediately take action. I'm tipsy but not drunk. I never allow myself to be drunk, but I can put on an act, and make everyone think that I've loosened my leash on life for today. Just for today.

"Well, there's my two favorite girls." I step into their conversation and change the subject, making sure to send it into a detour that will never be retraced.

I make a big show out of asking for their help with the birthday cake, even though I have it all under control already, as I always do. "Can you girls gather the crowd and make sure the birthday girl is seated at her special chair while I get the cake?"

"Of course." They both jump at the chance to help like I knew they would.

"Is it time for the festivities?" Ryan passes by just in time. He pulls me into his side and plants a kiss on my head.

The cake is a perfect ten. I assess the cursive purple writing that contrasts nicely against the pale pink swirls that rise upward and blend into a unicorn head. It's only big enough to serve twenty, but I have several matching round cakes for the remaining guests. I push in the eight candles, so they are evenly spaced and a safe distance from melting the yellow frosting that swirls down the head of the unicorn into one swirly mane. "Is it time?" Ryan cranes his neck around the edge of the doorway, the doting father and husband that he is.

"Yes, start singing!" I step forward as if I'm walking on eggshells, out onto the patio where Lily is primed in a chair embellished with crepe paper and balloons at the head of the table, circled by her friends, but it's Jack who is closest to her. They've made a couch out of the chairs, and he is so close to her it looks as if their bodies could be joined.

As the crowd sings happy birthday to Lily, I set the cake in front of her and take in the scene. My little girl looks up at me with pink cheeks, a smile spread so wide across her face it turns her eyes into two slits. This is the moment that I love so much, but it's the moment that I don't deserve. She is my star. She is my second chance to make my life right. I want her to be the me I should've been all those years ago. The one with the big dreams of leaving Flagport and carving out my own path, away from the confines of the McCue family name. She'll go far in life but not too far away from me so I can always have one eye on her every move, making sure she doesn't slip up and make a mistake that could change how she sees herself forever.

7

After

APRIL 2021

Lauren

Across from me, Piper is watching some YouTube video about obnoxious kids playing pranks on each other. I can't bear to think that kids make money on this crap, but right now it's making me feel a sense of peace to be mad about it. They can take all my money for their advertisements, they can post whatever ridiculousness they want, as long as it means my daughter is alive. I take it a step further and repeat a silent prayer. *Please God, pull Lily out of this, please God, I'll do anything to make sure my daughter is okay.* This isn't the first time I've prayed while in a hospital. It's not the first time I've made deals with God. Today, I'd exchange anything just to know that she's okay, that we can go back to simpler times. Like yesterday.

Yesterday, when I badgered Lily about working on listing out the pros and cons of the three colleges she had gotten accepted to. All three her top choice schools, it had been a hard decision to make and involved some color coordinating in true Lily fashion. Red was for best academic program, blue was for social opportunities, and green was locations of the educational institution. When the acceptance letters started arriving, one after the other, Ryan and I weren't surprised. There was no doubt Lily would get into her top choice, which happened to be my top choice. Boston University. She'd be at a top school only forty minutes away. I already had our weekend visits planned out and the decor that would go best in a dorm room of that size. Lily, I knew, would go on to do great things, especially if she had my hand on the small of her back steering her in life, protecting her from making mistakes. She'd always been the easy child, naturally motivated and driven, a rule follower. The fact that she was incredibly beautiful with thick, dirty-blonde hair and striking blue eyes added another flame to the fire that she would be able to spread in the world one day. Her eyes were her most noteworthy physical feature, cat-shaped like my own, but more of a pale blue that gave her face an angelic appearance. We used to have a porcelain doll that looked identical to her, minus the gaudy mauve dress and pageant hair that coiled in burgundy curls. It was just the face. Lily has a memorable face, one that I always knew would leave a mark on people.

"Coffee?" Ryan sets a Styrofoam cup on the table in front of me, beside an old magazine with torn edges.

I bring up the elephant in the room again and direct the question to Matt, who is sitting diagonally opposite. "Why would Evie be in a car with Lily in the middle of the night?" The question has been circling the room since Matt arrived at the hospital with Jack and Liam, moments after we did. My daughter and his wife are being treated for injuries that are still unknown, resulting from what a nurse confirmed was the same car accident. The two patients arrived at the hospital at the same time. While there was still no official police report on the collision that occurred just one mile from our home, it was confirmed that they were in fact together, in the same vehicle. Evie as the driver and Lily as the passenger. More details would follow, the nurses and the police department promised.

"Lauren, I have no idea." He raises his head from where it's settled in his palms, his forearms fall slack on his lap. "I'm just as clueless as you."

From the other side of the room, Liam comes to life. "Maybe they were friends." It's not lost on me that he uses the past tense, the *were* jolts me with a sick sensation. *Is my daughter going to die?* Liam is fifteen and the things that come out of his mouth make him sound like he's in kindergarten. He's been that way since he left the toddler stage and entered boyhood. All these years later and it's as if his mentality has never developed beyond that of a five-year-old. Evie and Matt repeatedly talk about how smart he is at math. "He's at the top of his class, a boy genius with numbers," they liked to boast, but I saw the concern in their eyes. The curiosity about why their youngest son is so much different than their oldest. The embarrassment they laugh off when Liam says something as off the wall as he just did. I had seen the counselors make home visits and the speech therapists and tutors that they've hired over the years.

"Liam, stop!" Matt snaps.

We've been neighbors for twelve years, best friends for ten. Our houses are on each side of a private road, both perched on the top of the street. Matt is always the happy-go-lucky guy who wears his heart on his sleeve. Always one to show an interest in everyone else's life with questions that are laced in a generous curiosity. It's probably why he's been so successful in sales. When Matt is with you, he's always listening, interjecting at just the right moment, tossing engaging head nods in, and riding out the conversation with patience and undivided attention.

"What? It's true. They can be friends too."

Jack looks up from his phone, a mask of angry red blankets his naturally bronze skin. "Shut up, Liam!" Much like his father, Jack rarely shows anger or frustration. But today is an exception. He falls in line right behind me, Ryan and Piper when it comes to people who are closest to Lily. The two have been best friends since they met, and managed to maintain their friendship through elementary school, the awkward junior high years and now, as seniors in high school, they are as tight as ever. But apparently not as tight as we thought considering he wasn't the one driving Lily home last night. The two of them have served as each other's shoulder to cry on when inevitable teenage breakups surfaced.

They were a team. And now his favorite teammate and his mother are in the hospital with diagnoses that we have yet to receive.

A nurse wearing Red Sox scrubs pushes the door open. The fact that it's opening day for the team is completely lost on me, but that explains the news show that has been interviewing players on a constant loop on the television hung on the wall. We are close to Boston. That would make sense.

"Mrs. Rivers?" The nurse looks through black-rimmed glasses as she pulls down her mask. Ryan grips my hand and glides up to a standing position beside me. A silent agreement fills the air between us. We are in this together.

Piper arrives on the other side of me, closing in on our threesome. I let my gaze fall toward Matt who is now standing, waiting for his name to be called. "Is this about the accident? My wife...my wife was in the accident too." He runs a hand down his face and itches his chin, a nervous tick.

The nurse looks down at a clipboard, lifts a sheet and nods. "I only have the information on Lily Rivers right now. I'm sorry, sir."

Ryan steps forward sensing the woman's confusion. Two separate families in the waiting room, one major accident. What are the chances the patients were together? Knowing a little bit about how a hospital operates, I know that she may not have been here when the intake forms were filled out. That nurse, may be long gone, sleeping off her midnight shift and having nightmares about the accident victims she treated the night prior. "Ma'am...Nurse—" Ryan searches for a name tag.

"Jane McGuinness." She smiles patiently.

"Jane, thank you. This is probably really confusing but...we're neighbors." Ryan waves a hand around the room, covering the section of the waiting room that they have taken over as their own. "Matt Sullivan is Evie's husband, and she was in the accident with our daughter Lily."

The information forms a rising wave of emotion over Jane's face. First confusion, then a pause to calculate the situation, and finally, understanding. "Oh, okay. Well, I'm sorry, Mr. Sullivan, I'm only assigned to Lily Rivers' case. But I'll let the other case manager know and you should be hearing from the doctor soon."

Matt wipes another hand down his face, looking around the room frantically, waiting for my approval. He wants me to give the go-ahead that it's okay for him to join us for the update. He wants to be with us when we find out Lily's status. But for the first time in our lives, we have to do something on our own. I can't help but think that this is the start of a long line that will be drawn between our two families, a forever boundary resulting from an unexplainable accident.

"I'm sure they'll be out soon, man." Ryan places a palm on Matt's shoulder and pulls him in for a man hug that spans longer than the one slap on the back kind of embrace they normally give. This night will either make or break our relationship with the Sullivan family, I can feel the gloomy anticipation thick in the air.

I pull us forward, my cue for the nurse to move along and bring us back to see the doctor. Once we are in the long corridor of the hospital, Piper, Ryan and I walk so closely to one another, it's as if our ankles are tied together in one of those relay races we used to do at the kids' birthday parties.

8

Before

JULY 2011

Evie

It's only eleven o' clock but we've already put in a full day of activities. The day kicked off at nine, with red, white, and blue mimosas at the Rivers' house. Then we all walked down to the town's annual Fourth of July parade. Pulling wagons decorated as tiny ships, our group of adults were dressed in anything related to the ocean. I held a red Ariel wig in place with a gloved hand while pulling Liam in a ship embellished with blue and white crepe paper and a cardboard sail spray-painted white. FYC for Flagport Yacht Club was painted in red letters diagonally down the sail, matching the shirts Lauren snagged from the special events office. Lily and Jack marched ahead with a gaggle of other children, all wearing sailor caps and holding a mishmash of props including fishing poles, nets, lobster stuffed animals, and the infamous sea creatures from The Little Mermaid. It was as if Disney, the Flagport Yacht Club and the movie The Perfect Storm crashed together and spit us out and onto the streets of Flagport.

The parade was everything I had imagined of a small town. Old military vehicles driven by veterans, a group of kids driving mini cars mimicking the Shriners, and every community group in town marching in the parade or on the sidelines waving mini flags. Lauren's status in town earned us a spot at the front, right behind the town council members who were tossing full-sized candy bars to the crowd, after they gave our kids first dibs.

"You'd think we'd been living here for decades." Matt leaned into me as he walked, smiled and tossed candy toward the sidewalks that wound through town.

We'd only been in Flagport for just over two years, but we were already blended in with the Flaggers thanks to the neighborhood we landed in. "I wonder where we would be right now if we opted for that house on Peach Ave."

"The one with all the old people?" He joked and nodded toward the intersection we were headed toward. "We'd probably be in the back of that Humvee with the World War II vets."

"True story." I thought about how close our little families had gotten over the past year. Not a day went by that we didn't talk. The Rivers and the Sullivans. It was when we spent all day on a group text during last winter's storm that I knew we were more than just neighbors. We weren't just talking because we were conveniently placed or passed each other by while taking out the trash. We were talking because we enjoyed each other's company, were at the same stages in life and had similar senses of humor. Although, I'd learned in that short amount of time that Lauren valued perfection a lot more than I did, always making sure everything had to look perfect and at times I thought she was a little too involved in Lily's life. The girl was only eight, but she seemed to have everything planned out for her, from the clothes she wore to her detailed schedule, every hour accounted for and filled with a sport, a task, or an activity. Lily, the good girl that she was, went along with everything her mother said, but part of me worried that maybe it was because she didn't know any better, and one day it would come back to haunt Lauren if she kept up the tight grip she had on the child. I know a thing or two about being controlled by a parent on some level.

Now, as we walked up the hill to the top of the street where our two houses sat like guards of the private road between them, I was already exhausted. The early mimosas and the full-sun forecast provided nothing for my energy levels, but I was looking forward to the rest of the day's activities. Anything planned by Lauren was a success and was bound to wake me up.

"What can I help you with?" I ask between gasps as we reach the edge of our driveway.

"Honestly, everything is taken care of," Lauren says, not the slightest bit out of breath. She is a solid fifteen pounds lighter than me, her arm muscles evidence of the daily hour she spends on her Peloton and her weekly Pilates classes at the posh boutique gym in town.

"You always say that."

"That's because she stays up until one a.m. the night before she plans these shindigs, making sure everything is in place," Ryan adds as he catches the end of our conversation.

"For your information I was up because Piper wet her bed and I needed to make sure her sheets were changed, and she was sleeping in the right position, so she didn't do it again."

"Is there a certain position that prevents bed wetting?" Matt interjects, naturally curious and showing his gullible side.

Ryan pulls Lauren into his underarm, swaying side to side with her. "According to Lauren there is," he teases, looking down at her rolling eyes. "According to Lauren there is a sleeping position, a rule, and a time and place for everything with our children."

"Enough! You spend all day with them and then tell me how my rules are holding up," she demands.

"I didn't know you were so type A," I chime in adding to the teasing.

"Only when it comes to the kids." Ryan raises a finger, correcting my reference as Lauren pulls his arm out from around her. I notice a faraway glaze to her eyes as we stand in a circle between our homes. "You're looking at future helicopter-mom-of-the-year award right here."

Lauren is unfazed by the ridicule and straightens her posture out. "Someone's gotta take control around here," she says.

Jack tugs on my hand. "Mommy, Lily has a Slip n' Slide! Why can't we get a Slip n' Slide?"

"Speaking of…Evie, why don't you help me set up the Slip n' Slide. That's something I haven't done yet."

"My pleasure, as long as that means we don't need to get one." I laugh as I look down at Jack, who is now grinning ear to ear.

"Our yard is your yard, Jackie." Lauren reaches for Jack's hand, and grips Lily's hand with her other, and the three of them lead us to their backyard.

The Rivers are expecting eighty people throughout the day. Some staying all day, others stopping by between other events, and then a group of late arrivals would come just for the fireworks. We aren't oceanfront in our neighborhood, but the Rivers have a second-level deck that overlooks the town and offers a view of the fireworks just as they are at their peak explosion in the sky.

By the time the Slip n' Slide is lubed up, there is a line of kids clad in red, white, and blue swimsuits, ready to take a turn on the extra-long, banana-yellow chute that reaches nearly the entire length of the yard.

"What did you do, tie five of those things together?" Matt arrives behind where Lauren and I are standing, amid several other moms.

"Just two." Lauren looks ahead, hands on her hips, proud of her work. "I promised Ryan I'd only duct tape two together this year." She turns to me and winks, and I can't help but melt at the sense of belonging I feel. I look around the yard, taking in the social circle that we've been dropped into, and I'm happy. I'm happy my children will have friends within walking distance to grow up with. My childhood as a military brat didn't allow for long-term friendships. Everyone was moving and shifting directions at a nonstop pace. So, when I see my kids building their own friendships in our neighborhood, I'm beyond happy. They will have what I never did. And if the last year and a half has shown me anything, maybe it's not too late for me to find the friendships I missed out on.

46

"She doesn't mess around." I elbow Lauren and laugh, just as someone tugs on her other elbow and hands her a cocktail. A girl I've never met before pulls Lauren into a hug and the two of them release screeches of delight. It's clearly a surprise visit based on how Lauren is giving her a friendly interrogation about when she arrived and all the details surrounding her flight . I notice a resemblance and it takes me thirty seconds to realize it's Lauren's sister. The one who moved to New York after she graduated high school. The girl's hair is the same texture but with fatter streaks of blonde, opposed to Lauren's more natural dirty-blonde tones. It's shorter and cut into long layers that land at her chin and fall back into her face after she pushes it behind ears that hold tiny turquoise balls. She grabs Lauren's shoulders, assessing her from head to toe, like two long-lost friends. It occurs to me that I haven't heard of a visit in the two years we've been living here, and I've been pretty privy to the Rivers' life highlights, always allowed in on their calendar of events, whether I'm attending them or simply learning of them. A visit from a sister was never mentioned.

I stand there like the outsider that I am. Having a sibling is something I always wanted. As I watch Lauren and her sister rehash their lost time together and catch up in a way that only siblings can with inside jokes and covert language, it's clear to me what I'd been missing out on my entire life. A built-in friendship, a safe space to talk about a shared past, while keeping a pulse on the present with the joint effort of two colleagues adhering to the same mission statement.

As if on command, Lauren's dad enters the yard. He's a man that can't be missed, with the height of a giant. I was introduced to him as Michael McCue, and directed not to call him Mr. or Sir, when I first met him. Much like Lauren, her dad made me feel welcome, with his natural curiosity about what landed us in Flagport, accompanied by warm eye contact and attention to detail. Every time since then, he's greeted me like an old friend, checking in on my sons by name, and priming our conversations about my landscaping business and Matt's sales work.

The two girls turn toward Michael, and I notice that Lauren's sister got his height, as she stands at least a half a foot taller. "Well, looks like the band is back together." His baritone voice cuts through Bruce Springsteen's Born in the USA lyrics.

"Hi, Dad." Lauren's sister leans into her father, embraced by his bear hug.

"What's this?" He points to the luggage that sits upright at her feet.

"Well, I thought I could stay here tonight." She turns toward Lauren. "Of course, if it's okay with you. You know, maybe we can have some late-night sister bonding."

Lauren's eyes expand into two saucers, and they sink into a level of confusion I've never seen in her before. "Of course. You know you never have to ask."

"Yeah, but she has to ask me." Michael winks. "I'll allow you to leave me for one night, but I want you sleeping under my roof for the remainder of your trip. There is nothing I love more than having my girls back in our home." He pats her on the shoulder and pulls her into his side, before he leans over and drops a kiss on her head. "It's been too long, kiddo. But I'll let you girls catch up."

Michael turns toward me on his way to the bar. "Well, hello there, Ohio...Megan, have you met our new friend? This is Evie."

Lauren steps forward, taking over the introduction. "Evie, this is my little sister Megan, and Meg, this is my friend Evie, from across the street."

"Friend!?" Michael bellows. "The Sullivans are practically family now." He pulls me into a side hug and scans the property for Matt, who is fully immersed in timing the kids as they race down the Slip n' Slide in what appears to be a contest. "Where's that good-looking husband of yours?"

Just as I point in Matt's direction, Lily races up the yard, wet strings of hair whipping left and right held at the top by the swimming goggles that are pushed onto her head. She jumps up and into Megan's arms, wrapping herself around the woman like she's climbing a fire pole. "Lily Lamb!" Megan spins her around, unfazed by the wetness that presses against her from the striped one-piece patriotic swimsuit. Megan sets her down and assesses her dripping body. "When did you get so big?"

"I'm eight now!"

"I know…have you been getting my monthly presents?"

"I'm pretty sure she's wearing one now," Lauren interjects, as she plucks one of the straps on Lily's suit, letting it snap back into place.

"And it looks beautiful on you."

"Lily, your turn!" She is summoned by Matt, who is at the bottom of the slick yellow slide, pointing to the timer on his watch. Ryan stands by, flagging her down with one hand and clutching a beer hugged by a red *Raging Rivers 4ᵗʰ of July* Koozie.

"Gotta go, Auntie Meg!" She pulls her goggles down, spins around and rockets down the hill, and without pausing, bellyflops onto the slide as effortlessly as an Olympic diver.

"That kid is amazing." Megan stands beside Lauren, arms crossed over her chest as she takes in Lily's antics. "Where's the other little angel?" She looks around the yard, searching.

"Being not so angelic." Lauren points to Piper who is pulling a popsicle out of another toddler's hands with fierce determination. She races toward her, ready to correct Piper's behavior, leaving me side by side with Megan.

"So, you live in New York?" I turn toward Megan.

"I'm currently living in Parkchester in the Bronx. Can't quite afford Manhattan." Her smile reaches her eyes and I notice a slight gap between her two front teeth, different than the perfect rows that sit in straight lines in Lauren's mouth.

"Yeah, I hear it costs a fortune to live there." As I say the words a wave of confusion washes over me. Megan comes from the same family as Lauren and it's obvious the McCue family is steeped in money; this is not only headlined on the name that is on nearly every billboard and flyer in town but confirmed by Lauren herself. While she has never openly bragged about her family's finances, she did mention that Ryan loves being part of a quasi-small town rich family and he fits in well. And I'm certain this entire yard was paid for by Michael McCue himself.

"Drinks, ladies?" Michael is back with a tray covered in drink concoctions that are layered in red, white and blue and accented with a skewer that stabs strawberries, blueberries, and mini marshmallows. "I figured I'd help the bartenders out a bit. Maybe we can get this party started a little faster." He winks and waits for us to select a drink from the tray.

"Thank you." I push the glass to my lips and taste the blend of pineapple, cherries, and vodka.

Megan waves the drink off. "No, Dad." She responds in a way that says he should know that she doesn't want a drink. She presses the water bottle to her lips and ingests the liquid with force.

Michael turns his back on Megan and smiles at me. "Don't forget to eat the fruit after it soaks in the booze." Another wink, before he turns himself around and weaves through the groups of adults, passing drink after drink, until he disappears.

"So, what landed you in New York?"

With one arm across her chest and her gaze steady on the yard below, she responds with a lack of enthusiasm, as if during the last five minutes she was deflated of air. "Oh, I...I left. Just wanted to go somewhere else, so I picked the big city."

I had made the assumption that she went to the city and stayed the same way everyone else did. College, followed by a big job opportunity, aspiring actress. Seldom did you hear about someone sticking around into their early thirties when they weren't still dreaming of being on Broadway or working for one of the many major businesses that mark the city. My interest was piqued. "What do you do for work?"

"I'm a freelance writer." *Okay, maybe she is an aspiring artist.*

"That must be interesting. I had some writer friends back in the day. Do you work for any of the literary agencies or publications? It's certainly the place to be for that kind of thing."

"No, I dabbled in the whole agency thing, but I settled on keeping it simple, so I write for random companies that hire me for newsletters, blogs, that type of thing." She let out a light giggle. "Actually, oddly enough some of my most loyal clients are in Boston. Go figure."

Just as I'm about to pry further, she's sidetracked, lost by a familiar face in the crowd. "Evie, I'm so sorry, but I think I just saw my old high school sweetheart." She turns toward me, resting her fingertips on my forearm. "If I don't come back in ten minutes, promise you'll come pry me away from him?" she pleads, a new side of her shining through.

I watch Megan march toward a gas fire pit that is surrounded by four Adirondack chairs, all filled with moms who are much younger than her. There is no one that fits the description of what I imagined as an old flame.

BY THE TIME the fireworks start, everyone is buzzed from the hours of endless bar service, conversations have transpired from defined and friendly to erratic and forgetful. Lauren's softer side has come to life as she's squeezed my elbow while passing by as she addresses party affairs and mingles with guests. A squeeze on the arm as I walk by, her head leaning away from her conversation and into my side as though she'd rather be conversing in a quiet room with me alone. A moment by one of the fire pits where we sat solo talking about whether or not we would've been friends if I had grown up in this town too. *Yes, yes, we would have.* We'd come to the obvious conclusion tipping our heads back in laughter and clutching arms. Although, I'm not fully on board with believing that she and I would have been tight in high school. I'm pretty certain I wouldn't have run in the same, rich circles she did.

The only ones remaining at the party by this point are the diehards who managed to survive hours of socializing paired with cocktails and parenting in the hot sun. And then, a few stragglers who came just for the fireworks, after they spent the day bouncing from one party to the next. Every conversation is exchanged with blurry lines and unclear stop and start points. And that is when I conclude that the Fourth of July is the biggest party holiday in this town.

Matt walks sideways across the yard, the flames of the fire pit reflecting a glow on his face. "Where are my boys at, woman?" he jokes in an octave higher than his normal voice.

"Um, I thought you had them?" I survey the yard, on the hunt for two brown-haired boy mops of hair, but only see a blur of adults, teens, girls and boys that don't belong to me. "Where is Lauren?"

I hear her before I see her and she's directing everyone to the upper deck. "Fireworks up here, everyone! Come get your popcorn!" Lauren mimics the voice of a circus employee. I maneuver myself up the stairs, moving sideways when necessary to fit between the cluster of people carrying chairs. By the time I get to the top, Lauren has blasted Fire and Rain by James Taylor, swaying sideways along with a group of other parents, clutching their kids in front of them. Lily and Piper are nowhere to be seen and I quickly concoct an image of them running out into the street unattended, or wandering into the woods that meet the end of the road.

"Lauren!" I push myself between a beanbag filled with kids, outlined in kernels of popcorn, and an older couple dancing. "Have you seen Lily and Piper?" Something inside me knows that they are with my boys, the four of them having become inseparable.

"Yeah, my mom's got them." She tilts her head to the side, as if to say *I got this. Don't doubt me.*

Matt, who had followed me up the stairs, is now lost in a conversation with Michael and a guy I've never met before. I head back down the stairs and walk through the open sliding doors that spill into their open concept living room and kitchen. The interior of the house looks empty, everyone outside anxiously awaiting the firework display. I hear the tune of Twinkle Twinkle Little Star echoing through the house and walk through, following the sound until it gets louder. I step quietly on the white tiled floor, the scent of left-over hotdogs and pie hitting my nostrils as I pass by the colossal kitchen island that marks the middle of the kitchen. I tip-toe down the hallway, following the black and white photos that highlight the Rivers family over the years, the sound getting closer, until I land in the entryway of Lily's room. Even though the girls have their own separate bedrooms, they each have double-size bunk beds in their rooms for sleepovers, which often happen nightly when Piper gets scared and sneaks into Lily's room. Now, I witness a different use for the bunks. I step closer and recognize Jack's thick mass of hair protruding from a My Little Pony comforter on the top bunk, one hand beneath the side of his face, and opposite him Lily is the mirror image, facing him with one hand beneath a cheek and a curtain of blonde hair resting on her temple and spilling on the comforter.

Lauren's mom sits in a pale green glider in one corner of the room, so still I almost miss her presence. "Aren't they precious?" she says.

I step further into the room and crouch in front of the lower bunk, where Piper and Liam are sprawled out, two starfish lying still in a sea of rainbows. Unlike the older kids, they've tossed the colorful comforter off them, the bottom sheet a canvas for their tangle of arms and legs. "They are." I look over at Mrs. McCue, a blanket pulled across her lap, her shoulders covered by a white shawl that greets her navy-blue tank top. Still at her age, she is simply beautiful, always coiffed to perfection and anytime I've been in her presence I've only ever observed her emit a calm demeanor, as if she has life figured out. Maybe that is how people with deep pockets feel. As if they can catapult themselves to another, all-knowing level. "Thank you for keeping an eye on them." I lean forward and push a strand of Liam's overgrown hair off his forehead.

"Oh, it's my pleasure. It's not easy being a parent. The days are long as they say. So, every now and then, it's okay to take a break and let someone else do the heavy lifting," she says, and then seems to get lost in the colors of the afghan on her lap. "You know, Lauren isn't the easiest on herself, and things have a way of staying with you and coming out in your daily life, so any chance I get, I offer my babysitting services. I just hope that she takes enough breaks for herself, reflects on her life and how far she's come."

Her words line up in my head in order, but they still don't make sense. *Why did Lauren come so far? What is she referring to?*

I wonder for a moment if Mrs. McCue has had one too many

patriotic cocktails, but remember that she doesn't drink alcohol, a requirement from a medication she's on. And then, as I stand, a boom punches the air, followed by a crackling sound that dims in seconds, and then a dozen hoots and hollers from the top deck above us.

9

Before

JULY 2011

Lauren

"So, how are you doing?" Megan asks me after everyone has left the party. The hidden meaning is not lost on me. She's asking me because we're alone. Ryan is in the backyard picking up the remnants of the party, the kids are sleeping, my parents are gone and every ear that could pick up on her undertones is out of reach.

I brush it away like I always do. "I'm fine." I wipe down the countertop even though a crew of cleaning ladies were here throughout the night, hired to pick up dirty dishes, take out trash and keep things looking pristine. "You know... staying busy. The girls keep me moving nonstop." I change the subject as fast as I can. "How is New York?"

She catches on to my transfer of the spotlight, the shift that puts the attention on her. I don't want to talk about me. She's the only person who knows every little detail about my life, every morsel of my past that has made me who I am today "It's good. My apartment is tiny, but it fits. My life is pretty boring, but I like it that way."

Of course, she likes it boring because boring is everything the McCue family is not. No, the McCue's take every opportunity they can to flash their success, although what lies beneath is often covered with niceties and kindness, the charming ways of the family name.

"You know Mom and Dad would happily hand you some cash to get a bigger place, Megs." I broach the subject that has been broached a thousand times before.

"I'm good." Now it's her turn to change the direction of the conversation. "So, your new neighbors seem pretty nice."

"The Sullivans are great. A breath of fresh air really."

"I could see that." She dips a tortilla chip in a bowl of what is now hardened queso, and wrestles with the cheese until she has a solid layer on the chip. "I think Evie is good for you." She stuffs the chip in her mouth and uses a fingertip to wipe away the crumbs that cling to her lower lip.

I know why she is saying that. "Because she's nothing like the rest of our family."

Meg nods as she chews and passes me a look that needs no explanation. She would give anything to be part of another family and would trade in the McCue riches for rags in a heartbeat. We look great on paper. Born and raised in Flagport to a father who not only succeeded in selling properties on the north shore, but a man who has consistently dominated the Boston real estate market for nearly fifty years, his father before him founded the business that launched a snowball effect of successful property purchases and sales. My mother fits the part of Flagport wife with her perfectly coiffed hair and attachment to every committee in town, her polished smile that she flashes with care and concern to the other affluent families in town. The way she is soft-spoken with a layer of confidence that projects the image she wants the world to see...that she is both kind and capable. She loves nothing more than being seen with my children, being gifted the opportunity to look like a doting grandmother, her patience bubbling to the surface as if she is actually acting the part of dedicated matriarch instead of actually living it. Because if everyone knew the real truth about what my mother and father are capable of, how they can turn on someone on a dime, they probably wouldn't be so damn respected now would they? They are constantly doling out money for scholarships and fundraisers, nailing everything it takes to earn a stamp of approval in a place like this. And while Meg and I were raised in comfort and wealth, we weren't fed with silver spoons that made us appear entitled or pretentious. We were raised with values. We just had a lot of support for those values if one of them happened to slip here and there. We were never told no, but there were times when we were told 'not now,' so we built up our patience muscle enough to be able to blend in with the rest of the world. "So, when are you heading back?"

"Tomorrow. First thing." Meg aimlessly swirls the spoon in the big bowl of queso, her gaze trained on the thick yellow substance.

"Dad's not going to be happy about that."

"Well, I don't live to make dad happy."

The comment stings me. I know she didn't mean to direct it at me, but I feel it all the same. She sees my neck pull back, and my eyebrows raise.

"I don't mean that you live to make him happy, I just—"

"I know what you mean, Meg." I slap my hands on the counter.

"You don't have to stay and do this dance, Lo." She drops my nickname into the conversation just like she did anytime she was trying to reason with me as a kid.

I allow my bitterness to surface. "I don't have to stay?" I hiss, throwing my arms in the air. "I don't have to stay *here*? You think I can just up and move my family away from the town we're settled in? You know, Meg, not everyone can just leave, not everyone can tear themselves away from the surroundings where their best and worst memories were made. Maybe I wanted a family so I could try to right the wrongs in my life…to give back to my two children in a way I would've never been able to do if I up and left for New York on a whim because I was upset."

"Lo, that's not what I mean. I just hate to see you be their puppet."

I turn away from the counter and dig through the cooler until my hand lands on the last water bottle, its label now peeling off, the personalized sticker now smudge red letters. I'm mad because I know she is right. I shouldn't be here, giving my parents the satisfaction of having a daughter in town, especially one who attends all the events, hosts the parties, and dances from social circle to social circle, making all the right moves so no one questions why both of their children didn't pack up and move away all those years ago. Only one of us did. But, the only way I could heal was to recreate the life I should've had. Now, I have two daughters like they had, except I'm going to make sure they don't make a mistake that will stay with them for a lifetime.

"For me, this was the only way I could move on. By having a family and building a life to make up for the ones I ruined—"

Ryan pulls the sliding door open just as I say the word. "Ruined what, honey?" He smiles, thinking this is a fun-loving conversation, and I go along with it, because that is what I do.

"Oh, I feel like I ruined that queso. It's just not spicy enough." I take a swig of the water bottle as I catch Meg's gaze, her eyes searing into mine. I can see the thoughts spinning through her mind, her ideas about how I should tell Ryan about everything that happened in our past. To her, it would be an obvious conversation to have with your spouse, but we are very very different.

And then, I watch her eyes soften and settle into the role she always does even though she doesn't want to. "Yeah, it could've been a tad spicier, sis."

"I thought it was delicious, honey," Ryan stabs a finger into the bowl of queso and chews the hardened cheese before he takes two long strides in my direction and rests his hands on my hips, planting a kiss on my lips.

"Get a room," Meg groans as she walks by us and heads to the guest room upstairs.

10

After
APRIL 2021

Lauren

The antiseptic smell in the hospital corridor greets my emotions with a handful of memories. The birth of my two girls, each one the start of a hospital stay that consisted of bonding and settling into a brief stint of postpartum depression, followed by random bursts of joy. Lily, always one to calculate situations before stepping into them, and think before she speaks, spent days debating her arrival date. She teased me with contractions that lasted forty-eight hours, just strong enough to send a wave across my waistline, but not close enough to launch into labor. When she finally did arrive, she was a sturdy newborn, with an immediate penchant for breast milk, tugging on my nipple with determination, and content to fall asleep on me with a full tummy afterwards. That first time I held Lily I knew that there was nowhere else I wanted to be, and when she looked up at me and locked her gaze on my crying eyes, I was certain that this little girl would always know what she wanted in life. She was my one chance to make things right.

Piper, on the other hand, made a much different impression. Like Lily, she came on her own terms, but when she did, she bolted into our lives like a hurricane, accurately forecasted but with much more force than expected. Instead of the easy breezy hospital entrance Lily demonstrated, Piper came fast and furious, her peak contractions hitting just as Ryan and I were stopped in the Boston tunnels where construction was well under way. A blur of orange cones and police officers directing traffic twisted through my vision as the contractions came full force. A call was made to the hospital. *I think I'm going to deliver this baby now. What do I do?* And then cancelled when a lane opened up, pushing us through the tunnel at the same speed Piper was moving through the birth canal. With Lily, I chewed on ice chips and had time to settle on the hospital's TV channels, but with Piper, I had the help of a maintenance worker rubbing my back and guiding me up the elevator and into the birthing room, followed by a bout of vomit, just minutes before she came barreling into the world.

"Mr. and Mrs. Rivers, you can have a seat here, Dr. Keen will be in shortly." Jane stands in front of a small empty room, both hands stabbed into the front pockets of her scrub shirt. "Is there anything I can get you in the meantime?" she asks as we file into the room and take a seat on the mauve cushions anchored by wooden arms and legs. It all looks bland. Even the rainbow mural painted on the wall opposite where our party of three is sitting, looks dull and colorless. I won't be able to see the pigmentation of blues and violets, greens and yellows, until I know that Lily is okay.

"No, I think we're good," Ryan answers for us. His grip on my hand hasn't slackened the slightest, since we ventured out of the waiting room. On the other side of me, Piper leans backward, the crown of her head resting on the wall, her neck bent like Silly Putty.

"Mom?"

"Yeah, honey." I keep my eyes trained on the door, afraid that I'll miss the doctor entering. As if he'll just blow by the room, forgetting to update his most critical family members. I assume we're his most critical and I tell myself that it's not a fact. Lily could have a broken arm for all I know.

"What if she's dead?"

The word lands flat on my heart and I unravel at Piper's blunt words. I turn to my youngest daughter and hiss, as Ryan grips my hand tighter. "How dare you say that? Do you have no heart?" And in that moment, I want to strangle her, ramble off a million inappropriate words because what she said is what has been torpedoing through my mind since I got the call. What she said is my biggest fear.

"I'm just—"

Ryan rises from his seat, letting go of my hand and trading me in for Piper. He crouches down in front of her like he used to when he coached her softball team, and she struck out. The same crouch he dropped down to when she got in trouble for putting Comet in Lily's shampoo as an April Fool's Day joke. He's always had to explain things to her that were obvious to everyone else. *You never bring up death when your sister could quite possibly be dying in the hospital. You never put a substance that could blind someone in a shampoo bottle.* Common sense was never Piper's strong suit. She was great at living in the moment, spying the magical snapshots in life that passed most people by, and she was a born artist, creating beauty out of nothing on blank canvases. But she was not someone who walked through everyday life armed with natural common sense that drove her decisions and actions.

I sink deeper in the chair and turn my body away, dropping my head in my hands and slouching like a bored teen, trying to avoid hearing the niceties Ryan is coddling Piper with. She's heard them all before. He's always been the one who has had more patience with her, and if our family was made up of two sports teams it would be me and Lily against Ryan and Piper.

When I see a flash of white between the partially open blinds on the door, I forget the last five minutes, and push myself upright, my body heavy with emotion, as if I'm physically weighed down from the pressure of the unknown. The doorknob twists with a click and a middle-aged man appears in front of us.

"Mr. and Mrs. Rivers?" He takes two steps forward and turns toward Piper. "Would you happen to be Lily's sister?"

"Yes, yes, this is Piper." I rocket from my chair, readying my body for an emotional bullet.

"Please, Mrs. Rivers, take a seat." He sits down, turning his chair so it's angled toward us. *It's never good when they sit.*

Ryan is back at my side, gripping one hand, while my other one slides into Piper's, the three of us a newly defined team, the past slice of discomfort from Piper's question all but forgotten.

"I'm Dr. Keen. I've been with Lily since she arrived last night." *Please tell me you weren't with her when she died too.* He crosses one leg over the other, a gesture that only confident, older men do. His black full head of hair is speckled with gray slivers and his skin is tan with etched lines that extend from the outside of his eyes. He has the eyes of a golden retriever, deeply brown and pinched together on the edges. "I apologize for the wait. We're understaffed as I'm sure you've noticed, and for whatever reason, last night was a record-breaking busy night in the ER. But, I assure you, your daughter is in good hands."

I'm overcome with a wave of confusion, unsure whether I'm lightheaded or if I just discovered that I'm dreaming in one of those rare events when you can wake yourself up if it's bad or keep yourself in REM if it's a really good dream. I inhale with my entire body, squeezing Ryan and Piper's hands tighter, as Dr. Keen continues.

"When Lily arrived in the ER last night, she was still conscious, however; she experienced severe head trauma when the cars collided." He clears his throat as I push the picture of Lily being tossed around the inside of a vehicle out of my mind. "The impact caused swelling in her brain, and to ensure she remains stable, we had to put her into a medically induced coma."

As soon as the words register, a wave of nausea crashes over me. I bend forward and dry heave. Seconds later, Ryan is holding a trash can in front of me and I'm vomiting up last night's chicken dinner, the meal I ate while sitting across from Lily as I lectured her to be home on time that night. She was going to an end-of-year party, just a group of friends celebrating their college acceptance letters. She'd been to gatherings like this dozens of times, always with me lecturing her and instructing her on the importance of being safe and being home at curfew. So why am I here learning that Lily's brain is swollen? I've always gone above and beyond to protect my children, to prevent them from having to face a situation that could drastically alter their life path. Ryan has always teased me that I was a helicopter mom because of my stringent rules and the obsessive tabs I've kept on my children. The word "coma" spins through my head, pinching every emotion along the way. Anger at myself for letting my daughter go out, frightened by what this means, but the one that lies thick and heavy in my heart and more prominent than the others is sadness. A deep sadness that is laced with some semblance of karma.

11

Before
SEPTEMBER 2012

Evie

I always expected it to be a sad day when I sent my baby to first grade. I know that I had a tough time leaving Jack, my first baby, going off to a new school in a new town. But he carved his path in the hallways of Flagport Elementary School and had a handful of playdates lined up within the first week of school. For Liam it's different. I'm less sad and more nervous. Less melancholic and more fearful. He's the wild card in this family, the one who requires more structure, more rules, and overall, more attention.

So, when I meet Lauren at her front steps where we plan to take our annual first day of school photos, with the four kids, I don't share the tears that are cascading down her cheeks. Instead, my emotions parade through my body differently. My hands twitch with nervous energy, my mouth is dry from the fear of the unknown. *Will Liam act out in class? Will he make friends, or will the other kids think he's weird? Will he say something inappropriate?*

No, I'm not sad. I'm scared.

"Why is this so hard for me?" Lauren embraces me in a hug then steps back and swats at her tears with one hand while gently dabbing her nose with a tissue in the other hand.

I feel guilty for not shedding tears, but I'm afraid that if I do, it will throw Liam off course, and he will be pulled into my emotions. He, out of all kids, doesn't need any more emotions causing turmoil in his mind. First grade isn't like kindergarten. He's going to have more stringent rules and less free passes. It's a full day instead of a half day. It wasn't rare for me to be pulled aside at kindergarten pickup to be informed of a complaint, followed up by a passive aggressive suggestion. *He's been having trouble focusing. Does he spend a lot of time in front of the television? He was a little too aggressive with another boy in class. Is he watching shows that have violence? He doesn't seem as interested in the curriculum as the other kids. Have you been working on his letters and numbers at home?*

"Because your baby is heading off to school," I answer Lauren.

"Then why aren't you crying?"

For a plethora of reasons, but I don't share the one that is front and center in my mind. "I'm not a big crier," I say.

"I'm literally just learning this about you, and we've known each other for over three years!" Lauren allows herself to laugh, and then takes a deep breath in and rolls her shoulders back. "Get it together, Rivers," she says to herself, as she heads toward a black bag at the bottom of the steps. "Okay, kids, time to lineup. You know the drill. Babies in the front, big kids in the back." She ducks her head through the open strap of the pricey professional camera she always pulls out for these occasions, letting the beefy piece of equipment land on her chest.

"Mom, we're not babies, we're going to first grade," Piper retorts.

"You're still a baby!" Lily rests her hands on a chagrined Piper and plasters a perfect smile on her face, tilting her head the way she's been trained to do.

Liam, the shortest of the four kids, is still pressed against my side. I have to physically move him to the front of Jack, who is clinging to the straps of his backpack with a big goofy grin stretched across his face. He looks like a silly schoolboy compared to perfect little Lily. "Lily, I need you to tilt your head a little to the left more and then twist your neck, so you are looking right at the lens. But lift your chin some more. Look proud."

Lauren's demands on Lily are par for the course. She's always angling her and positioning her like she's a doll, making demands of her activity calendar and triple checking her homework, as if she is some sort of windup doll. Truthfully, I'd always admired the attention she gives Lily. I wish my own mother had been that attentive to me. But there is something happening right before my very eyes. I watch as Piper shifts uncomfortably. She looks to her mother as if she's awaiting the same instruction that is being fired at Lily. *Why doesn't Lauren focus the same attention on Piper as she does Lily? Is it because she is older?*

Per Lauren's suggestions, we get to the Flagport Elementary School early. "It's always a zoo there on the first day," she says as we all pile into her SUV, another one of her suggestions.

She navigates her way through the town, and we pass by the police department, a brick block that sits on the corner of one of the main roads of town and across the street from the baseball field, where Lauren told me she had her first kiss when she was thirteen. In what feels like a minute, the town has stripped itself of its summer sheen, and is now dressed in a full-on business suit. Kids dot the sidewalks, all walking with more of a purpose than they had just two weeks ago when summer was in full swing. Brand-new backpacks bouncing on their backs like loose turtle shells, some hold tight to a parent's hand while others move a few paces ahead on bikes and scooters maneuvering the bumpy, in some places crumbling, sidewalks. I watch as a kid with too much confidence, races his scooter over the cracked cement that surrounds a tree. He flies over his handlebars and hits the pavement. "Wipeout!" Jack yells from the way back of the SUV, where he and Lily are sitting. They upgraded to the 'cool seats' at some point this past summer, on their mission to get space from their younger siblings during our joined family trips to the beach.

Lauren pulls up in front of the school, in a section of the

driveway that isn't outlined with parking lines. As we all tumble out of the car, I notice that no one else is parked in this section. It's a prime spot five feet in front of the bus parking and directly in front of the sidewalk that greets the row of first-grade classrooms.

"Bye, Mom!" Jack says as he heads down the sidewalk toward the fourth-grade classrooms.

Lily starts to follow him but is stopped by Lauren grabbing her arm. "Lily!" She crouches down in front of her so she's eye level with the girl. "Remember what I said about using your manners and make sure you raise your hand and answer questions when Mrs. Bowen asks, okay?"

"Yes, Mom." Lily starts to turn but is stopped again by Lauren.

"And make sure you eat all the fruit I packed you. Do not trade your lunch for sugary treats."

"Yes, Mom!" Lily lets out a long sigh and turns again, trailing behind Jack.

Piper and Liam stand in front of me, and I can't help but notice how Lauren's neck cranes up and out like a giraffe as she follows Lily's every move, until she blends in with the swarm of students entering the door that leads to the fourth-grade classrooms.

12

Before

SEPTEMBER 2012

Lauren

Sometimes when I look in the mirror, all I see is Lily's face. She is a spitting image of me, with the same dramatic cat-like eyes, the strong jawline. Even our hair matches, although mine costs a fortune to maintain the gentle streaks of blonde against the light brown backdrop that is currently falling forward in my face when I look back at myself in front of the mirror. The middle part I'm currently wearing provides two curtains for my eyes. I push them back, and my emotional wreckage becomes evident in the puffy bags that sit below my eyes, which are now two angry slits, a repercussion from my tears. I've never been a pretty crier. My Irish descent shows itself when I shed a single tear, forming bubbly puffs of red on my cheeks as if I'm allergic to something. In all the irony there is in the world, I'm pretty certain I'm allergic to myself. I dig the pads of my fingers into my shoulder, a habit I've incurred over the years, anytime the pain acts up. It tends to grow painful when I'm in the midst of an emotional state, as if my inner-energy drums up my painful past, resulting in a physical sensation. I remember how that cast felt on my arm and all the way up to my collar bone. It was so confining, but oddly enough I remember liking it, because it made me feel trapped, and that was how I knew I deserved to feel. Deep down inside I knew I should be in jail. Any other person would've gotten sent to the slammer. Sure, I was too young to actually go to a real jail, but even if I had been of age, I know I wouldn't have been put behind bars. It's one of the perks of being a McCue, after all.

As I watched Lily trail behind Jack today toward her new fourth-grade classroom, I was weighed down with the reality that she is getting older. And with that comes this idea that I'll need to put a tighter leash on her to keep her safe. Piper will be fine, I have no doubt about that. She's like her father and she'll skate through life swaying with every new friendship and job, adapting easily as if she is a chameleon changing color to fit in with their environment. But, Lily, she'll need me to protect her and keep her safe. She'll try to please people much in the same way I have my entire life, she'll give up herself so she can blend in with others and in that process, she'll lose who she really is and was meant to be. Great. Unless, of course, I steer her in the right direction.

I pat the pillows that frame the underbelly of my eye and dab some moisturizer followed by the best under-eye cream on the market. This magical cream cost a fortune, but it's as necessary as the organic food we eat in this house and the top-of-the-line furniture I've selected for every room in my home. It's yet one more opportunity to conceal who I am and show the world what I'm not. *Perfect.*

"Hello! Hello! Hello!" Several voices all at once pull me away from myself for a moment. I smooth my hair and blink my eyes multiple times, confirming the cream has done its job. I pull the bottom of my boutique top down and ready myself for my next act of the day. Hosting a group of moms for the annual "Mommy Mimosa Morning." It's something we do every first day of school, a tradition that started long before my children were in school, but an annual event I took upon myself to lead. After all, if I'm not busy doing things and controlling situations, then I think about the past. Quite frankly, the idea of having mimosas first thing in the morning is a tad ludicrous but it helps me keep up appearances, and it makes me feel as if I'm just like every other mom out there unattached to a haunting past.

I pad down the stairs and see Evie and a handful of other moms surrounding my kitchen island, lifting quiches onto plates, pouring orange juice and champagne into their glasses. Some like to imbibe on this day, others do not, which is why I have a selection of boxed coffees brewed from Flagport's best cafes, lined up alongside the delicate white cups engraved with an R.

"Helllllo, ladies!" I march toward the crowd and go to work pulling other items out of the fridge. Gourmet cheeses for a break-fast charcuterie board.

"We are free!" Annie Whitcomb raises her hands in the air and pops a quiche in her mouth, following it up with one giant swig of the mimosa that is balanced between her French manicured fingers. She's always loved the freedom of sending the kids off to school. I suppose if I had five children, I'd feel the same way. But I'm never sure I'll feel okay with having Lily out of my sight.

"Amen to that!" Several other moms shout as they clink their glasses together in celebration of what they believe is a joyous occasion.

I smile and slice the cheeses, nodding my head when appropriate.

"Lauren, relax!" Annie says, attempting to take the knife from my hand. "You're always moving, always doing. Take advantage of the deep breath you can take now!"

"I know, I know. I guess I'm just a bit sad about it."

"But they love school." Another mom, Whitney Ford, speaks up, "At least my kids do. I think they actually enjoy being away from me."

I think about Lily wanting to be away from me and it fills me with blackness. I don't know if I'll ever be able to handle the day she wants to be away from me.

"And besides, Jack and Lily are together in class and Liam and

Piper are together," Evie interjects. "They have each other." A ripple of confusion stops her train of thoughts. "Speaking of, how did that work out anyways? What are the chances both our kids would be in the same classes?" She pushes her eyebrows together, a question forming on her face.

"You're joking right?" Annie says as she refills her mimosa glass, topping it off with extra champagne. "You don't know Lauren Rivers very well, do you?" She twists her neck toward Evie, and I know exactly where she's going with this.

Evie, the naive newcomer to town, widens her eyes like an innocent schoolgirl.

Whitney slaps her hand on the table. "Lauren made it happen!"

Evie turns to me, and I'm instantly filled with guilt. She's the only one who still sees me as somewhat genuine. Not someone who cuts corners by using connections. Surely, she's seen some perks of my McCue name, but I didn't tell her just how many favors I could pluck from this town. "You did?" she asks.

"I'm sorry." I raise my eyebrows and put on my best innocent face.

"Sorry!? Why are you sorry? We gotta keep our kids together!" Annie adds.

Evie sidesteps and I see it in her face before she responds. She's uneasy about this. I should've checked with her first. But, she'll never tell me she's mad. I know that about her too. "Oh, oh that's fine." She looks around and smiles at the other moms, showcasing her approval of the situation, but there is something unsettling in her gaze when it lands back on me. "How did you pull that off though?"

Before I can answer with a response that makes me look more innocent than I am, Whitney steps in. "How does our Lauren do anything she does? With those fine McCue connections!" She dances toward the other side of the counter and adds some ice to her glass.

"Yeah, Evie, I figured you knew Lauren better than that," Annie says. "Not a single thing happens without her having a say, and I'm proud to call you my friend!" She leans toward me readying her glass, so it clinks with my coffee cup. I smile back but I want to sink into our natural-stone flooring and disappear. I'm doing exactly what I promised myself I wouldn't do with my life. I'm using my McCue connections as my get-out-of-jail-free card, controlling every situation that comes in my path. I wanted Jack to be in the same class as Lily so I could hear about any updates whether she told me or not. I wanted to be able to keep tabs on her, and this was an extra layer of me being able to do that. And then, I had to ask Mr. Reid, the superintendent of schools, to also keep Piper and Liam together. It was only right. Not that it mattered much, but I caught him at a good time, when he was on the golf course with my father.

13

After

APRIL 2021

Lauren

"What exactly does that mean?" Ryan steps forward, taking charge. I'm completely incapable of accomplishing anything right now. Words can't even surface. All I see is my little girl, and every single perfect piece of her. Her timid yet confident ways, her remarkable intelligence and willingness to accept everyone for who they are and what they believe in. She's nothing like the family I grew up in, and I made sure to instill these values in her. Even as a teenager she is an easy child to have. Forgiving to a fault, and more loyal than anyone I know. I can't live without those things. I can't physically walk through a future that doesn't include Lily's laugh. I can't bear to move through life if Lily is not in it...or if she's not the same human she was last night when I saw her walk out the door. Images of my daughter bed-ridden and limited, ripped of everything she's worked so hard for, taken away in a moment. I know that I'm not being rational, and I should be strong and sturdy like Ryan, but my body starts doing something I have no control over. I convulse, my insides shudder with every breath I try to take in. I don't know if I want to hear Dr. Keen's response. Maybe I'm safer in this in-between zone, unknowing.

Dr. Keen waits until I gather myself, and with Ryan's help I sit up straighter, my body going against everything it wants to do right now. "It means that we wait and watch. We monitor her 24/7 and when we feel like she's ready, when the swelling has gone down and the intracranial pressure has lessened, we gradually withdraw the drugs that are keeping her in the coma and, she hopefully regains consciousness with little to no brain injury."

"Little to no? What does that mean?" I ask.

"It means that she could walk away from this accident completely fine, back to her normal self, but we always have to consider that there is a chance that the accident caused more brain damage than we can see now." Dr. Keen's leg slides off the other leg and drops to the floor. Two navy-blue Brooks running sneakers peek out from beneath his baggy scrubs and I'm reminded once again of what I'd be missing if Lily doesn't come out of this the same. Will she ever run again? Since she was nine years old, she's been participating in fun runs, taking the sport more seriously when she got to high school and made varsity track and field as a freshman. She had planned to focus on her studies when she went to college in the fall, foregoing the sport but she'd made sure to announce that she would always be a runner. *It's the only thing that keeps me sane, Mom.* So young and she already understood what brought her joy, committing to never giving those things up. Anytime she was pinched with pain or stress, she would hit the streets running. "When she wakes up, we'll be able to administer a series of tests on her to determine her mental and physical capabilities." He pauses, steepling his fingers together in his lap and continues. "Mr. and Mrs. Rivers, Lily is young and healthy, so you have that going for you. I know that it's easier said than done but try to stay positive. And I assure you we have an amazing team in there watching over her. I'll keep you updated with every new detail we receive."

The word *accident* repeats itself in my head. For the last several minutes the only words I could register were "brain injury," and I forgot the entire reason why we are here.

"What happened?"

Dr. Keen gives me a curious look, considering the question that lands between us out of order. It doesn't take him long to register what I mean. "It was a two-car accident. Based on the information we have so far from the police department, the car Lily was in, was t-boned by another car in the middle of an intersection. I have no doubt that the blunt force of the car's impact is what caused Lily's head trauma." He says the word trauma, reminding me of the severity of my daughter's injury. The word trauma isn't used for broken bones, cracked ribs, and whiplash.

"What happened to the other passenger? The other driver?" I ask. I want someone to blame, someone other than myself for allowing her to leave the house at all last night. I'm her mother, I make the rules. This is my fault.

"I'm afraid I don't have that information. I'm Lily's doctor only. HIPAA laws don't allow me to share information on other patients even if I did know."

"It's just that, our friend, our neighbor is here too. He got a call his wife was in an accident," Ryan intervenes, knowing exactly what I'm trying to get at.

Dr. Keen gives him an understanding look. Two neighbors in the same accident even though their families had no idea where they were. "I'll try to get some information for you."

Ryan gives my hand another squeeze. "Thank you, Dr. Keen. When can we see her?"

"Does right now sound good?" His golden retriever eyes turn upward on the edges.

"Yes, yes please." Ryan sounds like a potential buyer following a realtor into a new house. He tugs me up to a standing position. *Yes, honey, let's go see our dream home.* The only difference is that this is more like a nightmare and hesitance runs through me when I think about seeing Lily in this state. How will I react to her unmoving body? Piper stands on the other side of me and grips my hand, and the three of us walk down the antiseptic hallways once again, this time armed with more answers that may have aged us a decade.

The route to the intensive care unit passes by the window that leads to the waiting room and I catch a glimpse of Matt, his head in his hands, with Liam and Jack bookmarking him. I forget that he is in the same situation as us, except it's a wife and mother, not a child and sister. He is steps behind us, still not knowing what state Evie is in, and my heart goes out to him, but I have to look out for my family first.

We follow Dr. Keen deeper into the dungeon of the ICU, his small talk with Piper marked by beeping machines and doctors being paged over the intercom. An older man walks in the opposite direction as us, with his arms around a woman, likely his wife, consoling her. He's holding on to the words the doctor beside them is spouting off, medical terms and diagnoses, that likely meant nothing to this man until right now. Is it a daughter or a son they are here to visit? A sibling? Surely, it's not a parent. If it is a child of theirs, at least they are older, their child likely a full-grown adult who has experienced life. My Lily has an entire life ahead of her. She has mistakes to make, lessons to learn, love to experience, fun memories to build. There are so many pieces of her that still need to be built and put together to make her whole. So many firsts that need to be had.

When we get into the room, I focus on the nurse who is adjusting the IV bag. She changes the fluids out as if she is changing a trash bag, a simple, everyday task. The sucking and beating sound of the ventilator breathing life into my effervescent, always-very-much-alive daughter, infiltrates my insides and forms a boulder in my throat.

But, it's not the multitude of machines circling her bed that I notice, it's not her limp body that catches my attention. It's the gauze that is wrapped around her head, covering her long dirty blonde hair, that has fallen down her back and whipped in her face since she was a little girl. I step forward when my arms are tugged ahead by Piper's and Ryan's steps.

Even when she's asleep she's beautiful. It's a thought I first had when she was two years old and her eyelashes had stretched and darkened, framing the same cat eye that I inherited from my own mother. When she slept, those lashes would rest delicately on her skin, her lips would part like an open heart, just like they were doing right now. Except now, from where I stand, several feet away, I can tell her lips are cracked as they circle the ventilator tube, chapped from the stale hospital air, the dehydration her body is likely going through. Sick people always seem to have chapped lips.

Ryan starts to sit on the side of the bed. "Are we allowed—"

"As long as you don't disconnect any of these machines, you can sit down there," the nurse, predicting what he's going to ask, answers him, as she adjusts the opposite side of Lily's body, raising a limp arm and placing it gently on the mattress. I wonder if they take such care when the family isn't in the room, or do they drop limbs, and turn the body with less caution. "I'm just doing my hourly adjustments on this beauty, so she doesn't get any sores," she says matter-of-factly, before she pats the side of the bed that she just worked on and looks at me. I make up my mind that this nurse is a good one and I'm immediately drawn to her deep brown eyes, her smooth brown skin, her full lips that manage to smile without her having to move them, as if her face is in a naturally happy and calm state at all times. I wonder if that's her way of conveying to us that everything is going to be okay. She takes pride in her job and I can tell this by the way she keeps one eye on the monitor beside Lily's bed, and one eye on us while she speaks.

I step forward and drop into the spot like a feather landing on the ground, with Piper tight to my side.

The nurse starts to walk out of the room, then turns. "Oh, and talk to her. From what I've experienced, talking to the patient helps." She shrugs her shoulders and I catch black cursive words that I can't make out from where I sit, tattooed on her forearms.

And this is the moment Piper's reality sets in. She leans into me and manages to fit her bottom on the small space of bed between me and the tubes that coil like snakes.

"No, no, this isn't right." Piper's voice is louder than I expected, and I have the natural inclination to quiet her down, as if Lily is sleeping and will get rudely woken up at the sound of her sister's voice any second. For years I watched Lily stumble out of her bedroom in the morning, angry about her little sister's screeches waking her up too early. What I would give to see that miffed eye roll that would make its way across Lily's face on those Saturday mornings, her hair matted down on one side. It was always the left side, ever since she was a toddler, curled up in a fetal position with her left cheek pressed to the pillow and hands tucked beneath in prayer position. "She hates things on her head." Piper leans forward and I stop her before she reaches for the gauze that adheres tight to Lily's skull. Ryan erupts from his side of the bed, vigilant of Piper's growing grief. He knows I don't have the physical strength to keep her off this bed, and one wrong move and she could detach any one of these mystery machines that pump and beep all around us. Piper has always moved slowly, and she's usually last to catch on to a joke, but in the handful of times I've seen her emotional about something, it's as if her body takes on another personality. It moves at a faster pace than normal, erratically catching up with reality in a way that is so opposite of who she is at her core.

Ryan's face tenses, he knows what he's about to be up against. It was similar to how she reacted when her beloved baby bunny died when she was nine. He hugs her from behind, pinning her arms to her sides before she can reach for anything with careless arms. Her thin lips are made even thinner, as they pinch together in one straight line, while tears cascade down her blotchy cheeks. Her shoulders shimmy as she tries to escape Ryan's arms. "She's not supposed to be here!" Her scream pierces the air, muffled between the gasps and sobs, but I can make it out. "Lily, wake up! Wake up!" She recruits the help of her legs and starts to kick, just as a nurse walks into the room. By the look on the nurse's face, this isn't a reaction she's ever seen before. She jumps into action and throws her burly body between Piper and Lily, she's a barricade protecting the delicate machines and wires that keep Lily alive. She presses the call button somewhere on the wall. Ryan moves backwards, continuing to pin Piper's arms to her sides, but she's still in a state, throwing her body in every direction, spitting with every word she yells. I'm not sure who she's fighting with but I guess she's angry at the world right now, angry at the sight of her older sister who was always the protector, the ultimate fort maker, the straight-A student, the admirable athlete. She thrusts her head back and hits Ryan in the nose, sending an immediate river of blood over his lips and down his neck, just in time for the security guards to come in and assist. He reaches for his nose and accepts a box of tissues from the burly nurse.

I'm dreaming. I'm dreaming. This has to be the worst nightmare I've ever had. Wake up, Lauren, wake up.

There was only one other time in my life when I felt that the situation at hand simply couldn't be real. This only happens to people in movies, sad movies that are made to evoke emotion. This can't be real life. Maybe that's why I'm frozen in place, still sitting on the side of the bed, unable to move, unable to help my husband with his bloody nose, or calm my younger daughter down. I've lost every ounce of control and I no longer know who I am.

14

Before

DECEMBER 2013

Lauren

The Sullivans front door is dressed up in a massive wreath, embellished with holly berries and poinsettia leaves. I expect nothing less from Evie. In the four years since we've known each other, every holiday has involved something handmade with flowers, plants, and succulents. The woman is the Martha Stewart of landscaping, constantly wowing our circle of friends with the elaborate centerpieces she manages to make with only a glue gun and flowers handpicked from her garden. Everything I have hired someone for in the past, Evie can seem to put together effortlessly. Sure, I can come up with fabulous ideas for memorable events, thinking up wild entertainment themes and seat placement, but Evie has this innate ability to recycle products and plants to create gorgeous pieces, most of which can be used more than once. The first time the Sullivans joined our group of friends for our annual Friendsgiving, Evie ended up giving the ladies a private lesson on how to make pumpkin centerpieces. While the men circled the fire pit, and the kids roasted marshmallows in our backyard, Evie demonstrated how to carve a pumpkin and use it as a vase for an array of autumn-colored flowers. She handled the carving tool with such ease, it made the rest of us look as if they were slaughtering a chicken. Which for many of us, it was similar to that—a foreign act—a do-it-yourself project. Flagport women were experts on hiring help for every little task from watching their children, to paying bag boys at the grocery store, from lawn care to private chefs.

"Why are we entering through their front door again?" Ryan asks, his two arms weighed down by four Christmas gifts. The question is an obvious one, as we typically use the side door that greets the driveway.

"Because this is our first official time at their house for an event," I say the words matter-of-factly.

Ryan raises one brow, and it hovers above his round blue eye, a signature move he used to seduce me back when we first met. It started out as an expression that he unintentionally used to get me in the bedroom, but over the years it transformed into a new meaning. *Whatever you say, boss.*

The sound of the deadbolt clicking back and forth several times is followed by the pitter-pattering of footsteps on the other side of the door before it swings open. In the entryway, Jack and Liam bounce up and down like jumping beans, the grinch faces on their matching pajamas peer at us with disapproval. "Yay! I knew it was you guys. You wore them!" Liam says, referring to the matching pajamas that Lily and Piper are wearing. The two girls push me and Ryan aside and squeeze into the front door, ready to get the annual Christmas exchange started.

I hold a platter of bacon-wrapped scallops with one hand and a bottle of Cabernet with the other. As I'm about to step up and into their living room, Matt appears from the kitchen, accepting the plate and wine, allowing my hands to free up so I can remove my long, white peacoat. "Front door...seriously? I thought we were better friends than that." He raises his eyebrows in sarcastic disapproval.

"Her idea." Ryan points to me as he drops the bags by his feet and leans into Matt for a repurposed man-hug that is free of the grip, pull, hug movement and replaced with a gentle shoulder bump, both cautious so Matt doesn't disrupt the plate of appetizers.

We both present Matt with a little jig to accompany our matching footie pajamas. Ryan pulls on his zipper, bringing it down just far enough to show off his hairy chest and Matt blocks his eyes. "Dude, I've seen enough."

The four kids are already on the floor at our feet gathered around the gift bags and pulling out the paper. "Hey! Stop it you vultures. That's for later!" I lift the bags up and march them over to the tree on the other side of the living room. After I set them down in the back of the tree, making sure the kids have to struggle to get to them, I find myself standing in front of the display, consumed by the ornaments. It always feels like getting a sneak peek into someone else's life, the ornaments from the past telling a story. My mother always had our house in pristine condition, and she never held onto the outdated ornaments. Instead, they were replaced every year by whatever was trendy. Some years it was all white bulbs and others it was blues or strewn beads and popcorn. Looking at Evie's tree, I'm envious. I pinch the bottom of a ceramic frame clearly made by a child. At the bottom of the frame, red puffy paint spells out the year 1988. Being a tad younger than me, Evie must've been around seven when she made this. The plastic that normally covers the photo is gone, but the picture is still tucked into the homemade frame. Evie sandwiched between her two parents in front of a Christmas tree. Surrounding that ornament are dozens of others that hold different memories. A piece of construction paper, yellowed on the edges, and made into a snowflake dated 1986 and then several made by Liam and Jack, marking every year of their lives. Seeing this makes me bubble with resentment. My mother never liked knickknacks, she didn't hang our art projects on the wall or clutter the fridge with our drawings. Everything had to look perfect for everyone besides the people who lived there. There was no place for scribbled paper on her gleaming countertops where she set rows of embellished martini glasses during her Flagport Women's meetings. There was no place for our sloppy clay sculptures on the white doilies that dressed the table centered in the dining room. The only photos that made the wall in my mother's home were those that were professionally done. A canvas painting of Meg and I, where we are wearing matching blue dresses clung to the wall above the intricate fireplace. Meg and I always joked that we looked nothing like the painting. Instead, the massive portrait that took up several feet on the wall, appeared to be showcasing two dolls, poised properly with tilted heads and perfected smiles.

A Christmas tree tells a story. But stories must include a full plot, and in my family, we have a tendency to remove bits and pieces of plot lines, switching up characters and heroes and minimizing the inciting incidents where we should be held responsible.

"Hey, stranger!" Evie walks up behind me.

"Merry Christmas!" I pull her into a hug, taking in the scent of peppermint in her hair, feeling the soft flannel of her pajamas. Evie feels like home. A home I never knew.

"Merry Christmas." She steps back. "You know why I'm calling you stranger, right?"

I offer her a confused expression.

"Because only strangers come through the front door." She circles her head and expands her eyes into two brown saucers.

"I thought I'd be professional and make a *real* entrance." I follow Evie into the kitchen, the blended scent of savory and sweet getting stronger with each step.

When Evie steps into the kitchen, she turns around with raised brows. "Is that because this is our first official time hosting an event?" She rests her hands on the red apron that billows out at her hips. She's all curves where I am not, all bronzed skin where I am more of a pale rosy, that is often covered up by a very pricey bronzer.

"I did not say that!" I laugh at the ongoing joke between the two families. They are always over at our house, and it's not because they haven't offered up their home. It's because I always insist on it. I love being in control of an event, and all the steps that go into preparing and putting on a show. They think it's me being friendly and giving, but it's really me having to have control. "What can I help you with?"

"Absolutely nothing. You just sit down and have yourself one of my signature cocktails." Evie waves a red and green snowflake patterned hand towel in the direction of a large crockpot and a self-serve cooler.

"Ohhhh, what do we have here?" I sashay over to the counter. I lift the lid on the crockpot and inhale, taking in the scent of cinnamon and apples. "Gosh I can practically taste it." I use a nearby ladle to fill a glass mug. I would've had this themed and labeled accordingly, but that is why Evie and I balance one another out.

"Is it too strong?" I take a sip, letting the rum hit my palate, burning my throat as it goes down. "Not too strong for me."

Evie fills her own glass with the concoction in the cooler, a Manhattan mix of some sort. "Did your family serve this for the holidays growing up?" I ask. Sometimes I think I know nothing about Evie's background, the mystery of her not being from Flagport serves as an added layer of intrigue. Ryan has often accused me of being the biggest presence in a room, and I make it a point to put the spotlight on Evie for once, even if it's just the two of us in the room. It's not by choice that I take up space. According to Ryan, my family just takes up more space than anyone else. *It's not that you talk a lot, it's just that people are intimidated by your name, and they let you lead.*

"My dad would always make Manhattans. He wasn't a big drinker but he loved a Manhattan around the holidays and since we were always living in different places, we had to change up the type of whiskey we used," Evie says. "So, when we were in the South, well, there were a lot better options of whiskey than say when we were in California." She winks. "He even made me virgin Manhattans so I could clink glasses with him and Mom."

"That's so nice. Your dad sounds like a great guy," I say as I picture a young Evie celebrating with her two loving parents in the comfort of a home that isn't tainted by money and prestige.

"Yeah." Evie holds my gaze longer than normal, pausing as if she is dreaming about being back in her memories.

I let out an exhale, which brings her back to the present. "I'm sure my holidays were nothing compared to yours growing up." Evie passes me a genuine smile, unlike the envious ones many of my other friends share. "I just love your family so much." She leans against the counter, her new highlights shimmering against her natural brunette hair beneath the overhead lights. Again, she turns the conversation over to my family and life. Over four years into our friendship, and I know little about Evie's background besides her ability to transform yards into beautiful works of art and her parenting skills. And of course, her loyalty. She's been utterly loyal to me in a way I probably don't deserve. It's what makes her stand out from my other friends. She could give or take my name and my money, but the others...well, I know they use me. I'm okay with that. I suppose it's the least I could do.

"Mom! Liam is opening the presents!" Jack's voice slices through the room.

"Oh crap!" Evie sets down her drink and marches into the living room. Ryan and Matt are sitting on the couch with pints of beer in their grips, unaware of what is going on only ten feet in front of them. "Liam!" Evie drops to her knees, gathering up the green and red tissue paper that Liam has pulled out of the bags we brought. Seconds before she reaches his arm, he removes the inside of the gift that was wrapped for Jack. A piggybank in the shape of a basketball I had specially personalized for him. It only takes another three seconds for Liam to lift it over his head and with the anger of a manic monkey, he slams it on the hardwood floor. Pieces of sharp orange ceramic slide in different directions, spinning and settling into place in slow motion. It's as if we are watching an accident unfold.

Matt rockets up from the chair, lifting Liam with one arm and swinging him up to a standing position. "Get in your room... NOW." Each word coming out as sharp as the edges of the broken pieces, that now sit stagnant. Tiny crumbles stick to the gift cards I added to the piggy bank before I wrapped it. Without showing an ounce of remorse, Liam stomps up the stairs and marks the next moment with one loud slam of his door.

"Oh my gosh, Oh my gosh, I'm so sorry." Evie shrinks to the ground, gathering up the pieces and putting them in the front pockets of her apron. She looks up at me. "I'm so sorry." Then, her attention turns to Jack. His lower lip quivers, his tan skin now a blotchy red, as one tear escapes his eye.

"It's okay, Jackie, we'll get you another one," Lily, sweet, perfect Lily says, as she takes his hand in hers.

I bend down, setting my drink on the nearby coffee table, and help Evie gather the pieces. I seldom get mad, but in this moment, I'm real mad. This isn't the first time Liam has acted like an out-of-control toddler. Even at two years old, both of my girls were better behaved than he is at seven. I breathe in reminding myself this mess is not Evie's fault and there are six other people here who are innocent. But that child is a monster. I am well aware that we don't get to choose what blend of DNA our offspring gets, but this moment solidifies any questions I've ever had about something being off about Liam.

I force a smile on my lips. "Oh goodness, it's okay. No worries." And I wave a hand in front of me like it was no big deal at all.

15

Before

DECEMBER 2013

Evie

After three more Manhattans, I'm at my peak buzz and I've numbed some of the anger I feel toward Liam. When he smashed the piggy bank on the floor, I was beyond embarrassed. Something like this would've never happened in Lauren's house. Her daughters are well-behaved, well-mannered, and seemingly perfect all around.

The kids are snuggled in one of the beds upstairs, watching Rudolph, while the adults are sprawled around the massive sectional that takes up our entire living room. I glide my fingers along the silver chain necklace that Lauren gave me. It has one simple wave charm and matches the one that dangles from her neck. After we all recovered from Liam's piggy bank massacre, we exchanged gifts and nibbled on an assortment of holiday staples. Pigs in a blanket, meatballs and pork pie, followed by cheesecake and a green mousse decorated with M & M's like a Christmas tree.

"Have I told you how much I love this necklace?" I announce for the fourth time over the past hour.

"Yes!" Matt and Ryan's voices blend together in one loud syllable that hisses at the end. They've spent the majority of the evening poking fun at the newfound "friendship necklaces."

"Should I check on them?" I start to push myself up from the deep couch cushion and fall back when they all object.

"No! It's quiet, they aren't breaking anything, so just leave them alone," Matt lowers his voice to a whisper.

"Haven't you taught her anything about never waking a sleeping baby?" Ryan twists toward Matt, exasperation layered on his face. It's always me and Lauren on one side and the husbands on the other, these were the habits we'd created in our little social circle, naturally slipping into patterns at all of the gatherings.

"Well, you know what they say about quiet kids. That's when they're up to no good," I say.

"Let's savor the moment when they can all be in the same bed together without us having to worry about what's going on under the blankets," Ryan says, ducking just in time from the pillow Lauren hurls across the room at him.

"How old does all that stuff start now anyways?" Lauren asks, and I can't help but be surprised that she doesn't already know the answer to this question. Since I've known her, I've been impressed by how she has a pulse on things before they happen. School vacations are always readily planned out, she has the 411 on every town activity involving the kids, and I'm pretty certain she had Lily's life mapped out from the day the girl started kindergarten. There are charts dictating goals that are strategically color-coded on one massive marker board in their kitchen, which makes me feel like I'm one of those free-range parents who lets their kids run around with zero rules attached.

"Change of subject...I'd rather not think about our children fooling around together. So, Ryan, how did you and Lauren meet?" Matt asks.

The story was an old one, they rehashed how they met on numerous occasions. "Well, you see, we met at a college diner. I was there late night, drunk and Lauren was looking all cute, reading away in a booth in the corner."

"Surely she was drunk too if she let you talk to her," Matt pipes in.

"Nope, she was as sober as a judge." Ryan sits up proudly.

"What were you doing in the diner alone in the middle of the night?" I ask.

"Oh, you know…reading," Lauren says nonchalantly.

"What college did you guys go to?" I ask.

"Kline College," Ryan answers for them. I don't show it but I'm surprised. I always assumed Lauren would've gone to one of the top-notch Boston schools. Surely she had the connections.

Ryan continues, "So, I slid into her booth, ordered a coffee and the two of us talked until we got kicked out the following morning at seven. The rest, they say, is history." Ryan crosses his ankle over his knee and smiles.

"And you graduated college and moved in together that following spring?" I recount the details I remember.

Ryan, again, as proud as a peacock, says, "Yep."

"Ryan had no qualms about moving to Flagport and becoming part of the McCue clan," Lauren teases.

"I don't blame you." I say louder than I intend, the Manhattans catching up with my inhibitions. "The McCue's are awesome. I want to be a part of that clan too. Will you adopt me?"

"They're not as perfect as you think," Lauren retorts, and I can't help but catch a sliver of resentment in her voice, as I notice her smile coming to an abrupt halt before it reaches her eyes.

16

After

APRIL 2021

Lauren

The sound of my own snores wakes me up. I look down at my watch and the date and time stare back at me. It's 5:15 a.m. I have to relive my reality all over again. The puzzle pieces slide back into place as I take in my surroundings. The cot beneath me creaks, as I roll onto my back and take in the yellow stain on the ceiling. It's the shape of a cloud. For a second I question whether I'm dreaming, but the smell and the dryness in my eyes presents me with my truth. I'm in a hospital. The smell of flowers and bleach hits my nose and the beeping of monitors and pumping of machines stirs my emotions. Lily. I'm here because Lily was in an accident. I wasn't supposed to fall asleep. I look back at my watch and do the math in my head. I fell asleep for two hours. It's no longer the day of the accident, it's the day after. The minute hand on my Garmin watch blocks the day, but I can see the date clearly. April 13. *The day Jessica Milburn took her last breath.*

The last thing I want to do is leave the hospital. It's bad enough I fell asleep for two hours when anything could've happened to Lily. She could've woken up reaching out for me, needing her mother. Or she could've struggled to breathe, and I may not have woken up in time.

I push myself up so fast, the cot legs slide on the linoleum floor and screech. "Ry?" I whisper. Ryan sits upright on a chair on the opposite side of Lily's bed, swiping through his phone. It's a Monday and I imagine he's checking work emails, rescheduling home viewings with potential clients, and that's when the thought strikes my mind. *My parents.* I haven't told my parents about Lily's accident yet. I fumble around beneath the blanket on the cot until my hand lands on my phone. And there, as I expected, are a dozen missed calls and texts from them. Of course, they found out about the accident. It happened in our town, *their town.* On a street I'm certain they frequent daily. The residents on that street are likely spreading the news like wild fire, filling the Flagport Facebook group up with comments and announcing their knowledge of the accident in the coffee shops and restaurants that serve as gossip hot spots.

Before I do anything else, Ryan answers the questions that are circling in my head. "Hey, honey, your parents are on their way. They've been calling. I tried to put them off until you got up, but I really wanted you to sleep." He stands up and makes his way over to me. "I had to answer and tell them what happened."

I nod. Of course, he did. He's their son-in-law, just as much a child of theirs as I am. And he adores them as much as he does his own parents, possibly more. Conflict sets in, and a tug-of-war plays out in my head. I need to get out of here, but I can't bear to leave Lily.

"Hey, do you mind if I go home and get some fresh clothes?" I ask.

I can tell that Ryan is shocked that I want to leave and remove myself from the space that holds my daughter. He may be part impressed by my release of control, but it's hard to tell as his own anxiety is pulling down on his skin, concealing the expressions that I've grown to know. The scowl he produces when he's angry, a rare emotion for him. The fluttering of his eyes when he is nervous about something, like the time he first met my parents. The way his eyes light up when he feels particularly connected while he is conversing with someone. All of those little traits seem to have washed away overnight, replacing my husband's face with blankness. "Sure, of course." He sets his phone on the ledge that greets a window leading into the belly of the hospital. "I'll handle your parents."

Those were the exact words I wanted to hear. I am in no mood to deal with my parents' assessment of the accident, pulled back into my own past. I am in no condition to deal with my father's likely demands on the doctors, requesting better treatment because of his name. I'm certain this doctor has no idea who he is considering we're outside the bubble of Flagport, in the closest nearby city that isn't quite as far as Boston, but my father, when he is determined, doesn't take no for an answer. And while it will kill me to leave Lily, I need to go to Jessica Milburn's grave, a pact I made with myself and committed to every April 13th for the past twenty-four years of my life.

I push myself off the cot and look down at Lily. For a second I question whether her head was slightly tilted to the opposite side last time I looked at her. Maybe she moved during the two hours I slept. But I'm reminded that I set my cot on this side for a reason. Because Lily was ever so slightly tilted to this side, and I figured I'd be more likely to hear her move or breathe or do anything if I was positioned on the side that her mouth was facing. These are the games you play with yourself when your daughter is on the cusp of life and death. I pull her slack hand to my lips and kiss it gently, brushing my lip on a piece of white tape that secures an IV to the vein beneath her middle knuckle. I make circles on the spot I kissed and make a mental note to get lotion to spread on her dried knuckles. I'll get her favorite. Bath and Body Works eucalyptus stress relief.

Ryan is now standing beside me. I lean into him, and I'm jostled when I think of the ticking clock. "I'll just go get some clothes for all of us. Piper too, just in case." After Piper's incident, we had her best friend's mom come and get her. In the past, I would've called Evie to come collect my panicked child but I'm not sure if I'll ever be able to do that again.

"Okay, take your time. If you want to lay down at home for a while, you could use some more sleep."

I'm not going to lay down at home. In fact, I'm only going home for show, to gather the items I said I would. The rest of my time away will be spent praying at Jessica Milburn's grave. Praying for her and begging her ghost to somehow give my daughter another chance, a chance that I certainly don't deserve.

17

Before

FEBRUARY 2014

Evie

The halls in Flagport Elementary School look as if they got taken over by the Valentine's aisle in the Dollar Tree. Red construction paper hearts tattooed with glittery names are strung along the walls with sparkly twine. Strands of pink and white crepe paper frame the hearts in two loopy lines. "Wow, they go all out here for the occasion. You'd think it was Christmas."

"Well, think about it…it's kind of a big deal." Lauren twists her neck toward me as a giggle spills from her lips. "It's the one day that these kids get to confess their love to their crushes."

"Isn't that awkward enough at this age?" I ask as I pause to adjust the box in my arms. Craft contents are piled high threatening to escape.

"Ahhh, I remember my first Valentine. Bobby Edelman." She sips in a breath of air and slows down her stride as if she's suddenly floating, mimicking a helpless schoolgirl.

"And where is Mr. Bobby Edelman today?" I turn toward her, as I lift a strip of cartoon heart stickers that escaped the roll and are coiling over the edge of the box.

My question pries her out of her dream state and snaps her back to reality like a boomerang. She swats a hand between us and scrunches her nose up as if a bad scent hit the air. "Oh, Bobby didn't turn out to be my knight in shining armor. Last I heard he's still living at home with his mom and dad over on Turner Road. And I'm pretty sure a lifetime of living on cigarettes and fast-food didn't do anything to help him maintain his football player physique."

"Oh, was he the high school jock?"

"Something like that." Lauren switches gears. "But I lost interest long before high school. He was a fifth-grade crush. I had a lineup of other guys to date after that." She winks in my direction, flipping her hair off one shoulder. "What about you? Was Matt always your one true love?"

The question splits itself in my conscience, as if I have a devil on one shoulder and an angel on the other. Like every time I've been asked prior, I lie. "Yeah, pretty much. I mean, there were crushes in each school I attended, but does that really count?"

Before Lauren can respond or dig further, we are greeted by Mrs. Leavitt. "Girls, thank God you're here. You two are a lifesaver." The teacher ushers us into the classroom, as the chatter rises. "Are you Liam's mom?" A little girl with two pigtail braids shouts.

I nod and smile. The energy of twenty-two excited kids seems to create extra heat in the space. Kids make me nervous. I don't have the same natural way with them that Lauren does, and then my nerves shoot up a level as a boy in the room yells loud enough to stand out among the escalated chatter. "Liam is a troublemaker. My mom says that he's a bad egg."

It takes me several seconds to register what the boy said. And another several seconds to adjust my jaw and close my mouth. I go from being hot to sweating beneath the red sweater I'm wearing for the occasion. I realize I'm no longer holding the box, but I'm clutching it to my chest, as if it can save me from the embarrassment this little boy has caused.

And then Lauren saves the day, like always. "Graham Pendleton." She tips her head to the side calmly. "I know your mom, and I know she would never, *ever* say something like that about our friend Liam."

Mrs. Leavitt, evidently well-versed in elementary school antics, shakes her head side to side, maintaining a stern, yet unaffected look on her face. "Graham, what do we say about not saying anything out loud if it's not nice."

The class, without any instruction, recites the saying in sing-songy, uneven voices. "If you can't say anything nice, don't say it at all."

I want to cry for Liam, but when I look over at him to gauge his reaction, he's smiling as if the boy has just complimented him. As if being deemed a troublemaker is the best title someone could attain. My mom guilt goes into overdrive and before Mrs. Leavitt lists out the rules for the class project, I've already paraded a series of questions through my head. *Is my son the class troublemaker? How would an eight-year-old kid know the saying 'bad egg?' Is my kid the one with the bad reputation? What have I done wrong as a parent? Am I not giving him enough attention at home, so he has to act up in class?*

As if Lauren can read my mind, she stops pulling the containers of colorful glitter glue out of the box and squeezes my elbow. "That kid is an asshole. I'll talk to his mom."

I was always the good kid, a role model student with perfect grades and a quiet disposition that every teacher loved. So, to hear that my kid is potentially a brat, has me fired up, but I wave it off like it's no big deal.

"Don't worry about it and please don't talk to his mom. I know kids will be kids." I recite the words as if I'm reading from a script. I laugh it off in front of Lauren, but my heart feels heavy in my chest. This isn't the first time I've physically felt my emotions churning inside my body. I feel it almost every time I look at Liam. It's not just when he's done something wrong or off-the-wall weird. I feel the weight of my emotions when I watch him sleep, when he interacts with others, and even when I take him for his annual checkup at the doctors.

Between Mrs. Leavitt and Lauren directing the class to the cookie decorating stations and the crafts, the students have forgotten the comment that still stings my insides. "Hey, buddy," I crouch down beside Liam and pour some Elmer's Glue into a Dixie cup.

"Hi, Mom." He sticks a finger into the glue and smears it on the back of the heart-shaped card stock. I take in the conversations going on around us, all of the other girls and boys seem to have a buddy to banter with, a friend who is laughing alongside their glue jokes and sharing in their messy fingertip delight.

I squeeze his shoulder as I stand up and walk toward another table, keeping my eye on him the entire time.

After the kids have completed their project and the cookies are decorated and half eaten, Lauren and I say goodbye to Mrs. Leavitt, who I have now deemed a saint for having to deal with twenty-two children she didn't conceive, on a regular basis. That woman should be paid millions.

"So, what the heck was that all about?" Lauren walks beside me, her tote bag bumping into my shoulder as she uses her hands to talk. "That kid is a brat. I knew he was a brat. How dare he say that?"

"It's no big deal. He's just a kid being a kid. Kids say that stuff." I say the words with more confidence than I feel.

Lauren hisses. "Well-behaved kids don't shout such things in front of a class like that! Do you think any of our four kids would say something like that?" I hide my curiosity that rises in me from her question. Liam is a wildcard and I never know what is going to come out of his mouth, but I don't need her to know I feel that way about my own son. I read between the lines. Lauren doesn't realize what she said, probably because it was unintentional, but I get what she is saying. Kids don't say things out loud like that, but everyone could think it. She's seen enough fits spun by Liam to know that he's not a well-behaved angel at all times.

She catches me lost in thought and she stops mid-stride. She grabs my shoulder and leans in. "Eves, he didn't mean it. Liam is a good boy."

The boulder in my throat has moved upward and it's pushing tears to the surface of my eyes. I try to stop them from coming but my lower lip quivers, giving way to the first of the tears to cascade down my cheek.

I'm about to confess everything I've worried about with Liam, I'm ready to pour it all in her lap, when an older woman waddles down the hallway, her gaze held steady on Lauren. "I think that woman might know you or something." I swat at the tears on my cheek, pushing them away like an embarrassed child.

Lauren twists her neck toward the woman, who is now making a beeline for us. "Lauren McCue, I thought I'd never see you again!" The woman beams.

"Hi, Mrs. Sacco." Lauren backs up slightly as the woman steps into her space, staring at her as if she's a ghost.

"My goodness! I never thought I'd see you again. It's been years!" Mrs. Sacco claps her hands tighter. "After you left Flagport High, I was certain you'd end up coming back. But it was like one day... Poof! Lauren McCue disappeared. And as you can see, I'm now teaching at the elementary school level. Can you believe it?"

As someone who has rarely seen Lauren misstep, or struggle with conversation and confidence, the fact that she looks rattled with nerves is not lost on me. *Was this teacher hard on her as a student? Did she forget to hand in a paper that she still hasn't forgotten about?*

"Mrs. Sacco, this is my friend Evie."

The woman turns to me, but only for a brief second to be polite and then she shines a light back on Lauren and her alleged disappearance. "So, what happened? How come you left Flagport High? You were doing so well! You were a cheerleader and gosh, I think you were at the top of the junior class back then."

"Oh, um...I finished up school at Pembroke Academy and—"

"Oh yes, that's right. I think I may have heard it through the grapevine that you were there."

Lauren's gaze wavers and her face flushes in response to the woman's words. And just as she's about to speak again, the bell rings, and kids skitter out into the hallways like marching ants, all headed toward the double doors that spill out onto the playground.

"Well, duty calls!" Mrs. Sacco shouts over the chatter in the hallway and Lauren grabs my arm and pulls me toward the exit, just as the woman's lips are moving and she's saying something else that I can't quite make out.

18

Before

FEBRUARY 2014

Lauren

When Evie asks me about my abrupt move to private school, I lie. I tell her that my parents were disappointed with the educational levels of the public school system and since we had the finances, they sent me to the best private school in the area... Pembroke Academy which happens to be two towns away.

"Wow, that must've been tough. Moving at the end of junior year like that."

"Says the girl who moved every two years as a military brat," I retort. It's a good comeback because there is nothing she can say about it. She knows the drill. You pack up your life and move to another school, rebranding yourself for a whole new group of friends. At least that's what I did. Flagport High was among the top five public school systems in the state for testing and quality of education, but I'm certain Evie hasn't had time to really ingest these statistics yet considering our kids aren't of testing age yet.

"Did you have to wear a uniform…like one of those skanky schoolgirls?"

I give her my best eye roll and change the subject. "Do I have glitter in my eye?" I turn toward her in the parking lot, as I swat at my under-eye with a pinky finger.

She leans in and investigates. "Hmmm, not that I can see."

"So, are you going to let me talk to that jerk's mother?" I ask, successfully changing the subject.

"Maybe that kid is right."

Evie's suggestion shocks me. "You can't be serious." I come to a fast stop and that's when I realize her face is steady, removed from expression. "Oh my gosh are you serious? You don't really think that Graham's mother said that."

She shrugs, defeat settling in her shoulders. "I don't know, I guess I just don't know about Liam sometimes." An uneasiness settles on her face. I know she's always been irritated by Liam's erratic behavior, but I suspect something different this time. Instead of the loud exhales and frustration of an aggravated mother, I see a severity in her features, as if she is actually debating whether Liam has a serious issue.

I tuck a strand of Evie's hair out of her face, offering a gentle touch when I see more tears bubbling to the surface. "What do you mean, Eves?"

A sheepish expression forms on her face as she says, "It's just that, Liam is so different than Jack and I don't know how to handle him sometimes."

She's not wrong. I've witnessed Liam say some awkward things and he's had more bouts of uncalled-for anger than I consider normal, but a bad egg? I don't know if I'd go that far.

"Well, my girls are different from one another," I add as an act of kindness. They are very different but not to the extent that Jack and Liam are. They are different in the way that Lily is exactly like me, and Piper is like Ryan. I've kept my mouth shut about how different the two boys look. Jack is a spitting image of Evie and I'm not quite sure where Liam fits in. Besides the smattering of freckles and lighter skin like Matt, the boy's other features don't seem to lean toward either one of them. I've witnessed other parents observing the differences between the two boys, but I've stayed away from offering my opinion on that topic. After all, I look more like some of my cousins than I do my own sister. I learned from personal experience that it's never fun to be compared to another person. Most of my childhood was spent trying to be like my older cousin, Kristen. I tried to dress like her, act like her, and do everything she did, until I realized I couldn't be her no matter how hard I tried.

"I know but not like Jack and Liam." Evie pauses, a light bulb going off in her head. And then she continues as if she was reading my mind. "Were you and your sister different when you were younger. I mean, you guys don't look a ton alike now, besides the lighter hair. But did you two act alike or were you opposites?"

She's looking to me for advice but I'm not the one to give it. I can't let her know very different we are. How when my family did the unthinkable, Megan left and basically never turned back. Besides the occasional visit, Megan is not a regular in my family's life anymore, and even though she points the finger at my parents, I take full blame for her absence. And here I am, fully immersed in the Flagport lifestyle, opening my palms when my father offers me money to solve a problem, and sharing in the same jovial conversations with the people of the town who look up to him, the same people who look up to us.

"We used to be a lot alike actually. But not so much anymore." I think about how Megan and I used to spend countless hours building forts in the woods behind our house, going against our mother's desires that we remain clean and tidy at all times. I think about how our bond only grew over time and unlike many sisters, I actually enjoyed her company and let her tag along with my friends, who were always older and cooler than she was. When she got into high school, I walked her to her first class and helped her navigate the hallways that were filled with intimidating upper classmen, and I enjoyed every moment doting on my little sister. Until she transformed from the happy-go-lucky tag-along teen to someone who was determined to stay away from our family forever. Unlike me, intentional wrongdoings were unforgiveable in her eyes.

19

After

APRIL 2021

Lauren

I head straight toward the cemetery, hoping to get there before a scheduled funeral begins. I always arrive there no later than six a.m. on April thirteenth, knowing that there are few, if any grieving visitors who arrive this early. Most people come when the sun is fully shining so they can lay flowers upon graves, knowing they will catch a ray of sunlight in the process, as if that is enough to rid them of the pain they feel from losing a loved one. This is my own assumption, of course. In the twenty-four years I've been partaking in this anniversary ritual, mostly on my own, but there were times when I brought Lily along before she was old enough to know where we were, I'd only seen walkers getting their morning exercise in the hilly cemetery.

I arrive five minutes after six. I made good time, considering I came from the city. Normally, I just have to drive through two towns and a lot of stoplights to get to the town of Bridgeton, where Jessica Milburn is laid to rest. I pull my hair back in a ponytail and tuck my loose layers behind my ears before I put the Red Sox hat on. The rearview mirror shows me a woman who is barely recognizable. Puffy pillows shrink my best feature, transforming my cat eyes into two slits, the whites no longer the perfect backdrop for my blue irises, and instead they are a map of red veins.

The irony of my daughter being in an accident the day before Jessica Milburn died, is not lost on me. I've lived the past twenty-four years walking on eggshells, waiting for karma to get me, filling my schedule with anything to take my mind off my past and using Lily as a focal point to somehow step beyond my grief. Now, as I look through the dew drops that run down my windshield, and take in the cemetery ahead, I am drowning in pain, layered in fear and a dozen other emotions. I reach over to the passenger seat and gather the bouquet I purchased in the hospital gift room, knowing that if anyone I knew saw me, I could say they were for Lily. I push the door shut with a hip so it doesn't slam loudly. I don't want to alert the residents in the houses nearby, their backsides facing the graves. I move ahead, keeping my gaze focused on the cracked pavement and patchy grass. Unlike the cemeteries in Flagport, this one seems to have skipped a few maintenance appointments. I take in a few purple flowers poking through the grass, the first signs of spring and I'm naturally brought back to all the Aprils when Lily and I planted bulbs in our yard. That may be one of the only times I allowed her to do something without me hovering over her. Looking back, I now realize that is why she seemed to love the annual activity so much. "Mom, when are we getting the bulbs?" She'd always ask the question around the time change in mid-March. I'd purchase several bags of bulbs from the Flagport Garden Center and drop them around the yard, letting her dig and bury them wherever she pleased. It didn't matter what type of plant or flower they were. What mattered was that Lily had free rein of something and we both celebrated when a surprise plant would inevitably sprout from the grass. Sometimes they were in the middle of the yard, and other times they would rise from the dirt that outlined the fence before the rest of the spring plants were placed by landscapers.

The idea of landscapers naturally causes a shift in my thoughts, and I think of Evie. Where I once had feelings of warmth at the sight of her smiling face, I feel pain. I cannot imagine how I can forgive her for picking up my daughter. How will I get past this? How will I move on when there is a glaring reminder every time I look out my window and see their side door through the space between the trees. Forgiveness is a tricky thing. After all these years, the only person I've really had to forgive is myself, and I have yet to do that. Instead, I cover up the hate I have for myself with perfection. They say that when you are hard on yourself, you're even harder on other people. Maybe that's why I've put so much pressure on Lily, because inside I'm beating myself up. Planting those bulbs may have been the only time I felt free of the jail cell I've put myself in.

I catch a tear slide down my cheek at the memory and swipe it away. The cement path that leads to Jessica Milburn's grave is crumbling in some sections, creating an obstacle for my feet. I make a mental note to make another anonymous donation to the cemetery, one of the many commitments that I've made to make myself feel better over the years. Throwing money at pain and brushing things under the carpet is such a McCue trait and I've somehow seamlessly adopted this way of life.

For the first time, I look up, gauging the distance from where I am to the grave, and that is when I catch an unexpected visitor crouching down at Jessica Milburn's plot. I'm caught, is all I can think, and I react quickly, diverting to the grave that is closer to me, just a few feet away from where the man is crouched.

I panic, and I set the flowers on the grave that reads *Greta Fortier.* Although he is a good ten feet away, I hear the man move, letting out a sigh as I watch his body rise to a standing position from the corner of my eye. Greta Fortier is old enough to be my grandmother, her life bookmarked between the years 1935 and 2020. She was eight-five years old when she passed, not far off from my own grandmother. I hear a sniff and the swishing of a jacket, followed by the man's voice, which sends my nerves into a game of bumper cars. "It never gets easy, does it?" His voice hits my ear. It's friendly, like someone making small talk in a grocery store checkout line.

I turn to him and that's when I realize who it is. I've never seen him in person, but when the internet sprung to life in the early two-thousands I searched for him everywhere. It wasn't until two years ago when he finally had some semblance of an online presence for his business, that I actually got to see his face. *Jeffrey Milburn.*

He looks more casual than his LinkedIn photos, where he is in a full suit, the face of a non-profit he founded. Assuming he was the same age as Jessica when they married, he would be around fifty-five now. "Yeah." I pause taking in waves of sandy brown hair with flecks of silver. He's attractive, even in his mid-fifties, and I'm certain he and Jessica turned heads when they were younger. I feel a lump expand in my throat, thinking about all the life she lost. "You're right about that." I try to act casual. Even though he'd likely never recognize me, I'm petrified he'll discover who I am and come charging me. He'll pull out a gun or a knife and kill me, in an eye-for-an-eye type of exchange.

I don't know what to say after that, but luckily, he continues for me. He wants to talk. "I still blame myself." He maintains his gaze on his wife's grave, and I take in the dates one more time, as if I haven't thought about them every single day since the day Jessica died. *January 27, 1965-April 13, 1997.* "I was the one who was supposed to pick up Katie from the sleepover." I let him continue even though I know his words are going to create more turmoil inside me. The least I can do for this man is listen. "She was only six. She was too young to sleep over a friend's house and we knew that her friend's mother would call us at some point, when Katie came to terms with the fact that she wasn't ready to be away from us for a night quite yet." He runs a hand down his face. I take in the lines that are deeply etched in his skin as if he spent decades of his life on a boat in the sun. "I made a mistake. I opened a beer, and by nine, I assumed we wouldn't get the call and maybe she was brave enough to stay for the whole night. So, I had a few more. I was fine when the call came in at 10:30, but Jessica, being the good mother she is…was—" He catches himself. "Sorry, I still sometimes think she's still here." He drops his head in his hands and I step closer when I see his shoulders shudder. I lay a hand on his shoulder, compelled to make him feel better while my own heart is crumbling, witnessing the pain that I caused. "I knew that she had trouble driving at night. She had this thing with her eyes where she couldn't see in darkness. Everything just blurred for her, is how she always described it." He sniffed and looked down at the ground, as if he was talking to Jessica instead of me. Or maybe he felt embarrassed by his tears, and he couldn't look me in the eye.

"That's not your fault." I find myself saying the words out loud, hiding the guilt that crashes over me.

"Oh, it's taken me a long time to forgive myself but, it still stings. Like if I could go back to that night. If I didn't open that beer, I would've been the one who went to pick up Katie in Flagport, and the roads and signs wouldn't have blended together. That's a forty minute drive, it's not like we lived right around the corner. She wouldn't have gone the wrong way down that one-way and crashed."

Jeffrey Milburn doesn't have to finish the story. I know what happens next. "We can't change the past." I preach the words that I should be telling myself.

"Yeah, and I'm just so grateful that Katie wasn't in the car. At least I still have her." I catch a glimmer of gold on his left hand and see a band. He answers my next question. "As weird as this sounds, I think Jessica would be proud of the father I became and I hate to say this, but sometimes I feel as if she's watching over me, even though I didn't watch over her that night." He clasps his hands and drops them on his worn jeans, and for the first time I take in the work boots he's wearing, and I remember his non-profit. The mission statement said everything I needed to know. He helps build homes for those less fortunate, an organization he launched when he felt the need to give back to the community of Bridgeton. "My therapist has helped a lot. I no longer think about the 'what-if,' and instead I put my energy toward the 'what now?' How I can help the living, and all that, you know. It's probably why I'm standing here talking to you. I've gotten used to talking to strangers about my pain. I suppose my therapist is right…it really does help."

Jeffrey Milburn is essentially a stranger, tied to me by the death of his wife, but sometimes it's a passing stranger who offers you advice that has the potential to change your life. "Well, I think I've used up enough of your time." He offers me a mock salute and turns away. I wait until he is pulling away from the cemetery in his beat-up work truck before I move the flowers from Greta's grave to Jessica Milburn's.

20

Before

Evie

Growing up, I didn't have a lot of quality time with my father. The majority of my weekends were spent doing chores, helping my mom run the household while dad was deployed or attending to military duties.

One week every summer, however, my parents would take me camping. We would pack up our van and make the trek to the nearest mountain wherever we were stationed. In California, it was the Sequoia National Forest, where the trees were massive giants that always made me feel like I was a miniature human, so small in comparison. We would always stop at quirky country stores along the way to collect souvenirs. For that entire week the three of us were free to talk, laugh and eat together as a family without the constraints of being interrupted by the sometimes unpredictable obligations of the military.

I roll up my green hooded sweatshirt, its edges tattered, and the print faded, a souvenir from one of my camping trips as a kid, and I tuck it inside the duffel bag that our family of four will share. "Liam! Jack! This is the last time I'm going to ask. Do you have anything else to add to the bag?"

My question goes unanswered but seconds later I hear the sound of plastic slapping against our hardwood floors, getting closer to the master bedroom. I squeeze each side of the bag together and start to pull the metal zipper along the track. "Mom, should we take these?"

I look up to see Liam standing in the doorframe wearing swimming flippers and the headlamp he got for his last birthday. He continues to walk toward me but trips on the flipper and falls flat on his face, letting out a squeal that is recovered by laughter.

"Yes, to the headlamp, no to the flippers."

"But Piper is bringing flippers!" he says from the floor, where he is lying down sprawled out like a starfish, his eyes glued to the ceiling.

"Well, here's the deal, buddy. Lauren has never been camping, so I'm guessing she is going to bring everything." I heft the bag on my shoulder, the weight of it causing me to lean against the wall for balance. We're only going camping for two nights, but the contents of this bag say otherwise.

"Fine." He continues to make a snow angel on the floor, with his flippers and bathing suit bottoms on, his headlamp pointed at the ceiling.

As I turn the corner on the staircase, I nearly smack into Jack, who is racing up the stairs. "Um, Mom, you might want to look out the kitchen window."

I don't ask. Instead, I roll the bag down the stairs, step over it and stand in front of our open kitchen window where I have a clear shot of the Rivers' driveway. "Oh geez."

Matt walks up from the basement maneuvering his way around grocery bags and sleeping bags, while he holds a red cooler. "What?"

"Come see this." I lean forward, peering closer.

He stands beside me, and we both watch as if we're about to reach the climax of a movie. Lauren is trying to hoist a hammock into the back of their SUV, her body bending backwards from the weight of it, as Ryan jogs over, lifting the bar from her and setting it down. We watch as he raises his hands and drops them down as Lauren punches him in the shoulder and tips her head back in laughter. He scoops her up and carries her back down their driveway. I watch in awe. They are the perfect couple. Lauren can be strict with the girls, set in her perfectionist ways and a bit over the top when it comes to throwing parties, but Ryan balances that all out with his fun-loving nature and tolerance for her antics. I know she's over-the-top, but I also know she wants this trip to be perfect, a gleaming memory for her girls. She's the best friend I've ever had and has easily filled the friendship void I've had my entire life. In fact, she's also managed to fill the sibling void I've had, and I now think of her as a sister. Her generosity alone is something I've never witnessed in a human. She gives of herself so deeply and treats me with this unconditional friendship love that I never knew was possible. Just the other day she stopped by with a beautiful handmade pot from one of the boutique shops, engraved with our last name. "You're a landscaper, you should have a special pot to showcase your beautiful work," she said through her matter-of-fact smile as she placed the pot on our front steps. Remembering that makes me smile while I watch Ryan set her down at the side steps of their house.

"I thought you said she's been camping before?"

I wince. "Girl Scouts when she was nine and they tented out on the beach."

Matt rolls his eyes. "Oh boy, well, hopefully she will let us take the lead." Matt bends down and lifts the lid of the cooler open, making sure he has everything packed to perfection.

He doesn't have to explain further. We both know that Lauren can be a bit controlling when it comes to plans. She needs a time and a place for everything, or she'll spin out of control like a tornado. I've witnessed it getting worse over the years, mostly with Lily, maybe because she's the oldest. She tries to have such a tight grip on her life, leaving zero space for the girl to grow independently. Now that Lily is twelve I've started to see her frustration in her mother's ways. Any new friends outside of the trusted circle are deeply scrutinized. Once when Lily asked permission to go to a new school friend's house, Lauren asked more than a dozen questions about the girl. *Who are the parents? What does the girl do for extracurricular activities? Do they have pets? Will the parents be there the entire time, or will a nanny be at the home?* I'm pretty certain she Googles and drives by the homes of any of Lily's and Piper's friends. Matt, Ryan and I have learned to expect her controlling tendencies and we brace ourselves for it anytime there is a new event or activity that we're involved in. It balances out my lackadaisical approach to life and makes me grateful to have boys. I've always assumed the fact that Lauren is controlling has a bit to do with having daughters. She's just trying to protect them from making decisions that could hurt them later in life and adding a layer of caution that doesn't seem to be as warranted as much in boys. That's my guess at least.

21

Before

JUNE 2015

Lauren

I never in a million years thought I'd be sleeping in a tent. I ordered two queen-size air mattresses for the occasion and scoured REI for the best camping gear on the market, but still...sleeping in the woods overnight is not a bucket list item. I'm doing my best to make everyone think I'm enjoying every second of being out in nature though. I comment on the soothing sound of the birds, the fresh air, and even the unexpected comfort of the mattresses. I do like nature, but not quite to this extent. Nobody has to know that though, I'm a good secret keeper.

The sound of the river finding its way downstream as it swims over the smooth rocks serves as the perfect backdrop to our conversation around the fire. I take mini sips of wine from my tumbler and keep one eye on the children who are hunting for sticks in the patch of woods that separates the camping spot we're sharing with the Sullivans from the spot beside us. The spot closest to us is filled with a handful of college-age boys whose voices seem to be rising along with the number of crushed cans on their site.

Evie, wearing a t-shirt that says, "Camp Hair Don't Care," drops into the beach chair beside me, newly purchased for the occasion. She stabs a marshmallow for Piper and says, "slow and steady," as she turns the stick over a blue flame with the ease of a Girl Scout leader.

I feel incredibly unqualified for this experience, and it shames me that I don't have the tools to teach my girls how to live in nature. Another thing my parents did wrong for us. Our entire lives revolved around looking good in front of the Flagport community, showing up at events and having a constant presence in the town. But what about the rest of the world? What about life outside of Flagport? I watch as Evie effortlessly moves in nature. Earlier, she unpacked their supplies and set up shop, placing them on the picnic table in a sensible manner, while I had trouble finding a simple paper plate in the giant Tupperware bin I packed.

I watch as Piper puts her mouth around the marshmallow. Her eyes grow wide in satisfaction. "This is amazing, Evie." The words manage to get past the gooey white substance. "You're the best."

The comment bites me and I take a gulp of my wine. "You're so good at this stuff, Eves."

"She learned it from all those military boys," Matt says as he cracks open a beer and sips sideways from the can.

She rolls her eyes and laughs, but there is a mystery behind her life as a military brat. Having lived in the same town my entire life, I'm naturally curious about the secrets you could hold onto when you move every few years. I've always wondered if Evie has a cannon of unrevealed moments that she has yet to release. I've jokingly asked, and she brushes it off but there is a mystery behind those brown eyes.

"Is that true?" I ask.

Evie furrows her brow, and the topic is changed when Lily and Jack come running toward us, piercing the air with their squeals, stopping fast before they run into the fire. Jack holds his hands out proudly and Lily looks on uneasily. "It's a toad!" she yells.

"Let me hold it!" Liam steps in between Lily and Jack prying the creature out of his hand. And then a battle begins.

"Hold on a second," Jack says as he pats it like it's a puppy.

"No, give it to me!" Liam tugs at his arm and the toad falls to the ground.

"Look what you did!" Jack's face contorts when the toad heads toward the fire. He drops to his knees and reaches for it just before it takes its final leap into the flame. He makes a cave out of his hands for the toad, picks it up and runs, with Lily and Liam following behind.

Piper, uninterested in the amphibian, goes back to practicing her marshmallow roasting skills, this time making one for Ryan. It's not rare for Piper to disengage with the other three on occasion, opting to be by herself or with the adults. She rockets upward when the marshmallow is heated to her liking and presents it to Ryan. I watch as she pauses mid-step, her eye catching a handful of college-aged girls walking by, their laughter spilling onto our campsite. The vintage bug zapper that Matt hung over our sites emits enough light that I can make out their bikini tops and shorts, and the way they walk with a drunken sway. With hands gripping tumblers not much different than mine and Evie's, they sip and laugh, passing friendly elbow bumps into one another.

"Why are those girls acting so weird?" Piper asks as she cautiously nibbles on her next marshmallow, savoring it. When satisfaction of the flavor hits her taste buds, she attacks the remaining piece like a ravenous raccoon.

"Oh, they're just having fun," I say as I continue watching the girls walk toward the water's edge, where several massive rocks are positioned in a way that looks intentional, as if God created furniture out of them. Two rectangular pieces fit together, one higher than the other, making a perfect couch, perched on a smooth sand path that spills into the river.

"To be seventeen again," Ryan says, as he and Matt both look at them in a way that is free of sexuality but layered with longing of their own youths.

"Seriously," I say. "To do it all over again." The words accidentally spill from my mouth. If I could go back in time, I would specifically want to skip ages seventeen and eighteen, erase all memories from those years, and redo them like a clean slate. It's why I'm on high alert when a teenage girl is in my presence. This isn't the first time I've found myself keeping tabs on teen girls in public settings. Mabye it's because my subconscious is moving through me, making me see other girls as I saw myself, and trying to prevent them from making the same mistakes. Last summer, while we were at the town carnival, I saw a group of girls get dropped off by an Uber. Beneath their blankets I could see tumblers that I knew were filled with liquor, some mishmash of juice and vodka or rum and soda. As they walked by, I could smell it on their breath, I could see it in the sway in their steps. Between bouts of doling out money to Lily and Piper for food and rides, I kept one eye on the girls, watching them flop onto the blanket and tip their heads back as they gulped from the tumblers. Everything is fun and games until someone gets hurt.

"You'd want to do it all over again?" Ryan asks. "You grew up in the best town in the world." He asks, taking a swig of his beer.

"Yeah, I'd give anything to have a childhood in Flagport, where at least I wasn't moving around everywhere," Evie adds.

"Well, first of all, I think those girls are older than seventeen." I don't know for sure, but I'm hoping they aren't seventeen because that was the age I was when Jessica Milburn died and every time I see a girl that age, I'm taken back to that night, back to the darkest memory of my life. I can still see the look on Megan's face, the fear in her eyes. I can still taste the vomit that erupted from my mouth on the side of the road, the smell of the appetizers blended with bile. I swallow the remaining wine in my tumbler, hoping it will numb the pain that is starting to surge within me.

The giggles get louder, and the sound is now shared with escalating squeals and the splashing of water. "Ouch!" one girl yells.

"Dang it, that's sharp!"

Then the sound of a splash and a ripple of gasps and screeches.

All four of us adults look at one another.

Without warning, my body skyrockets upward. I feel the chair tipping over behind me, as I sprint toward the direction of the voices. I go into fight-or-flight mode, where I no longer have control over my body. I want to help. I need to help to make up for the past. When I arrive at my destination, I see the girl splashing around in the water helplessly surrounded by her friends shouting her name and moving toward the water's edge. "Ellie! Ellie!" They yell in unison, although none of them are making the effort to help.

I surpass her friends and walk out of my flip-flops, submerging myself in the water toward the splashing girl. I hear Ryan's voice, mashed together with Matt's and Evie's, but it's too late. I made up my mind. I'm saving this girl. This young girl who has her entire life ahead of her. I'm not letting her drown because of one stupid decision she made to go close to the water's edge at night. It's only June in New England. The river water hasn't had a chance to warm up. This girl will die if she doesn't get out now. I recruit all the skills I learned when I worked as a lifeguard at the Flagport Yacht Club all those years ago. The freezing water makes my muscles go stiff, but I wrap one arm around the girl's waist, the other I use to paddle out of the deep hole of water that is framed by the jagged rocks. Her body feels limp, but I keep paddling and pull her to the surface. I feel other bodies around me, but I don't know who or how much they are helping. I hear Ryan's and Matt's voices punch the air, but I'm lost. It's 1997 again and I've been given the chance to save someone, to do it all over. To make a different choice.

"Don't die on me, don't die on me!" I yell. The young girl is a complete stranger, and while her early death would be a tragedy, I know how this looks. My attachment to this swimming victim is out of the ordinary. "Damn it, wake up!" My voice pulls from my lips. "I'm sorry, I'm sorry, I'm sorry." I'm in a trance now. I slap the girl's face and pump her chest, on autopilot. I activate all my lifeguard skills, the steps unfold before me as I put my mouth on hers, pump her chest and repeat.

Ryan steps forward first and drops to his knees, making demands for someone to call 9-1-1. It all happens so fast. A wave of shrieks hit the air as the other girls scatter to get their phones. Someone aims a flashlight on the girl, her body taut like a teenage athlete, flowery surf shorts cling to her upper thighs, and one of the triangles on her bikini top is pushed to the side, revealing a small nipple upon a tiny mound of breast. The reception is bad here, we were all just discussing that earlier. They'll never get through. I keep pressing down with the heels of my hand, like I was taught on the dummies in the CPR class I take annually.

And then, I hear a sound.

I roll her onto her side and water dribbles out of her mouth, her eyes wide with fear. She almost died. She's so young and she's already had a run-in with death. She gasps and a flood of relief surges through me.

Her friends, now back from retrieving their phones that also don't have a signal, gather around. Some stand a few feet back, as if getting near will push them that much closer to their own tragedy, or maybe they are afraid their presence will pause her progression and she'll slip back into an unconscious state, sipping more water and losing more breath. One of the girls stays close and kneels down beside her body. "Ellie...I'm right here," she says as she pushes the wet strands of hair off her face with one hand while resting the other on her shoulder.

I'm now standing, my mind and body fully connected once again. It was only two minutes, but I was gone. Far away and back in the past to a moment where things could've gone differently. "I'm sorry." I'm not sure why I say those two words.

"Why...are...you...sorry?" The girl, who I now know as Ellie, asks the question as she pushes herself up on her elbows and twists to her side, spitting out more water.

I look over at Ryan, Matt, and Evie and our children, who have all followed the noise and gathered around the commotion.

"Woah, your mom just saved that girl's life," Jack says to Lily and Piper, who are looking at me with confusion and pride, the same expression that is shared by Evie, Matt and Ryan.

And for about ten minutes I allow myself to be a hero, until later that night when I can't sleep because I keep seeing Jessica Milburn's face.

22

After

Lauren

Piper has always been a daydreamer, seldom miffed about anything, often unaware of her surroundings. The fact that her older sister is lifeless on a bed in a hospital is reason enough for an outburst, but it still surprised me when she expressed how upset she was when she first saw Lily.

The nurses and doctors that have become part of our lives in a matter of hours actually advise us to leave, which is why I knew Ryan wouldn't question my desire to leave earlier this morning. It was a white lie. I did go home and get a change of clothes like I said, I just also happened to stop by the cemetery on the way. I still hear Jeffrey Milburn's voice in my head. He unknowingly gave me a piece of advice that after all these years my own therapist never offered. *Focus on the 'what now' instead of the 'what if?'* Sometimes the answer doesn't come to us right away. For the past twenty-four years I've been wondering about the 'what if.' What if that night had never happened? What if Jessica Milburn wasn't out picking up her daughter from a failed sleepover? What if her daughter never had the sleepover to begin with? Would things have been different? Who would I be today?

Had I met Jeffrey Milburn before Lily's accident, I may have been able to think about the 'what now?' and really recruit his therapist's advice into my everyday life, but I cannot help but feel like this is just the universe's way of saying I deserve this. I don't wish these feelings on my worst enemy. The unknowns of my daughter's life. *Will I feel her body move while she's enveloped in my embrace again? Will I see her walk up our long driveway, the same pavement that she learned how to walk on, sixteen years before?* I've done everything I've known how to protect her over the years. I've preached to her about safety, about not falling for peer pressure, and believing in herself no matter what. I've been there for all the sporting events, the prom, the spring concerts. Showing up early and staying late, volunteering and pushing her in the right direction in all areas of her life. *So, why am I here in a hospital room? And why is Evie rooms away in the same hospital? Better yet why was my best friend picking up my daughter when it should've been me? What other secrets are they holding onto?*

Ryan is taking the opportunity to step out of the hospital while the nurses give Lily a bath. The thought makes me nauseous. I'm the only one who has bathed my daughter in her lifetime, and now she's being wiped down by a stranger.

The only other person in the waiting room is an older woman. She grips a leather bag to her chest as if there is gold inside it. Maybe her husband had a heart attack and she's awaiting the news of his state. As if on cue, my stomach growls. I haven't eaten since last night and that thought causes a lump in my throat to surface and another series of tears to infiltrate my eyes.

As I walk down the hospital corridor on a mission for a snack, I realize I can no longer tell the difference between the walls, floor, and ceiling. Everything blurs together in one swirling cloud, a dreamlike state.

Hospital employees move around me, intent on getting to their destination. A nurse shoves the remains of a bagel in her mouth and wipes away at crumbs on her lips before she twists a doorknob and walks into what appears to be a conference room. My legs propel forward pushing against the quicksand of my emotions and I somehow land in front of the vending machine at the end of the hallway. Like the corridor, the options in the machine are a blur. My stomach objects to everything that's in front of me, but my lack of energy is forcing me to press the combination of letters and numbers for some type of organic protein bar.

"Lauren!" The familiar voice pulls me from my haze as I use all my strength to open the wrapper and force-feed myself. Matt is run-walking toward me, followed by Liam and Jack. "Evie is okay." He's out of breath by the time he reaches me, his words coming out in puffs. "She's...got a...broken...arm...and a bad case of whiplash... but she's going to be okay. They had to pull her into surgery...her humerus was broken in several places...and I..." He runs a palm through his hair. "I'm just so happy she's okay." He catches himself after he says the words. Maybe he knows that he has no right to be happy in front of me.

"An arm...a broken arm that needed surgery? That's it?" I realize how I sound as soon as the words hit the air, but I'm just wondering why he wouldn't have learned this sooner, and a tiny slice of me is resenting the fact that his person is okay, and my person might not be. Because his person is a spouse, not a child. I could still carry on if I lost Ryan. People move on from the grief of a dead spouse, but people, at least not ones I've heard of, move on from a dead child.

He looks at me dumbfounded, and I continue, saving myself. "It's just...why didn't you know this sooner? Why did it take so long to find out her status?" I ask the question I already know the answer to. The same reason it took so long to find out my sister Megan's status in the hospital twenty-four years ago. Because hospitals take forever and there is changeover in staff. There is no time to wait and notify family members when an emergency surgery is necessary. I'm supposed to be happy about this news, happy that my best friend is alive, happy that her husband doesn't have to plan her funeral or set up in-home care to tend to her. But I'm numb.

"Don't even get me started on that. I already gave the front desk an earful. How dare they make us sit in fear all this time, only to find out she was fine. The boys—" he starts. Matt has always been teased by us for being naïve and a bit gullible, but he's quick enough to know when to stop. "It doesn't matter. We're fine. And I'm grateful for that. We're heading in to see her shortly. Do you—"

I know that I'm supposed to say *yes, I want to see Evie, I want to celebrate the fact that my friend is alive and she's going to walk out of this hospital in likely less than a day,* but it's hard for me to drum up the excitement when my daughter is in a stagnant state.

Matt takes my wrists in his hands. "Listen, I'm sorry. I shouldn't have asked. I'm sure this is incredibly hard for you. You don't have to come in."

"No, I want to come."

Seconds later, after I managed to shove the protein bar down my throat in a blur, I'm walking beside Matt, with Jack and Liam trailing behind us. Evie's room is much different than Lily's. There are far less beeps and tubes and there is a tray hovering over Evie's lap to show that she's eaten food and is capable of feeding herself.

She moves her head in our direction when we walk in the room, a half-smile slips out, but her eyebrows are crunched together painfully. Tears immediately hit the surface of her eyes and cascade down her cheeks as she grips Liam's and Jack's hands with the hand that is not hidden beneath a cast. "My babies. My babies." She gathers them in her one arm as Matt hovers over the three of them, a happy family of four reunited.

After what seems like hours of me watching their family reunion, Evie looks in my direction. "Lauren. Oh, Lauren." She shakes her head left to right. She can see the discomfort on my face. "I don't know what happened. I was driving and—"

"You were hit by another driver," Matt interjects. "It wasn't your fault."

"But what about Lily? Where is Lily?"

Matt looks over at me, a question mark on his face. He hasn't told her yet.

"Honey, Lily is—" he starts.

I finish for him. "Lily is in a coma, Evie. My baby is in a coma.

What happened last night? Why were you in a car with my daughter?" My words come out harsher than intended. Now that I know Evie is okay, I'm letting it all out, my anger at the situation, my fear of the unknown. I'm no longer a friend, I'm only a mother.

Her face crumples into a mishmash of features, and her gentle tears transform into sobs. "I'm sorry, I thought I was helping."

23

After

APRIL 2021

Evie

I understand why Lauren is mad. If I were her, I'm not sure I'd talk to me again either. It looks bad. I was the one driving the car in the middle of the night. With her daughter in the passenger seat. Matt asks me the same questions that are likely spinning through her mind.

"Honey, why were you in a car with Lily so late at night?"

I pick at the edge of the cast with my free hand. "She needed me." I answer his question matter-of-factly.

"Why would Lily call you for a ride in the middle of the night?" he asks. I would ask him the same question if he was in a similar situation. We are close with the Rivers, but our bonds have never spilled out into separate parent/child relationships.

"Because she was drunk." The response comes from Jack, who is sitting in a chair by the window, swiping across his phone nonchalantly.

I'm just as shocked at his answer as Matt is. "How?" I start but can't finish. Confusion ripples my brow.

"How did I know?"

I nod. My normally reserved and calm son is on edge. He bounces his knee and changes position two more times before he continues. "Because I was at that party."

"You left her at the party, knowing she was drunk and had no way to get home?" Anger rips through me, altering the calm and grateful state I had just moments before when I was reunited with my boys. That changed to sadness when Lauren stormed out of the room, and now I feel my face growing red with fury. I thought I raised my boys to be polite gentlemen, to look out for girls, especially girls they were best friends with. And then it dawns on me. "I thought you weren't going to that party anyways." It was the end of year celebration of college acceptance letters but the majority of the kids celebrating were the ones who would be attending mostly Boston area colleges.

Jack's gaze skitters away from mine. His head swivels and he looks everywhere but at me and his father.

"Jack? What's going on?" Matt, already standing, sidesteps with hands resting low on his hips. He's a pacer. He always has been. Never has he been able to sit still when the wheels in his mind are spinning. And I know they're spinning. In different directions and with varying speed, the wheels in his head are spinning, trying to figure out why Jack left the party early and why I, not Lauren, picked Lily up in the middle of the night from a party. I didn't think to check Jack's room before I left to go get Lily. I assumed he was out with his friends and his curfew was midnight. It was only 11:30 when I got in my car.

Jack huffs as he shakes his head left to right. He doesn't want to talk about it, but there is no way he's getting out of this without giving me an explanation and I make that clear when I escalate my voice and sharpen the edges of my words. "I'll ask you again, Jack. Why did you leave Lily at a party alone and drunk?"

He sniffs. "We got in a fight."

Matt raises his eyebrows, alerting his son to continue. There has to be more.

"There was…this video." Jack's face, normally the same bronze tone as mine, is now bright red.

"What video?" Matt and I ask the question at the same time.

Jack leans forward and drops his head in his hands. For the first time in years, I see him cry. His back is in the shape of a C, and I sit up as much as I can in my bed holding one arm out as if I can reach him in the chair he is sitting in. His back muscles twitch, his body gives way to sobs. And that's when I remember Lily's last words to me before the accident. *Jack and I are in love and I'm moving to California with him.*

As far as I knew, the two were always the best of friends, but I thought it ended at that. Over the years there had been random crushes that lasted a day or two before they moved on to other class-mates, but for the most part Lily and Jack were friends only. Sure, Lauren and I had joked about the two getting together so we could be in-laws and live happily ever after. But, as far as we knew, the two preferred a friendship and had no future plans of becoming more than that. Lily had always been the straight-A perfectionist student while Jack was just okay in school, and I always assumed my son didn't have enough drive to sustain Lily. It was why Jack was going to a mediocre state school in California and Lily was going to a top school in Boston. But now that I see my son so distraught, it's all become clear to me. He is in love.

Over the years, there have been moments when Jack has wanted just me in the room for certain occasions. Anytime Jack had an acci-dent as a little boy, he did everything in his power to hide it from his father. While he was no scholar in the classroom, he did have a penchant for writing and his teacher often applauded him for being a natural. Whenever he brought home a new essay, he always shared it with me, but never with Matt. I always wondered why and now it's a bit clearer to me. He doesn't want to show his father his soft side. I watch as this dawns on Matt too and he does what he always does in these situations and says, "Hey, Liam, I'm hungry…you want to go get a snack?"

Liam pulls his attention from the phone he is maniacally swiping and punching and shoots upright. "Sure."

When they leave, I say, "Hey, buddy, come here." I pat the bed beside me, not much different than I would have if we were at home. He's always been my more sensitive kid and I know he needs a more delicate approach to his feelings.

He gets up and swipes at his nose with the back of his hand just like he used to do when he was a little boy and cried about a missing toy or the dead hamster. He drops into the small space beside me and adjusts his position uneasily. It's in this moment I realize just how big he has gotten. His once-bony upper body has given way to broad shoulders and well-developed chest muscles. He pushes his brown hair out of his eyes in the way that's become a habit since he started letting it grow out, but he keeps his eyes trained on the floor. "What's going on?"

His entire body moves and causes the bed to creak when he lets out a long sigh. "I don't know...there was—"

"Honey, you can tell me. I'm not going to get mad." I use my free hand to push myself more upright.

"This video. All of a sudden everyone in the school had a video of me and Lily—"

This is a conversation I never imagined myself having. A conversation that I definitely wouldn't be having without Lauren by my side. *Lily and Jack? How did they hide it for so long? Or were they just two kids, two longtime friends experimenting?*

"It's nothing...I mean it was just under the covers, but everyone knows it's us. Our faces. I'm sorry, Mom...I—"

I'm not sure why he's apologizing. He and Lily are both eighteen, after all, and I was gosh, sixteen when I decided to try and make my own father angry by having sex with a neighbor. But, hearing my son, who was just a little boy not long ago, share this information, brings with it a bittersweet blend of emotions. He's in love. He's in love with a girl who I adore, but now, here he is reeling from an embarrassing video and heartbroken because the girl he loves may not live.

24

Before

MAY 2016

Evie

I've never been one to make a big deal out of a holiday. But when Lauren invites me to join her for a Mother's Day brunch at the Flagport Yacht Club, Matt urges me to go. *Take a day off. You deserve it.* Now, as I get ready for the outing, I'm filled with insecurity. I tug at the bottom of my blouse as I stand in front of the mirror and turn to my side. I've never been thin, but I've definitely lost a few pounds since I started taking Barre classes with Lauren. Growing up in a military community, I was never in the presence of wealthy people, which is why I'm scrutinizing my outfit right now. If past events at the Flagport Yacht Club have been any indication, the hall will be filled with high-end moms, doused in impeccable layers of boutique clothing, sparkling jewelry, and trendy hair perfected by pricey blowouts.

"You look gorgeous." Matt stands at the threshold of our bedroom.

I turn toward him, ashamed of myself for putting so much pressure on how I look. There was a time when I didn't care about how the world saw me. My old self would be laughing at what I've become since we moved here. It's as if it happened without me even knowing. I simply became the people I surrounded myself with and Lauren's lifestyle has somehow become my norm. Of course, without all the glitz and glamour. We don't have the built-in family money to afford home renovations every other month, interior designers, boats and yacht club memberships, but the shock factor has worn off. When we first moved here my jaw would drop when I heard the cost of one of those cute tops in the downtown boutiques. Now, it's the norm. I may not be purchasing them myself, but I no longer feel breathless when I hear the high price of things. "I do?"

"Yes, stop second guessing yourself," Matt says, having witnessed my internal transformation over the years. "And just have fun, okay?"

I step toward him and fall into the bear hug he is offering. "Moooom!" The sound of Liam's voice interrupts our moment.

I look up at Matt and pat his cheek with my palm. "If you say so. I'll start now. Go handle your son." I laugh, as I slide into a thin, white jacket I purchased online, after I walked by the boutiques and realized I could get the same product, minus the designer tag, for half the price.

"I'm on it." Matt passes me a mock salute. "I think I heard Lauren's car door shut a couple minutes ago, so you might want to head out there now."

My boys are sitting at the high-top table, each has a steady gaze on the back of a different cereal box. I slip by unnoticed as they slurp the milk from their bowls. "Bye, boys." I drop the words just as I open the door and I close it before they can ask me for anything.

As expected, Lauren is sitting behind the steering wheel inside her vehicle, talking into her phone. I slide into her passenger seat and take in the smell of the SUV's fresh leather seats. She winks at me and then continues talking into her phone, making demands into her note app. "Get gift for Lily's track coach, order gift basket for meet, review Lily's essay, order leggings for her last day of school outfit, have Lydia prep appetizers for—" she pauses and looks at me. "Shit, Eves, what am I prepping appetizers for?"

I let out a ripple of laughter. "Slow down. You're going too fast.

Take a breather and you'll get your memory back." I pop a piece of mint gum into my mouth and pass one her way. "But I think you're bringing appetizers to Noelle's baby shower maybe?"

Lauren shoots her index finger up in the air. "Yes! That's it!" She smiles and repeats the task into her phone. "What would I do without you?"

"Well, for starters you'd probably be going to this brunch alone."

Lauren sets her phone in the console between us and backs us out of the driveway. "Yes, you're right about that. Actually, no, I'd probably be stuck going with my mom."

"Hey, what's wrong with your mom?" I ask in a reprimanding tone.

"Oh, nothing. Colleen McCue is a perfectly perfect mom." She winks at me as she steers us toward the yacht club on the other side of town. The drive there is picturesque, especially now that the majority of boat owners have launched their vessels and the water is dotted with sails that bob in the light waves that shimmer beneath the full sun sky.

I roll my window down and sip in the ocean air when we drive over the bridge that leads to the part of town with the wealthiest homes, waterfront properties that are five times the size of our home. "Did you ever want to live in this area of town?" I ask Lauren.

"No, not really." Her response is clipped, but then I see her face softening and she continues. "I guess Ryan and I wanted to create our own space and build on what we had."

"Well, you've done a wonderful job," I say, thinking about the major improvements they'd made on their home. "Especially seeing those photos."

"I can't believe Ryan shared those." She laughs and my body jerks back, as I feel the SUV pick up speed.

"Hey, didn't you pass the street?" I ask, motioning toward Bellevue Ave, the one-way that Matt and I have always taken to get to the Flagport Yacht Club. When the boys were little, they demanded we take that street just for fun because of the two big humps for hills that naturally cause a belly-drop sensation. *Let's go to the roller coaster street!* they would shout whenever they were bored and looking for something for us to entertain them with. Admittedly it's been a cheap form of entertainment over the years.

"Oh, I have a shortcut." She continues down the main road that outlines the peninsula, and in what is definitely not a shortcut, she finally turns down a narrow street and enters the yacht club.

25

Before
MAY 2016

Lauren

The Mother's Day brunch at the Yacht Club is the same every year. The same pale pink linens cover the ten-top tables while a jazz combo plays music in the back corner of the space. The band members are the only men in the room besides the sole male bartender who is already in the weeds taking orders from the well-dressed women who form a long line that zigzags through the tables to the center of the room.

With Evie by my side, I scan the room and take in all the familiar faces. Only women attached to old money are invited to this event, which is why the ages range from those who are on their last leg of life, all the way down to the younger moms who just recently had babies. I fall in the middle somewhere, with my mother now as the matriarch of the McCue women, since my grandmother passed away five years ago. And one day, Lily and Piper will represent our family here. As long as everything goes according to plan.

I watch as my mother looks up from going over what is likely the speech she is giving later on. She makes a beeline for me and Evie, alongside Mrs. Beal, a longtime friend of the family who is of equal wealth and status. "Oh, well hello, ladies, don't you look beautiful." My mom rests one palm on Evie's arm and one on mine, sandwiching us closer together. I catch her gaze making a stealth trip to Evie's outfit, surveying her in a sideways glance from head to toe. Evie is naive to my mother's facade, and I don't have the heart to break the news to her that the woman isn't as perfect as she thinks. I love my mother, I really do. It's one of the reasons why I've stayed in Flagport and shaped my life in a way that fits in to the high society I was raised in. It's much easier to blend in than to try and start over and come to terms with my past. Or at least I think it is.

"Thank you, Mrs. McCue." Evie accepts the compliment as if it's a genuine one and I love her even more for that. "You look stunning." I watch as Evie looks at my mother in awe. She does look amazing for her age with skin that has a sheen that can only be achieved from regular trips to the spa. Her pink skirt suit is tailored to flatter the minimal curves that she does have, the tweed hugging her hips and the cropped jacket landing just above the bottom of her forearms, allowing for enough space for the human eye to catch a glimpse of the gold and diamond bracelets that tap against her wrist.

"Oh, please, honey...call me Colleen already!" She swats at Evie's arm and rolls her eyes, putting on her best modest expression, before she leads us deeper into the room and toward a server greeting the guests with mimosas. Evidently the women in the bar line either chugged their complimentary glasses already or they pushed their noses up at the selection and opted for their own spin on a martini or a pricey wine that can only be purchased. "Well, come in, ladies. What do you think?" She grabs us each a glass and hands them to us delicately.

"It's absolutely beautiful in here," Evie says, genuinely enamored by the decorated space. "Did you do all this?"

"Oh goodness no," my mom responds. "I mean, I manage the team of decorators, but I leave the artwork to the professionals." She winks at Evie just as another woman approaches.

"Why hello there, darling." My mom greets the woman by holding her hand in her own for a moment. "It's about time you make it to one of these shindigs," she scolds playfully. She tips her head back and her coiffed hair doesn't move an inch.

When the woman turns toward me, I nearly gasp. While her features have aged over the years, they all fall into place, and I remember. The way her mouth is permanently turned downward as if she's always sad, the tight brown curls that spring from her head, now with small specks of frizzy gray and not as shiny as they were the last time I saw her. While her mouth is naturally sad, her eyes make up for it and they tilt upwards on the edges thanks to her round pink cheeks, while her lips remain sad until she lifts those too in greeting. She's younger than my mother by two decades but older than me by one. "Oh my goodness, Lauren McCue. You sweetheart. How have you been all these years?"

I look to my mother to properly introduce the woman and receive the message she is silently passing me. "Lauren, honey, you remember Mrs. Kennedy? Robin."

"Oh my, she might not remember me." Robin's face turns sympathetic. "That was nearly twenty years ago."

"Have you been gone that long, Robin?" My mother, making sure not to direct any attention to the number of years that has passed, moves the conversation along. One month ago, made nineteen years since I last saw this woman.

"Believe it or not yes...well, actually nineteen." She pauses and passes an uncomfortable glance between me and my mother. "I left not long after I last saw you...Savannah..." She pauses and looks around the room. "Well I thought it would be good to move away for a bit. And it turns out we liked California more than we expected."

My mother changes the subject again. "Well, we are certainly glad to have you back in Flagport. And if you're up for it, I have some great committees for you to join." My mother forgets all about me and Evie and hooks her arm through Robin's arm and walks away. As their voices start to fade, I do pick up on Robin's response. *Oh, we're just in town visiting family. We're not staying.* I release a long exhale at her words, grateful I won't have to see her again, because just seeing this woman's face has brought me back to that night and stirred up a tornado of emotions in my head.

"What was that all about?" Evie asks. She's smart, privy to her own intuition, likely something she learned from all the strangers she met growing up. All the times she was thrown into new mixes of people, she relied on that instinct. And I have to stop her from relying on it again.

"Oh, I was friends with Robin's daughter a lonnnng time ago."

"Things didn't end well between you and the daughter, I take it?"

"High school drama," I lie, and I hook my arm through hers and lead her toward the line at the bar.

26

After
APRIL 2021

Lauren

The beeps and whooshing of the machines are the background to the conversations I'm having with myself and Lily. I couldn't stand to look at Evie any longer, after she told me that she was just trying to help. I left her room at those words. The last thing she was doing was helping, when she landed my daughter in a coma. It should've been me who was there with her, picking her up from the party. I didn't let Evie explain to me why she was driving my daughter around in a car while I was sound asleep in my bed. There is a part of me that doesn't want to know. Maybe I'm afraid it will unveil the guilt I feel as a parent. The feeling that I'm never enough, and sometimes I'm too much all at the same time.

"Hey," Ryan says as he stands in the doorway.

"Hey." I hold onto Lily's limp hand, circling my finger around the pale skin that surrounds her IV. It seemed like just yesterday I had an IV in my own vein, after I delivered her. It seems like just yesterday she made eye contact with me for the first time, immediately after the doctor handed her to me, as if she was saying, "Hey, Mom, I'm here, your life can begin." After all, it wasn't until I had children of my own that I felt like I was living, finally experiencing life for what it is and cherishing every moment. I had been through my fair share of pain, guilt and resentments. Being a mother was my second shot at life. Really my only shot at recovering from my old life.

Ryan steps into the room. A series of tubes and machines, a teenage daughter who is unmoving, has become our new normal. A life that changed in an instant, without even a sliver of warning. Just a simple phone call in the middle of the night. "I talked to Evie."

I look down at my lap, taking note of the coffee droplets that spilled on my pants earlier. Ryan slides a chair beside me, the sound of the legs scratching like nails on a chalkboard. He cocks his head to the side. "It's not her fault."

"How do you know that?" I hiss, twisting my neck in his direction.

He leans forward resting his elbows on his knees, his hands clasped in prayer position. "Honey, she's been our friend for years. I really don't think Evie did anything wrong. She was trying to help."

"Help by doing what exactly? Picking our daughter up from a party? Why didn't Lily call *me*?" The words hit me heavily, a new reality setting in. My own child was scared to ask me to pick her up from a party.

"Maybe Lily was scared you'd be disappointed in her."

Of course, this is all my fault. I'm the mother, the one who is supposed to instill the rules like a warden yet always be on, and ready to have fun at the drop of a hat.

"So, you're saying I was too hard on her?" My use of the past tense isn't lost on me.

"No, you're her mother, Lauren! All teenagers are scared of their mother."

Maybe I should've been more scared of my mother twenty-four years ago. If I had been, maybe I wouldn't be sitting here today.

Tears boil at the surface of my eyes, causing a steady stream to flow down my cheeks. All the memories from the past resurface, and I know, deep down inside I deserve this.

27

After

APRIL 2021

Evie

"Jack?" I ask the question again. "Why didn't you tell me about you and Lily? You know that I would've loved the idea of you two together."

"Lily made me promise." He sniffs.

"Why would she make you promise? I don't get it." I'm so beyond confused. For years we've been jokingly pushing the two of them together, mocking what it would be like if we were all one big family, joined together because Jack and Lily tied the knot.

"Because she was afraid of how her mom would react." His hands twist in his lap and for the first time I notice the calluses on his palms, tattoos from the little construction gig he's been doing on the side for McCue Real Estate. The job was a suggestion from Mr. McCue who was happy to take Jack under his wing and show him the ropes. He'd start out in construction, then maybe learn a thing or two about real estate. The plan was to give him a reference for the future, regardless of what field he chose to dive into or what area of the country he settled down in. He turns to me now. "Mom, you know how Lauren is."

"Yeah, but I mean…she's just protective of her daughter, that's all."

Jack looks at me like I'm an idiot. "Mom, it's more than that. She's psychotic about Lily. Do you know that she went ballistic on her for staying out one minute after curfew last week? *Literally* one minute."

"Well, she was probably worried."

"Worried is one thing, but I saw how Lauren reacted. She didn't get physical or anything with her, but she threatened to take her phone away for a week." He pauses and sips some air, allowing his breath to catch up. "First of all, she's eighteen so she can do whatever the hell she wants."

I'm guilty of forgetting our kids' ages too. I'm not sure if it's denial or an escape of time, but I've had to remind myself several times that Jack is an adult now. Still, an adult that lives under my roof, but nonetheless, he's an adult. "Yes, that's true, but…I don't know, honey, some parents are different. They like a tight leash."

"And look where a tight leash got Lily."

He adjusts his position so he's facing me. "Mom, what if she dies?" The first signs of tears hit his eyes. "It's all Lauren's fault. She hasn't let Lily breathe all these years." He pauses. "Do you know how many times Lily has told me she has felt like she's in a jail cell with her mother hovering over her at all times?"

I nod. I don't want to agree with him. I want to believe that my best friend has it all together, but when I look back on all the years I've known her, her obsession with Lily has been questionable at best. "Honey, she's not gonna die." I make a promise I can't keep as I pull his hand into mine. "We're going to get through this, okay?"

He nods and falls toward me. His stalky build is heavy on me, and I don't tell him that my weakened state is making it hard to breathe. Because all I want to do is hug my child and beg God to keep his love alive.

When Jack pulls back and I'm able to catch my breath again, I ask him, "How did a video get out to the entire school anyways?"

28

Before

AUGUST 2017

Evie

"Gotta love Lauren's epic lemonade stand bashes," Matt says as he carefully places his craft beers in a cooler.

"Hey, there is nothing wrong with celebrating all the little things in life." I toss a couple bottles of water into the cooler and pause at the window. I'm not sure if my timing happens to be spot on lately, or the boys are just always fighting. Liam, double the size Jack was when he was his age, has his older brother in a headlock. Just as he's about to press Jack's cheek into the cement patio, I scream through the open window. "Liam! Let him go, now!" He still holds him, squeezing his neck tighter. Matt drops the bag of ice he's holding, races to the sliding door, nearly tripping over the dog on the way.

"Liam! What the hell is wrong with you?" Matt rips Liam's arms apart, and Jack goes tumbling backwards, reaching toward his neck.

Liam has zero response. There is no expression of guilt, not an ounce of remorse in his straight stare. The therapist he's been seeing has chalked his behavior up to him just being a boy, but my gut is telling me it's something more than that, and the more I get to know my own son, the more I think that maybe he was born with a lack of empathy, an empty space where his emotions are supposed to be. Matt yells again, this time he's eye level with Liam. "I said, what the hell is wrong with you?" Liam responds with a shrug of his shoulders. "Apologize now!" He points toward Jack who is crouched down on the patio, still holding a hand on his neck. As Liam follows his father's orders and heads in his direction, Jack backs up like a scared puppy dog, now pressed to the foundation of the house. He's fourteen years old and he looks petrified of his eleven-year-old brother.

THE PARTY IS in honor of the annual lemonade stand the Rivers' family hosts. It started when Lily was four and wanted to sell cups of lemonade in front of their house. She ended up raising so much money thanks to the deep Flagport pockets, that little Lily became a philanthropist overnight when she had the idea of giving it to home-less people. Lauren met her halfway there and decided to donate it to a local non-profit. Even Megan, who I haven't seen in over a year, made it home for the occasion to dote on her niece.

Lauren stands in front of the custom-built lemonade stand at the back of the driveway and takes pictures of Lily and her friends posing while pouring the yellow liquid from a vintage glass container into blue and yellow striped cups. Each cup is labeled with "Lily's Lemonade," alongside a photo of the smiling girl wearing an apron that matches the blue and yellow theme. Signs dot the edge of the driveway in addition to the signs that have been hung around town for the past week. It's another Flagport tradition that seems to be spun from Lauren's imagination.

"Can you tell Lauren is proud of her daughter?" Ryan sips from the craft beer in unison with Matt, the two having formed a bond over unique, local-brewed beverages.

I watch Lauren as she moves Lily into certain positions like she is a puppet, while she snaps photos with her professional camera. You know it's a big event when Lauren has the big camera. Parents mingle in the driveway, sipping on a spiked version of Lily's concoction while the older kids help Lily man the stand which now has a line that reaches the street. Some people come by for a quick cup and drop shockingly big bills in the square box, while others stick around longer and let their younger kids slip into the backyard to play on the water bounce house rented for the occasion. "No, no I cannot tell at all," I say sarcastically as a sting of curiosity pinches my thoughts. Why is Piper not involved in this? It's strictly Lily who is in the spotlight. It's a thought that has crossed my mind often over the years, but I assumed it was that break between the two children. Piper and Lily are as different as Jack and Liam. They need different things and so we have different relationships with them.

Megan stands on the other side of the men, her eyes trained on the lemonade stand, a look of longing on her face that I never witnessed before. Maybe she wants children of her own? I try to pull her from what appears to be a sullen mood.

"Hey, good to see you again. Glad you could make it back."

She turns to me, seemingly pulled out of a trance. "Yeah, well, the city isn't so great to be in during a heat wave." She allows a smile to spread across her face as she turns to me.

"How are you, Evie?"

"I'm good." I remain quiet for a few beats before I continue. Megan is a mystery to me, and I have so many questions. I want to know everything about her. "I meant to ask you...did you also go to Kline College? How did you end up in New York?" One question spins off the other.

Her eyebrows raise at the impromptu interview. "Kline?" She scrunches her nose up and for a moment I can't decide if she is offended or confused at the question.

"Yeah, didn't Lauren go there?" I'd heard the story dozens of times. Ryan and Lauren met in the campus diner. Ryan was drunk and Lauren was studying, and the rest was happily ever after.

She furrows her brow and I watch as if she is doing a math equation in her head. "Um, did Lauren go there? No, I...ah...no I didn't go to Kline. I just picked up some community college classes along the way in New York."

I PULL my shirt over my head, happy to slip into something more comfortable. Being out in the hot sun all day has caused a rare burn to form on my shoulders. I push against my skin with a finger and watch the white circle disappear. That's not the only thing that has been burning since I left the party at the Rivers. "Hey, Matt," I pad down the hallway toward the bathroom. He's brushing his teeth and topless, and it looks as if he's wearing a white T-shirt, his arms and neck are burnt, and the rest of his skin is as white as baby powder. He uses his free hand to present his farmer's tan to me before he spits out the toothpaste.

"Hey, what," he says.

"Didn't Ryan go to Kline College?"

"Yes, sir." He pulls the navy-blue hand towel from the rack and wipes the white toothpaste foam from the corner of his lips. He puts it back on the rack lazily and I move into the bathroom and adjust it.

"What about Lauren? Did she go there too?" I sit on the toilet and watch him floss, noting the food particles that are flying from his mouth to the mirror. Another thing I'll have to clean later.

He turns to me, with the string dangling from between two teeth. "Um, yeah, where have you been all this time? We've heard their little love story repeatedly since we've known them."

"Yeah, I know but I got a weird vibe from Megan when I asked her if she went to the same college as Lauren."

Matt holds the used floss over the trashcan and swats at it until it falls into the bin. "I don't know if I'd trust everything you hear from Megan." He says the words so matter-of-factly, which throws me off.

"What do you mean?" I follow him into the bedroom.

"Well, I don't know." He grabs the edge of the comforter and nearly tosses it on the floor. Typically ten degrees warmer than me at all times, Matt never sleeps with covers in the summer. "Ryan has just alluded to her being kind of odd."

"How so?" I pull the sheet up on my side of the bed and slide under it.

"Well, nothing specific. He just says she's very distant and he gets annoyed because, well, you know how close he is with the rest of Lauren's family."

"Yeah." I think of the way he is like an actual son to Mr. McCue, how the two go out for coffee nearly every morning and work together all day.

"Well, I guess he's a bit offended that she doesn't...I don't know...come around more. And why doesn't she anyways? According to Ryan, she lives in like, a closet in New York. Don't you think that's a bit odd, when your father is a real estate tycoon and has loads of money to spare. Seriously, did you see the size of the check he put in Lily's lemonade stand fundraiser tonight?"

"No, and how did you see it?"

"I happened to be standing next to him when he wrote it for..." Matt's eyes grow wide, and his mouth stretches to emphasize his next words. "Ten *thousand* dollars."

I'm suddenly pulled from thoughts of Lauren's potentially fake alma mater, to the amount of money Mr. McCue donated. "What? For real?"

"For real." Matt turns on his side, resting his head on his elbow and looks me in the eyes. "Allegedly, the amount has been going up every year since Lily was four."

Matt kisses me on the forehead before he falls onto his back. "That's definitely a guy I want on my side."

29

Before
AUGUST 2017

Lauren

I don't count the cash in the box until everyone in the house is sound asleep. After I've picked up the empty lemonade cups that were strewn about the driveway, I carry the box to the office and start counting. I line the bills up by dollar amount and then create several piles of coins starting with the quarters from pocket change to the pennies that were mostly contributions from little kids who stopped by just so they could use the bounce house. Lily's lemonade stand draws a crowd nearly as big as our annual Fourth of July party and I'd have it no other way. Over the years the collection has grown, and more people have been added to the list, the event itself having built up a solid reputation that piques the interest of both kids and adults.

I use my phone to count out the total. We surpassed last year's lemonade stand by nearly five hundred dollars, making a total of $19,500. This is a minuscule amount compared to what I donate to the Katie Milburn Fund annually, tucking away hundreds here and there without Ryan seeing. I conceal my anonymous donation by telling the town guests that it's going to the Flagport Children's Fund. When I created the fake fund, I knew that Flagport residents would not take the next step and actually look up the made-up name. My own father doesn't question it as he's been upping the amount of his donation every year, believing that he is supporting a children's organization. I suppose, in some sense it is a children's organization, at least in the singular sense that it supports one child and not the entirety of Flagport's children. We all know that Flagport's children don't need any more money, but that doesn't stop people from doling out hordes of cash thinking it's going toward building up the recreational activities in town. As if we need more of that. Not one person has questioned my creation, and if I ever got outed, I would just launch into a Robinhood story about stealing from the rich and giving to the poor. Not that Katie Milburn is poor. Part of it is just me throwing money at a situation in an attempt to make myself feel better. It puts a Band-Aid on my pain for a day or two, until I slip back into my old, tormented thoughts.

30

After
APRIL 2021

Lauren

The police station hasn't changed in twenty-four years. I take baby steps toward the front desk, Ryan's hand at the small of my back. Instead of tapping on the glass to get the receptionist's attention, I stand, waiting. That's all I've done for the past three days. I'm waiting for my daughter to wake from a coma, and I'm waiting for my life to return to normal so I can go back to the things that once stressed me out. Like the kids' sports schedules, hiring workers to upkeep the house, the stresses of everyday life. Lily's impending transition to college being the biggest stressor as of late. I had been dreading the day I had to say goodbye to my oldest daughter, the day my nest would start thinning. And now, I was waiting to see if my daughter would even be alive to pack a car full of household items and clothes for her freshman dorm room at Boston University, still in New England but still out of view when it came to keeping an eye on Lily. Although, I thought I had been keeping a close eye on her for the past eighteen years and look where that landed me.

The woman behind the desk looks up, two squinting eyes behind black-rimmed glasses. Her short mousy-brown hair is pulled back into an efficient ponytail, showcasing a few strands of gray at the crown of her head. "Lauren McCue!" the woman says, as she shoots up in her seat. It went without saying that I would run into someone I know at the town's small police department, but I wasn't in the mood to catch another person up to speed on my family's tragic event. My mother and father were already spreading the word, making sure the McCue family had a support system in place. It's what townies did, after all. They brought casseroles and offered large donations if there was a GoFundMe page in place. They'd be there to mourn alongside me if there was a funeral, but how long would they stay? There was no GoFundMe page in place for this particular tragedy because it was known that the McCue family had enough money to handle the medical expenses, a funeral and years of therapy. But this time, money wouldn't help heal my broken heart.

"Hi…" I look at the woman's gold nameplate on her uniform. Sergeant Gilford. Betsy Gilford, who I remember as an aunt or cousin of one of my high school friends. Like every other small town in America, everyone knows everyone in Flagport which means that everyone knows everyone's business.

Betsy disappears for a moment before she opens the door that leads to a hallway. "The whole family is praying for Lily." She pulls me into a bear hug and I feel my own heart pounding in the woman's embrace, at the sound of my daughter's name slipping from someone else's lips. She sets her hands on my shoulders and holds me at arm's length. For a moment, I think the woman is going to break her straight militant expression and erupt into tears, but luckily, she doesn't. "We're here for you." She squeezes my shoulders. "Whatever you need, okay?" And then she drops her arms by her side.

"Thank you." I muster the words. It is all I can manage to say when I receive sympathetic hugs and prayer offerings.

Betsy leads me and Ryan to the interview room, where we're scheduled to meet with the officer who responded to the accident. He was also the officer who would get the process started if we want to press charges on the teen driver who allegedly crashed into Evie's vehicle when she was driving Lily home from the party.

"Take a seat. Officer Wright will be here shortly." Betsy waves a hand in the direction of plastic chairs that flank the rectangular table.

"Thanks, Sergeant Gilford." Ryan speaks for both of us.

"Please, call me Betsy." She passes us a tight-lipped smile and closes the door gently.

"Hey." Ryan grabs my hand between his clammy palms. "Look at me, Lauren."

Since the accident, I've been hesitant to look into my husband's eyes. While Lily doesn't resemble Ryan, I see all the memories I've ever had with Lily reflected in his eyes. She is half me and half him and it's hard to face the one other person on the planet who has a front row seat to Lily's life, as if every time I look at him, I'll be reminded of what I lost if I do lose her forever. I now understand why marriages sometimes crumble after a child is lost. It would be impossible to sustain a relationship with Ryan if Lily were no longer in the picture. Now, as I look into Ryan's eyes, against my will, I'm prepared to unleash a new collection of tears.

"It's going to be okay. All right? We'll get through this." He uses his index finger to lift my chin up ever so slightly.

Just as I'm about to let a flood of words spill out of me about all the ways we won't get through this if we lose Lily, there is a one-knock warning on the door. Officer Wright pushes himself through and turns gently to close it.

"Hi, Lauren. Ryan," Officer Wright says as he gently drops into the chair opposite us. The guy hasn't aged since he was a teen. His full head of dark hair is free of any gray and parted on the side like a modern-day Don Draper. I remember him being a heartthrob in high school, but he was never my type. "He's too rigid," I told my mother all those years ago when there was an attempt at setting us up. Mr. and Mrs. McCue ran in the same circles as Mr. and Mrs. Wright, and it was no surprise when he ended up marrying the daughter of another couple they hung out with. Jake Wright and Jenny Cramer were made for each other.

She was the head cheerleader, and he was the football quarter-back at Flagport High. The last I learned through social media, Jake went to a prestigious college, then he attended the police academy, before landing a job at Flagport PD. He did his four years, then married Jenny, his high school sweetheart and the two went on to have three sons, who look exactly like Jake, and are a smidge older than Lily. After I switched to private school at the end of my junior year, there were little interactions with the Wright family. As a married adult with children close in age, I've seen them here and there at town events and kids sports but nothing more than a simple greeting has been passed between us until now.

Now, Jake Wright is suddenly a critical part of our lives. He was the first person to see Lily after the accident, the one who called me close to midnight to inform me of the horrific news. He sits erect, his hands on a folder and I can't help but think, *"all my daughter gets is a single folder."* Based on the turmoil this has already caused us and how much space it is taking up in our lives, I feel like the evidence should be of colossal size. A giant box in the shape of a beating red heart maybe.

"Did you get the toxicology report back?" Ryan jumps right in. He's convinced the driver of the vehicle that hit them was a drunk teenager. So far all we know is that it was a girl.

"Yes, we did." Jake flips open the top of the minuscule folder and reads off a white piece of paper with small print. "She was found negative in every form of narcotic. The only thing that was detected in her system was decongestant."

A nineteen-year-old girl who I now know by the name of Vivian Whitfield caused an accident that uprooted my daughter's life. According to the grapevine in town, the girl was driving in from Providence College, planning to stay with her aunt and uncle who live in Flagport. Vivian is originally from Virginia but spent several summers in the town with her aunt, often working as a camp coun-selor at some of the summer camp programs.

Ryan exhales at the news and Lauren isn't sure if he is relieved that the girl was not intoxicated. "If the girl wasn't under the influence, then what the hell was she thinking when she went through an intersection without stopping to see if anyone was there?"

It's not lost on me that Ryan seems to be giving the girl a free pass in the event she actually was driving drunk.

"Well, considering it was later at night, we are assuming that it had to do with lethargy."

"So, because some kid was tired, she's going to get away with nearly killing my daughter!" Ryan slams his hands on the table, spurred by an anger I'd only witnessed when his sports teams were losing.

"Not necessarily. That's kind of up to you guys and why we're here right now." His words were softened on the edges, made gentler with an empathetic tilt of his head. "Have you thought about pressing charges?'

I had thought about it. I had thought about it while I sat alone at Lily's bedside, but the thoughts would often produce emotions laced in anger, hatred, and defeat. Pressing charges would never be enough if Lily didn't make it through this and return to her perfect self. Instead, I thought about how I wanted to take my own vehicle and drive into Vivian Whitfield repeatedly, how I wanted to grab her by the shoulders and shake her for driving when she was overtired.

"Yes, we're pressing charges," Ryan answered for the two of them.

"What good will that do?" I throw the question in between the three of us. "What good will that do if my daughter is dead?"

"Lauren." Ryan looks as if he wants to yell at me, but he stops himself and plasters an empathetic expression on his face. "She's gonna be fine."

"How do you know?" I can feel the start of tears again, the swell that forms in my heart before it rises to my eyes, releasing a flood of emotion that is rippled with anger and sadness, the two swinging back and forth like a pendulum on a grandfather clock. *Back and forth, back and forth.* "Tell me, right now, Ryan…how do you know that she's going to be okay? Did you somehow become psychic overnight, because the last I checked, her doctors had no answers for whether or not she would walk out of that hospital, or even be wheeled out, for that matter. We don't know what we are going to have for a daughter when and *if* she wakes up." As the words erupt from my mouth, I feel a surprising blend of relief and remorse.

"Lauren, we're gonna deal with whatever happens, okay?" Ryan tries again but it's too late. A wave of anger takes over my body, moving through me like a tsunami.

"I can't deal with this right now—"

"Lauren, I scheduled a—" before Jake can finish, I shoot up from my chair and make a beeline for the door. As I push through, I nearly smack face-first into Evie and Matt.

"Lauren!" Evie reaches for my elbow, but I flip my arm back before she can make contact, sending a painful surge through my bad shoulder.

31

After

APRIL 2021

Evie

I've seen Lauren mad over the years, but I've never seen her like this, and it constricts my insides to know that I'm the cause of it. I turn around and watch her speed out of the police station, her flip-flops smacking on the concrete floor. And then, Ryan pushes out the same door. Without any words, his face asks us why we're here, but instead of pausing to inquire, he walks around us and races after Lauren, releasing a loud sigh in his wake.

Officer Wright emerges from the room and directs us to two of the eight chairs that surround the table. "Sorry, I'll handle this. Just take a seat." He follows the same path that was just carved by Ryan and Lauren, and moments later the three of them are back in the room. Lauren and Ryan sit on opposite sides of Matt and me, and Officer Wright is at the head of the table with two folders.

"Okay, so I'm sorry if this is poor timing on my part, but there are some decisions that need to be made if you all want to press charges," Officer Wright says, his words shaky.

I feel the desperation inside me as I attempt to make eye contact with Lauren. Just three months ago, we were celebrating my fortieth birthday party, a surprise event planned and thrown by her, with everything I could've imagined. A cover band that played the nineties songs she and I always reminisced about, a dessert bar that had pastry's prepared and tattooed with my name, and she even took the time to buy me forty of my favorite items. Just two weeks ago the two of us were planted in the Adirondack chairs in my front yard discussing life. *What would we do when the kids left the nest? Were we prepared for the inevitable sadness that comes with no longer having our babies at home and were we ready to embrace it?* Me more than her, of course. While I would miss the boys something awful, I was at peace with them facing the world on their own, and I was confident that Jack would find his way. Liam, I still had a couple years to work on, but Jack was ready. When I expressed this to her two weeks ago, as we drank our coffee and watched the first signs of spring come to life, I saw something harden in her eyes. She looked down into her mug as if she was searching for something and that's when I realized this was going to be a much harder change for her than it was for me. I reached for her hand. "Hey, it's gonna be okay. Lily will only be forty-five minutes away. She can come visit you every weekend."

"She won't."

It was the first time I'd seen Lauren look defeated. Over the twelve years I'd known her, I'd witnessed her work a room like a trained sales professional, tipping her head back in laughter at just the right moment. I'd seen her execute an event flawlessly, not a single seating chart mistake for parties of five hundred. I've watched her attend every one of her kids' events and volunteer at half of them, a smile always spread across her face and intention in her every move. But, in the moment she confessed that Lily would never visit her, I had trouble not feeling the same way. And it was then that I realized that maybe Lily really did despise her mother for the years of control. Maybe Lauren had appeared to be the perfect mother from the outside, but she crossed a million boundaries behind closed doors.

AND NOW, here we are, sitting in a police station, deciding on the fate of the teen girl who crashed into my car and put her daughter in a coma. This decision is not up to me. Yes, I was the driver of what is being deemed as the innocent vehicle, but I'm not the one who has a life on the line. I look at Lauren's face from the opposite side of the table. She looks like she's aged a decade. Her skin is free of makeup, revealing the tiny dents and bumps that come from age. The only time I'd seen her without makeup was during our beach days, but even then, her skin had a nice glow to it, and her eyes were shielded by big sunglasses, concealing any potential sightings of dark circles. Now, there are two pillows that billow beneath her eyes, her cheeks are marked with red patches, a blend of dry skin and incessant tears, I imagine. The cat eyes that have always stood out on her face, with only a sweep of mascara, are now two sunken gems beneath her brow, which is now grown in where there used to be a seductive arch. That is what three days of grief and fear will do to a person.

The four of us remain silent as Officer Wright flips through the folders, although I'm not sure what he is looking at because the folders are bare, with only a handful of documents in each. He's nervous, I think. "So, do any of you have opinions on whether or not—"

The sound of the door hitting the wall interrupts his words and a cohesive ripple of surprise runs through all of us in the room. Michael McCue is standing front and center, the top of his head only inches from the doorframe. A rush of red brightens his face, and he throws an arm in front of him, extending an index finger in my direction. "We will be suing, Jake...the chief already has my attorney's information."

Lauren sits up in her chair, her eyes darting from me to her dad and back. She's just as confused as the rest of us. "Dad, what are you doing here?"

"Sweetie, don't worry, I'll handle it from here."

I hear Matt mumble, "what the fuck is happening?" as Ryan

seems to sink into his chair and Lauren rockets herself upright with an energy I didn't think she was capable of in her current state. "Dad, what are you talking about…the driver wasn't intoxicated… she was tired. That's not going to change anything if we press charges."

"I'm not talking about the other driver, sweetheart; I'm talking about this driver!" He points another finger in my direction and I feel as if a spotlight has just been placed on me. I'm on a stage in a dark room in front of hundreds of people and a light is shining directly on me. "Honey, she was never good enough for you and now look what she did. She put my granddaughter in danger and nearly killed her." The words come out in a growl, the skin on his cheeks move in rhythm to his head shakes.

"Hey, hey, hold on a second." Matt stands up, resting a hand on my shoulder, going to battle for me. "What are you talking about? Evie is not at fault here. Can we just sit down and talk about this?" Always the diplomat, Matt's voice is calm, as if he is simply breaking up a fight between Liam and Jack.

"What the hell was that woman doing driving my grand-daughter around anyways? I knew from the second you two moved into this town you were trouble. And now my sweet baby girl is on her deathbed—"

"Dad! Stop!" Lauren erupts in a scream.

"Michael—" Ryan starts.

"No, this conversation is over. We're suing you for being a negli-gent driver. I know that you were stopped in the intersection for a beat too long. That girl wouldn't have hit you if you weren't paused to do whatever it was you were doing…molding my granddaughter to be a piece of trash like yourself or maybe you were checking your phone—"

Heat swells inside of me, from the blend of emotions that are wreaking havoc on my insides. As if I didn't feel awful enough. Up until this moment I held firm to the belief that this accident was not my fault. But now I'm second-guessing myself. Is it my fault that I told Lily to move to the front seat when she was feeling ill? Is it my fault because I didn't walk over to Lauren's house in the middle of the night and let her know her daughter needed a ride? Maybe Michael is right. I could've handled this accident in a dozen different ways, and it could've resulted in a dozen different outcomes. I could have my best friend still in my good graces, the family across the street would still be my family, the family I'd grown so attached to all these years. I look at Lauren, and I see something I've never seen in her eyes before. This is the same face that has only offered me smiles and expressions of approval, and now all I see is sadness and disappointment.

"Hey! Hold on a second!" Matt holds a palm out in front of him. "Can we talk about this?"

Michael McCue has made his way across the room and pulls a now sobbing Lauren into his side. He holds her in the crook of his arm, and over her head he says, "There is nothing to discuss. We're done here."

32

Before

DECEMBER 2018

Evie

The Flagport Yacht Club is decorated with class. White lights cling to the outlines of the building, a massive wreath is adhered to the mahogany door, all professionally hung by the best decorators on the North Shore of Boston.

"I feel like we're forgetting something," Matt says, placing his hand on the small of my back as I step into the building.

"The kids maybe?"

"Is that it?" Matt looks at me with the naivety I've seen a thousand times before. I imagine it's his ability to speak so honestly that has him as the highest selling person in his industry. People have always been able to relate to Matt. He makes everyone feel human and listened to, even if he does sound a tad dumb in the process.

"It feels good to have a night out without them."

"They're sixteen and twelve it's probably time we get used to having nights out without them." I nudge his shoulder.

"I know, I know, they're growing up. I'm just...I don't know, it's a holiday event and I feel bad leaving them home three days before Christmas."

"I'm pretty sure they aren't missing us. The four of them are having a ball, and hopefully not getting into trouble," I say, picturing Jack, Lily, Liam and Piper doing God knows what at the Rivers' house.

"Are you kidding...Lily would never allow them to get into trouble. Lauren probably has her volume turned up extra high tonight on their home cameras, so she doesn't miss a beat on what is going on at the house," Matt says.

It wasn't the first time we let the four kids stay home alone together. We'd been out a handful of times, but never quite so late as I imagine we will be tonight. "That's exactly why I feel so safe leaving them alone. I'm pretty sure Lauren has cameras in all the rooms the kids have access to."

"At least they have each other." He repeats the thoughts that have been running through my mind a lot lately. The Rivers family has become our own. We do everything together and our kids are getting a sense of what it feels like to have extended family. With my only-child status and our distance from Matt's hometown, our kids will never know what it's like to bond with cousins. So, the fact that our children are spending the night with the Rivers' girls brings me a sense of comfort. Although, even after all these years, I still wonder why Lauren, with her status in town, has chosen me to befriend. I sometimes find myself allowing insecurity to slip in and I question whether I'm a charity case for her. Someone she has wanted to mold, to take under her wing and steer in a direction similar to her own. I'll never be a McCue, but I'm starting to feel like I belong somewhere, a far cry from how I felt bouncing from state to state, friendship to friendship. I've arrived in a town I never want to leave, and I look forward to the day my own children will have children here, a new generation that will officially have the Flagger title, as ridiculous as that may sound.

"Yeah, and I'm pretty sure we belong at that bar right now." Straight in front of us, is a wooden bar in the shape of a boat, decorated with lit up red and green buoys and lifesavers.

"Damn!" Matt says louder than necessary, making us look like newbies. This is our first time attending the annual Christmas party hosted by Lauren's parents. We've been invited in the past, but it always fell on the same night as Matt's company party.

I feel as if I've walked onto the set of a Christmas movie. A server stops in front of us, holding out a tray covered with cranberry and brie canapés, parsley sprinkled on them like fallen snowflakes. "Thank you." I pluck one from the tray and do my best to avoid my perfectly placed red lipstick as I push it into my mouth.

The smell of pine is confirmed when my gaze lands on the biggest Christmas tree I've ever seen. Across the ballroom, it's decorated with blue and white bulbs and sparkly white ribbon, staying in the yacht club color theme.

"Shall we?" Matt loops an arm through mine and leads us to the boat bar, where the atmosphere is bubbling with glee. Chatter and laughter punch the air as hugs and handshakes get passed around like gifts under the Christmas tree. The bar is three bodies deep, but people kindly move out of the way, toting their own drinks and making space for us to present our order. "For you, madam?" Matt is still going strong with his best high-falutin impression. We've lived in this town for over nine years, and like me, he still feels out of place in the circles we run in at times. We do well between Matt's steadily increasing raises and bonuses and my bustling landscaping business, but we don't come from money, and I sometimes worry that we have a red flag on our foreheads annotating this.

"I'll take a peppermint martini." I surprised him with the diversion from my normal cabernet.

"Woah. Glad this is open bar." He winks and passes our order to the twenty-something bartender who is wearing a scantily-clad elf costume with cleavage pushed together by a cropped red vest. The girl's flirty wink is lost on Matt.

"This is open bar?" I look around the room, my gaze naturally landing on the sparkly jewels that tattoo every woman's ears, the tuxes and jackets that fit in a way that is only possible with a hefty price tag. "I shouldn't be surprised."

"There you guys are!" As if on cue, Lauren struts toward us, a hunter-green dress hugging her body and landing just above the knees. We lean in for a hug, her nude heels giving her just enough height so she is equal with me in my kitten heels. I normally tower over her, but now we stand eye to eye. "You look beautiful!" she says, her cat eyes enhanced even more with a deep green shade on her lids and gold sparkles beneath her brow.

"*You* look beautiful!" We sound like two schoolgirls seeing each other at prom.

"Hey, dude, you look gorgeous," Matt says to Ryan as he takes him in for a hug and shoulder pat, clearly poking fun at our exchange.

"What can I say? I try." Ryan adjusts his tie and shrugs his shoulders. "What do you guys want to drink?" He looks at our empty hands.

"Oh, we got some drinks coming…from the Barbie elf," I joke.

Lauren lets out her signature one-syllable laugh. "Ha! I said the same thing. Clearly a man was in charge of hiring the help for this shindig."

"I had no idea elves had cleavage like that," I add.

"You and me both."

Ryan flags the elf and asks for a bourbon.

"Excuse me?" Lauren raises her brows at Ryan, accusingly.

"What?"

"Did you not ask your wife if she wants a beverage?"

Sarcasm spills from his lips as he says, "What would you like, dear?"

"Whatever my friend is having." She nods to the filled-to-the-brim martini glass that is being slid across the bar toward me by the elf.

"So, this is quite the bash," I say, taking in the effervescence that moves through the room freely.

"Best Christmas party in town…at least according to my parents." Lauren massages her shoulder with polished fingertips, a gesture I've noticed her doing more and more over the years. "It used to be kid-friendly too. As a kid, I saw my fair share of drunken adults passing around gifts. In fact, my grandfather used to play Santa Claus, and I'm pretty sure he kept nips tucked away in his suit coat."

"When did it change from kids to adults only?" Matt asks.

Lauren's face shifts, a look of discomfort passes over her expression, and the conversation slides off the tracks when Megan walks into the circle.

"Well, hello Sullivan family," Megan says.

"You made it home for the holidays?" I say.

"Only because my big sister begged me." She brings a glass to her lips, something clear and bubbly and garnished with lime, taking a tiny sip, while she winks.

I've always enjoyed being around Megan, and I think part of it might be because she has been a challenge to figure out, like sorting through a one-thousand-piece puzzle. She always seems to have it together, but her friendliness has rigid boundaries, where she lets you in just enough, without having to share too much about herself. As much as I've tried to dig, I've never found the answers I was looking for when it came to Lauren's younger sister. Why does she stay so physically distant when her family is so tight knit? Why does she always seem to have one eye on Lauren as if she's babysitting her when she is the younger sibling? Why has she never, as far as anyone knows, been in a romantic relationship? She's stunning, with big round blue eyes, and she always has her bright blonde hair cut into trendy layers, drawing attention in the way that blondes do. She seems to like her career as a writer, but not to the point where it overpowers her life. And I know this because on more than one occasion I've heard her preaching to Lauren about the importance of *me* time, and how it helps us reenergize when we separate ourselves from both family and work. So, she's not a workaholic who prioritizes her career over her family. So, what gives?

"And look at you four out on the town childless tonight."

"A rare moment indeed," Ryan says as he pulls Matt away in some sidebar conversation about another home project they plan on attempting together.

Just as I'm about to ask Megan how long she plans on staying in town, knowing full well it will be less than twenty-four hours because it always is, a hearty laugh echoes through the ballroom.

"Oh boy, is this happening right now?" Lauren takes a gulp of her martini, her eyes aimed at the entrance. Megan follows her gaze, then I follow, a rippling effect of attention. A jolly man in a red suit *ho ho ho's* his way across the ballroom, as a slow clap ignites amongst the guests.

"Is that—"

"Yep, it's our dad." Lauren turns to me and starts to step behind me as if I could hide her.

"Wow, I didn't know this was part of the entertainment," I laugh.

"Always. Every year, except—" Lauren starts.

"Except the year I...uh... had strep throat," Megan finishes her sentence.

We watch as Mr. McCue shuffles across the floor, a sack over one shoulder and a white, gloved hand extended in a wave the entire time. "Your dad is awesome. My dad would never do anything like that." I think of my militant father, attached to the Army lifestyle in every sense possible, rarely breaking his tight upper lip or allowing his upper body to fold into a real, genuine hug. Instead, every hour of every day was dictated by rules and routine, our schedules, and to-dos a finely tuned calendar.

"Ohhhh your dad is actually sounding pretty awesome right now." Lauren balances her martini glass between her fingers, with arms crossed in front of her chest.

I look at both girls and expect to see an embarrassed, yet joyful look on their faces, but instead I see something else that I can't quite figure out.

"You girls must've loved this when you were kids."

"Yeah, Dad was a pretty great Santa Claus." The words slip from Lauren's tight-lipped smile. "He's a good actor."

We watch as the guests part to make room for Santa's entrance. He waves and hands out gifts along the way, and at the end he is greeted by another scantily-clad elf holding out a martini to him. And then, Mr. McCue is gone. He's swallowed up by a crowd of men who I recognize as some of the town officials and police chief. They all clap him on the back and pull him into their circle, and the room gets louder.

33

Before
DECEMBER 2018

Lauren

Being at this place makes my insides burn. It's never gotten easier, but I've mastered my role as Lauren McCue, the lucky daughter of one of the wealthiest and most well-connected families in town. I simply slip into my metaphorical costume and work the room as if I actually like being me. I make sure that everyone thinks I'm glowing from the inside out.

"Excuse me for a moment, I need to check on the desserts." I gently tap Lydia Harrington's arm, interrupting the ideas she was spewing at me about potential future yacht club parties. It's not rare for me to opt out of a conversation mid-way. After all, I'm head of special events and I put this shindig on, so it offers me the perfect opportunity to exit on a whim. If I'm going to be immersed in this town, I want to have a say in what happens. I want to dictate what events get thrown at this snobby club, and I want to be able to drop out of a conversation whenever I please, especially when I'm feeling uneasy. Especially when I'm overcome with anxiety, afraid that just by being in this space I'll have to relive my past all over again.

I move into the woman's changing room, a space that was added at my suggestion a few years ago. With the caliber of events that goes on in this space, we needed a place for women to nurse. However, the truth is, I use it as an escape room when I get overwhelmed, when I feel the panic rising within. I drop down on the edge of the green couch, a piece that was donated by my mother, during one of her many redecorating splurges. I suck in a breath of air more aggressively than I intend and get mad at myself for the harsh intake. If my therapist was here, she would tell me to relax my shoulders and think of a calming place. "Focus on your breath. Focus on a place that brings you joy," she would say. The Flagport Yacht Club does not bring me joy, contrary to what I project on the outside. I've mastered the fake smile I present when I pose for photos, and spin from one conversation to the next while gripping the forearm of fellow Flaggers as I pass by and make eye contact that is so intense, you'd think I was really listening to what they were saying. I'm not. In fact, I'm reliving the moment I transformed from happy-go-lucky teenager with the whole world ahead of me, to a person who had to pry herself out of bed every morning, walking through each day without ease, as if I was stepping through quicksand from the time I woke up to the time my head hit the pillow.

The only thing that has managed to ease a portion of the pain was the birth of my daughters. Lily, being the first, has always had a particularly tight hold on me. Without even knowing it, I've put a heaping pile of pressure on her, at the chance that I can steer her life, make sure she doesn't screw up like I did. I will be keeping my tight hold on her as long as possible. I only have one chance at this parenting thing and since it is the only thing that has saved me, I've given it my all, thrown myself into it with every ounce of my being.

Now, as I sit in this small room, I push my chest out, sitting upright to better my chances of gathering full sips of air. I try again, sipping instead of sucking the air in this time. And then, midway through my inhale, I stop abruptly when the door swings open. I knew it would be Megan before she even makes it through the threshold.

"I thought I'd find you in here." She drops onto the cushion beside me. She goes to work making circles on my back with her palm, her cool skin hitting the space where my dress dips down and exposes my skin. "Breathe. Just breathe."

I fall into her side, allowing her to embrace me. The smell of her Burgundy perfume has been a comfort to me all these years, offering me a sense of peace when it hits the air, as my emotions swirl in an endless loop of chaos. Guilt and remorse and regret bump into one another and collect like a tumbleweed of insanity. As if my senses are aware of Megan's presence, they line up to let me know that it's going to be okay. Megan is here to calm me. It's all going to be okay. I grab her wrist and pull it into me, tightening her embrace as if the less space I have, the more protected I'll be from my own emotions. "Thank you, Megs."

"You know you don't have to come to these things." She says the words that she's been saying for years.

"And how would that look?" I ask, trying to fight off the throbbing ache that is forming in my throat. *Don't cry, don't cry, don't cry.* If I cry, they will see, and I'll have to make up another excuse about why I'm an emotional wreck.

"Lo, it doesn't matter how it looks." She uses a finger to move an escaped tendril from my view. "It doesn't matter what all these people think."

"Yes, it does."

"Lo, I can't bear to see you like this anymore. I can't help you if you keep slipping back into Mom and Dad's warped lifestyle. You're too good for this. You're too good for them. You don't need to hold up this charade. Why does it matter to you what all these people think?"

I know the answer to her question, but I can't bring myself to let it hit the surface, because if it does, it means that it is true. If I don't care what everyone thinks and I don't throw myself into my life, into the Flagport life, then what happened all those years ago will come crashing to the surface and push me into an emotional state I'm not sure I'm capable of living through. If I don't throw myself into Lily's life and maintain a determined focus on her every step, my attention will be forced to shift elsewhere, and I'll have to accept the one thing I don't want to accept. There are therapists for this type of grief and pain and remorse, but it's easier for me to become my own dictator of my emotions. Having a tight leash on my life prevents all those horrid memories from coming to the surface. "I just…I don't know." A tear burns at the inner corner of my eye, and it falls over the edge, drudging up a parade of a dozen more. My breath, now fully erratic, joins my tears and I sob, thinking about how different things could've been if I'd made a different decision all those years ago.

"I know that you're denying your feelings, Lo, but you need to accept them so you can move on."

"I have moved on!" A surge of anger pushes through me. I've worked so hard to move on. I've created a family and a career and social circles that show how I've moved on. "What do you think I'm doing every day of my life? I'm moving on. I'm doing everything in my power to move on, to create a nice life for myself."

"That's not the same as coming to terms with the past, Lo." She's moved past my outbursts. She always does. I suppose years of therapy has given her that patience. "It's never too late."

"That's just it. It's far too late." I feel it in my gut that my time is up to come to terms with what I did. I signed a silent contract the day Lily was born, and I set her life in motion. I can't go back. I can't let my children know what I did. And they will know if I lift off the veil of my attachment to making everything perfect. If I don't put on this act, if I allow what I did to seep into my consciousness, then I will have to adopt an entirely different identity. I will have to think about that night and talk about it. Megan knows this. She knows that it's easier for me to just remain, to just go on living in the costume I've been in. She pulls me into her side tighter and then the door opens. I look up from behind my mask of tears and see Evie staring at me as a thousand questions show themselves on her sympathetic expression.

"Oh, Lauren…I'm sorry…I—" She looks behind her as if she is

speaking to the closed door instead of me. She's my closest friend but she still doesn't know what to say in this moment. She's never seen me cry. At least she's never seen me really cry. Sure, I've shed tears at those parental milestones that she's been there to witness. Lily's first boyfriend, Lily's first dance, Lily's first period. And it dawns on me that I've only ever really shed tears for Lily's gains. I've ignored all of Piper's firsts. It's as if Lily has been the one on my radar all these years. Lily, with her near-identical looks as mine. Lily, as my chance to try and make myself not feel any of the emotions that aren't going away. Sure, they decrease to a slow boil while I'm focused on Lily's life, but they always bubble back up to a full boil in the quiet moments.

"No worries, I...I was just—"

"We miss our grandfather, and well, this was the event that always brings up memories of him," Megan says, so well-rehearsed I silently applaud her for an act that is almost as good as the ones that I uphold.

Evie steps forward. Her eyes dart between Megan and me and I'm certain that the wheels are spinning in her head. She's wondering why the hell I'm sobbing and Megan's face is as dry as chalk. I know the answer to this, but Evie doesn't. Megan's mind has come to terms with our past, to that fateful evening, and she has changed the course of her life.

34

After
APRIL 2021

Lauren

I hate leaving the hospital. Even if it's only to step outside for a breath of fresh air. So when I make the trek back to Flagport to shower and get some things, I feel out of sorts. My luck in life so far has shown that I have bad timing, and my biggest fear will be that Lily will have a change in her condition while I'm away. Her status is still critical. Nothing has changed. I look in the rearview mirror as I pull into our driveway. It's only been five days since the accident, but I look like I've aged a decade.

Piper looks at me from behind her phone, catching my eyes in the rearview mirror. She offers me a tight-lipped smile, but she's learned to stay quiet around me. I'm like a ticking time bomb lately. Everything has the potential to set me off.

"All right, Pipes. You can shower while I get some stuff done, okay?" I muster up a smile at the end of my words.

She nods.

I fall out of the car, my body heavy with the weight of emotion. I look around me, hoping to God no one sees me going into my house. I was afraid my father would be planted on my front steps, with his attorney and a document at-the-ready to sign. I cannot think about who to sue or what criminal charges to press right now. As a McCue, he is looking out for me, protecting his own, but that doesn't stop me from being disappointed in his reaction toward Evie at the police station. In all the anger I have boiling up inside me for Evie, I found myself reeling at his comments toward her and I wanted to jump at her defense and protect the only real friend I thought I'd ever had.

The mailbox is filled with bundled-up envelopes and catalogues as if we've been away on vacation for a week. Our mailman has always looked out for us, and he must know something is off since we haven't been home. I'm always here when he arrives, greeting him with a smile and small talk. When I push through the door, I'm welcomed with the smell of home. I expected to walk into a mess, but remembered that our cleaner, Nina, comes twice a week. I've forgotten so much of what my everyday life is, as if I've been pulled into some twisted time warp. I haven't looked at my calendar in days, forgoing all routine and daily activity and pushed into survival mode. My color-coded daily planner dictated my every move but now I don't even know what day it is. I look at the clock on the microwave. Eleven. Yep, Nina would've left an hour ago and she comes on Tuesdays and Thursdays. The doctor shared the painful reminder that Lily has been in a coma for five days, so today must be Thursday. The house smells like lemons and lavender, and for a moment I regret not cancelling Nina this week. I wanted to latch onto what the house was like before the accident. Before the dozen vases of flowers and well wishes landed on my countertop. Hours before I got the call from the police, the four of us were seated around the table, eating our favorite takeout from Sotheby's Kitchen, a local restaurant that is a Flagport staple for quality food. The empty takeout containers are long gone, the smell of the food no longer here to drum up the last memory of my daughter, because Nina likely opened the windows to let the fresh spring air in.

The sound of the shower upstairs serves as background noise as I make my way to Lily's room. It's picture perfect as usual. Even without Nina's visits, Lily keeps a tidy room. She has a place for everything. I sit at her desk and smooth a palm over the white surface, pausing to pick at the one tiny dent in the wood, another memory. When she pressed so hard on her pencil that it dented the wood, tattooing it forever. Lily was nine when we realized she was a good student. Her teacher classified her as borderline gifted even though she said that term is no longer used to describe a student's status. That was around the time when I really started to take on a bigger presence in her life. I thought that if I pushed her hard enough at a young age, it would set her up for success. She would excel in school and get accepted to all the big schools that I wanted to go to. She would never make the poor decisions that I was exposed to and have a life of regret. I so badly wanted this for her and look where it landed me.

I pull open the bottom drawer, fully aware of the mistake I'm making. I've read all the parenting books about how a parent is never supposed to snoop through their teenager's belongings. It puts a pause on trust, and it takes a while to build back up according to every book I've read on the topic. But Lily already didn't trust me if she was texting Evie to come get her, instead of me.

The bottom drawer is the deepest. It's where Lily keeps her study books. All the SAT supplies I purchased to give her the best chance possible of getting a top score. And it worked. I use my fingertips to pull up the books and decide it's a lost cause. If she was hiding anything, it wouldn't be in this drawer. I pull open the thin drawer that sits beneath the desktop. Colored pens line up like dead soldiers, fresh Post-It Notes in every color imaginable, some still in the plastic wrapping. I pull out an opened stack of pink and go to work writing a note to my daughter. With a blue pen poised in my hand, I think of what I want to tell her if I could and I write a dozen messages, sticking them on her desktop, the bulletin board above her desk, and the white headboard at the front of her bed. If she comes home, she will see how much I love her. I imagine her plucking them off one by one like she did when I created scavenger hunts for her as a little girl. I imagine her smiling and laughing when she reads my notes. "Mom," she will say, extending the last "m" and rolling her eyes in the good way, the playful way. Not the bad way when she got frustrated with me hovering over her.

I press my hand on her white comforter and push myself up when my gaze lands on it. The navy-blue leather-bound book I gave her for her birthday during her sweet sixteen celebration. It's wedged between two thick novels. I told her to start writing her life goals down, because seeing them every day would be like an affirmation and they would one day come true. Not like she has any deterrents from conquering her dreams. She has the perfect setup in life. Born into money, driven, and supported by a mother who loves her more than anything in the world. My hand lands on the book and I hesitate before I pull it out.

The scent of leather hits me as I open it and a wave of heat crashes over my body when I read the first page.

35

Before

NOVEMBER 2019

Lauren

"You are officially no longer a Flagport sports virgin," I tell Evie as soon as we step through the gates that lead to the high school football field.

"We're the real deal now." She bumps shoulders with me as we make our way toward the bleachers, now a sea of red and black.

Lily takes off on a mission to the bleachers and stops to chat with a circle of girls, hugging each one of them individually. I watch, taking in how Jack is standing awkwardly behind her and for the first time I realize that he might not be as popular in school as she is. They are sophomores in high school, a time when popularity means everything. I march over to the circle and tug on Lily's arms after I greet the girls with my best "cool mom" smile. When Jack and the other girls are out of earshot, I lean down and whisper into her ear, "Make sure you include Jack, okay?" I catch her eye roll, one of many that she's showcased since this morning already.

"Yes, Mom," she says, adding another eye roll.

I assess her head to toe and notice her top is dipping a little too low in the front. Not that she has cleavage. She's as unblessed as I am in that department, but nevertheless I don't need her showing skin. "And button this up, please." I tug on the button of her hunter green jacket and pull it across her chest.

"Mom!" she hisses and starts to march back to her friends.

"Lily!" I yell. She turns around, whipping her blonde ponytail like a competitive cheerleader. "Don't forget...we have to work on your geography project tonight." It's Saturday. I'm certain none of her friends will be doing homework tonight, but she has to keep up and stay at the top of her class if she wants a successful life. She passes me an embarrassed nod and turns back toward her friends. I see her grab Jack's wrist and pull him into the circle, and I'm satisfied that at least one of my jobs is done for today.

"So do you have like, designated Flagger seats or something?" Evie, who is now standing alone, having been ditched by Piper and Liam, asks. I point to the bleachers, now towering over us. Spectators stomp their feet and clap their hands in tune to the song the band practices at the base of the field.

The two of us maneuver our bodies up the bleachers to the top row, where there is a strip of metal seating visible amongst the red and black. "Do you think the boys won any money yet?" I ask as soon as I plop onto the bleachers, the cold of the metal pushing through my black leggings. Ryan and Matt won a night out sans kids when we lost to a game of trivia to them at a local pub, and they chose to play poker with a group of guys that regularly play. Evidently, it's a game that Ryan has always wanted to get better at, which was news to me when he shared this piece of information.

"Matt is definitely not winning any money." Evie laughs. "He couldn't pull off a poker face if he tried."

"Wait-has he never played poker before?"

"Ummm...like maybe once for a bachelor party like, ten years ago," Evie says sarcastically.

"Lauren McCue!" A voice pierces the air, two rows down and diagonal from us. A woman wearing a red and black Flagport winter hat twists her body toward me, long wavy brown hair spills from the hat and lands in the front pocket of her jacket. She looks familiar but I can't place her.

She leans in closer, clearly a little tipsy. "It's me…Anna Moulton!" she yells, with far too much excitement. And then it dawns on me. She was in my home economics class junior year before I left for Pembroke Academy and never returned.

"Oh, hi, Anna! How are you?" I put on my best facade and brace myself for the questions she will undoubtedly ask.

"Where have you been?" She starts firing them off. "I haven't seen you since you left FHS. I thought you left town forever, until Gracie Wellington mentioned she saw you at Montby's a few weeks back." Being in a relatively small town, I'm constantly running into people from my past, and the lies I tell about the years I left slide off my tongue easily. "I don't blame you for leaving…I just moved back here too," Anna says. The fact that the girl is completely oblivious about why I left is comforting.

"Oh, you know…busy with kids and stuff."

"Is your family still like, dominating this town?" Anna shouts. It's all coming back to me. She was always one who lacked couth. She ran in different circles than me in school, but I was friendly enough to her. She was funny, always looking for attention as the class clown. I hadn't seen her since high school and now that makes sense since she moved away for awhile.

I don't know how to respond. Is my family still dominating this town? While it's a dumb question to ask, it's also one that I've pondered over the years. I smile at her. "Oh, you know, everyone is doing the same old thing."

"Your dad is like, in the paper every week, girl! I love that guy."

I nod and pass her a smile that I'm hoping shows confidence, even though I feel small on the inside. "Yeah, he loves the spotlight," I say jokingly. Although, I'm not joking at all. Michael McCue loves the spotlight as long as he's perfectly polished while it's casting a glow on him.

When Anna is beckoned by a girl who has her same hairline, one that starts further back than looks attractive, and a nose that is slightly too big for her face, I'm grateful that I don't have to go into any more detail about my brief escape from Flagport.

"I take it you two didn't run in the same crowd." Evie picks up on my discomfort.

"Yeah, Anna's a nice girl, but truthfully, I would've never remembered her if she hadn't announced herself," I say.

36

Before

NOVEMBER 2019

Evie

I naturally slip into the comfort zone of supporting a team and I even find myself paying attention to the game, shouting in sync with the crowds when the Flagport High School quarterback makes a freakishly long pass to his teammate. My childhood was not marked with football games and town events. Instead, it was a constant rat race of moving, meeting new friends, and moving again.

"Mom, can I have money?" Jack tugs on my jacket, interrupting my mix of thoughts. He holds an open palm in front of my face, a greedy gesture that I don't remember ever teaching him. But my question is answered when I see a matching extended hand in front of Lauren. Lily waves her palm around, awaiting a bill that Lauren slips out of her pocket and places in her daughter's hand, seemingly without a second thought. My own mother would be appalled if she witnessed me, as I rifle through my purse and pull out a five-dollar bill, placing it in Jack's palm without a single word of protest. "Get something for you *and* your brother." The money is given freely, without the completion of a chore or a reward for an occasion. It's simply placed in his hands in a way I never experienced growing up. If my mother were here, she'd be piercing the air with her Italian intonations, listing out all ways giving money to a child so freely is cause for the creation of a spoiled brat. But I've learned to ease up on spending money since we moved to Flagport. Sometimes a place can change you. We've been here for over ten years and I'm now just realizing how my values have shifted. Before, I clung to the idea that money was something that you earned, and I had committed to myself that I wouldn't be one of those parents who gives so openly. I promised myself I'd teach my children the value of a dollar.

I watch as Lily raises her eyebrows, evidently disappointed in the meager ten-dollar bill, a cue to Lauren that she needs more. Jack follows suit, but I hold my ground and stand firm with keeping the limit at five, while Lauren produces another bill and presses it on top of the ten in Lily's hand. I get a dirty look from Jack but promise myself he'll thank me in the future when he values a dollar more than his less-thrifty counterparts in life. Jack and Lily hop down the bleacher stairs making a beeline for the concession stand. I watch as Jack does as he's told and waves at Liam, motioning for him to follow him to the concession stand, pulling him and Piper away from where they are leaning on the fence that outlines the field.

My pushback on being a human vending machine seems lost on Lauren. Maybe she is so used to being able to attain money easily that the lack of it in other people's lives is completely nonexistent. It's not that Matt and I don't do well financially, in fact, I'm doing better than I ever have thanks to Lauren's landscaping leads. It's just that I think it's much easier for her to spend and let go of cash because of her wealthy upbringing. She's generous to a fault though, often getting our boys gifts that outdo the ones that Santa brings and on more than one occasion she's offered to pay our way into an event.

"Can you believe that our babies will be in this high school someday," Lauren says to me as I take in the view. Flagport High

School sits in one giant rectangular block beyond the busy football field. I spent half of my high school years at one school that was smaller than this one, and the other half at one that was larger.

"It's going to be a lot sooner than some day," I say, as I do the math in my head. "Liam and Piper will be here next year."

"I can't believe how fast they grow up—"

I look over at Lauren and take in her crumpled expression. And just as I'm about to ask her what's wrong, a small section of the crowd below is pulled into a circle, a tangle of bodies in the middle. My eyes scan the area, landing on the concessions, where I see Jack, Lily and Piper racing toward the newly formed circle. *Where is Liam?*

Lauren and I shoot up from the bleachers and race down, the sound of metal popping beneath our steps. I keep my eyes trained on the circle and take in the trickle of comments that surface from the spectators. *Fight. Two boys. What the heck is going on?* Before I even get to Jack, I see the light brown hair that belongs to my younger son flopping with every movement, now free from the confines of the Flagport hat. "Liam!" I yell, anger boiling inside of me. *Who is hurting my kid?* With Lauren close on my heels, I push myself through the crowd. "Liam!" I picture an older kid bullying my little boy, a spectator from the other team having beef with my son's head-to-toe Flagport attire.

I make my way through the mosh pit of people pulling and pushing to get closer to rescue Liam, and that's when I see my worst nightmare. Liam is straddling another kid of equal size, a fist raised overhead and crashing into the boy's nose before a man in the circle has the chance to drag Liam off the boy, tossing him somewhere in the crowd. A stream of blood surges out of the boy's nose causing a chain reaction of screams and demands in the circle of people. *Someone get a First Aid kit! Does he need an ambulance? What the hell is wrong with that kid?*

And then I hear the injured boy point a finger at Liam. "He stole from the concession stand!"

"Liam!" I race to his side and turn him to face me as I crouch down. Before I can deny the boy's accusation, I see three candy bars and a pack of gum in his grip. My mental calculator is doing the math in my head. I only gave the two boys five dollars to split and I'm certain each of these items cost at least two dollars. "What did you do?" I grab his shoulders with more force than I intend, and without looking up, I feel a hundred eyes on me, and my cheeks flood with warmth. *I'm the parent of the bad kid.* And then the band goes silent, and the second half of the game begins, moving the onlookers back to the bleachers and away from the scene.

I feel a hand on my shoulder and turn. I can hear Liam catching his breath behind me, his sniffs of cold air and the sound of his hand swatting at his dirt-encrusted face.

"Mom, it's my fault," Jack whispers as he stands over me, holding a single bag of popcorn, guilt crumpling his features.

Lauren stands behind Jack, beside Lily, Piper, and a handful of other girls.

"What do you mean it's your fault, Jack? What happened?" I interrogate him as he tilts his head to the side, a signal that I follow him. I take Liam's hand and let Jack lead us to an area that is out of earshot of the girls.

Jack has always worn his heart on his sleeve and he's silently sensitive, the type of child who will never get away with anything because guilt sticks to him like glue. "I used the money to buy Amber a bag of popcorn and I didn't have enough left to buy something for Liam."

The confession nearly smacks me into the brick wall of the equipment room that is several feet behind me, and I brace myself. "What? You're joking right?" I almost laugh but I stop when I see Jack's crumpled brow, the tears that are adding a shimmer to his dark brown eyes that match my own. "Jack, are you serious?"

He twists his head to the girls who are now gathered in a circle chatting among themselves while Lauren talks to a tall man in a Red Sox cap. I watch as she tips her head back and laughs, tossing a delicate hand on the man's shoulder. *What is going on?*

"I...I wanted to make Amber like me, and she had no money so—"

"So, you traded her in for your brother?" I continue.

He nods. "I'm sorry."

"But that doesn't explain why Liam stole from the concession stand." I pause, registering the situation. "And how did you even do that?"

"I didn't have any money!" Liam responds confidently, as if he had a valid excuse for stealing.

"Liam, that doesn't mean you take whatever you want." I stand up and look down at him. "And why on earth were you fighting with that boy?"

"He told me he would tell on me."

"And you decided to beat him up for that?"

Liam shrugs the way he always does when he doesn't have an answer for something. He's always been quick to react, seldom thinking before he makes a move.

After I make Liam return the crumpled snacks to the concession stand and apologize to both the boy and the volunteer working the stand, I make my way toward Lauren to tell her that we're going to leave because both boys are grounded.

Lauren is still in what appears to be a friendly conversation with the man but stops as soon as I approach. "Hey, is everything okay?" She turns toward me.

"No, we're going to head out. Looks like both my boys are in trouble this time."

"Hey, we'll go with you. We should leave to beat the traffic out of here anyways." She rests a delicate hand on my elbow, and then turns toward the man. "Hey, this is my old friend Andrew Stuart."

I'm in no mood to schmooze right now, but I reach out and shake the man's hand anyways, putting on a false smile. "Nice to meet you."

"Just so you know, that kid's no good." Andrew says as he tilts his head back in the direction of the boy Liam tackled. "Comes from the wrong side of the tracks, if you know what I mean."

I don't know what he means. In fact, I had no idea there were wrong sides of the track in Flagport. I nod anyways and as if picking up on my confusion, he cups his mouth and says, "He's not from here."

"Okay." I have no idea what he means by this but something in me stirs with his next line.

"It was great seeing you, Lauren. I'll tell my dad you said hi."

As we walk away from the field and the noise grows distant with each step forward, I ask Lauren who Andrew Stuart's dad is.

She looks straight ahead, and in a clipped response says, "The chief of police."

37

After

APRIL 2021

Lauren

When the words register in my brain, I feel as if I've been hit by a bullet. My daughter hates me. She's described her dislike for me in surprisingly poetic words.

DEAR DIARY,

My mother is psychotic. Why won't she just leave me alone? She treats me like a five-year-old, always hovering over me in her ever-present ways. I feel as if I'm suffocating, my life constantly dictated by her obsession with having to be the driver in my life. I cannot wait to move away, to have some independence from this house.

BEFORE I CAN STOP MYSELF, I turn the pages and read more.

· · ·

DEAR DIARY,

She did the unthinkable today. She literally stood over me as I was writing my essay for my college application. Maybe I should intentionally do a bad job, so I don't get in. Maybe that would teach her a lesson.

DEAR DIARY,

Why can't she shift some of her attention to Piper. It's always on me. Why is she so obsessed with every move I make? Jack is the only one I can talk to this about. He gets it. He sees her craziness since he's been a witness to her helicopter parenting for years. I cannot wait to turn eighteen, so I'll be free from her grip.

MY FIRST THOUGHT is that she is eighteen now. She's been eighteen since October, one of the oldest in her grade. I slam the book shut and toss it on the other side of the bed as if it's about to bite me. I feel sick with guilt. This accident was all my fault. She didn't feel comfortable with me. I was too much for her, so she called Evie. Maybe hate is a strong word, but my daughter was scared of me. She didn't even feel comfortable applying to colleges. But why didn't she ever say anything? Besides the occasional eye roll, I always thought Lily liked my presence in her life. I thought she liked the push I gave her. I thought I was steering her in the right direction, I thought that if I could be there, monitoring her every move, then she wouldn't have an opportunity to get hurt. When did I start to go so wrong? I'm pretty sure that I was a controlling parent from the moment Lily was placed in my arms, dead set on my desire to shape her life. Obsessed with making sure she couldn't make a bad decision and hurt someone else or herself.

I peel back the past eighteen years of my life as a parent and a million moments are pushed to the center of my mind. Moments when I was too overbearing, like when she went to her first high school dance. Moments when I made far bigger deals over things than I should've like at her track party when I forced her into the spotlight when she told me she didn't want the party at all. The lemonade stands, the birthdays, the way I made her dress to perfection, the cameras I put up in our home so I could make sure she was never doing anything wrong when we weren't home. Half the time I didn't even check the cameras because I knew she was a good kid at heart. She probably got that from her dad. And then there were the everyday things like how I made her do so many weekly activities, so she didn't have an opportunity to get bored, and didn't have the chance to turn into a bad kid. In Lily, I saw myself and she was my opportunity to change who I was and create new memories, even if that was through the life of another person.

I drop my head in my hands and allow the tears to fall. It's only when Piper knocks gently on the doorframe, that I stir and lift my head. "Mommy." She crosses the room and lands in my arms. "She's going to be okay." My youngest daughter tries to console me, and I nod along, but she doesn't know what I know. That it might be too late. I may have already done too much damage.

38

After

APRIL 2021

Evie

As soon as I see Lauren's car pull into the driveway, I'm filled with nostalgia. In the past, I would've greeted her if I was out in the yard gardening. We would update one another on our days and discuss our next outing. I would likely follow her into her house, and we would have coffee or a cocktail while the kids played. We've had so many days like this and it's so hard to not slip back into our old routine. But I'm going to try. I'm going to tell her everything I learned from Jack.

"Where do you think you're going?" Matt asks as I attempt to use one hand to lace a shoe, my cast awkwardly hanging forward. He kneels down in front of the mudroom bench I'm sitting on and without question goes to work lacing up my sneakers for me.

"I'm going to talk to Lauren." I squeak the words out, my mouth still dry from my stay in the hospital.

He twists his neck toward the storm door that faces the Rivers' home. The act is one we've engaged in so many times over the past twelve years. Checking to see if our best friends are home yet, the boys spotting their car in the driveway, always initiating a playdate. I watch the thoughts roll over his face when he spots Lauren's car in the driveway, the splash of white that can be seen where two trees make a space for the path that was naturally formed over the years, by the kids coming and going. Over time the path formed itself with their growing footprints, the repetitive steps making a crooked line in the dirt, the natural momentum of friendship. "Are you sure that's a good idea?" he asks, in a steady, nonjudgmental tone.

"I can only try, right?" I use my good arm to push myself upward and fall into him from the weight of my cast.

"You can only try." He steadies me, kisses me on the forehead and opens the door for me. "Do me a favor though?"

I turn when I get to the bottom step of our side porch and look up, awaiting his request.

"Bring this." He holds my phone out to me and I accept. "Just in case. I'll be taking Liam to baseball." He winks. Liam isn't an athlete, although he tries.

I nod. I know why he hands me my phone. He's afraid Lauren might go off the deep end. I'm not going to lie. I'm nervous too. I'm her biggest enemy right now. I could've done it differently. When Lily texted me, I could've called Lauren and presented her with the opportunity to make the call on who should pick her daughter up. But I knew what Lily was going through. I'd watched over the years how Lauren's grip tightened on that poor girl. And if I'm being honest, I liked being the one who Lily confided in, even if she failed to tell me that she was in a relationship with my son.

I make my way across the street with slow, unsteady steps, feeling the aftermath of not moving my body for several days. When I step onto the dirt path, my eye catches the round colorful stone that was placed all those years ago. Four handprints pressed into the stone, each a different color and name. *Lily, Jack, Piper, Liam. 2011.* My heart grows heavy, weighing my atrophied body down even more. The memory of happier times forms a lump in my throat and my eyes well with tears. I turn around and contemplate going back, giving Lauren more space because I don't think I'd be able to bear it if she turns me down, if she sends vicious words in my direction. I see Matt watching me from the storm door as if he's watching his child go off to school. He's ready for whatever I decide. If I turn around or if I continue forward. I adjust my sling and continue to walk up the path, where two more steppingstones pull me back to the past with the messy scrawl of our four children.

The Rivers' home is more unlived in at this very moment than I've ever seen it before. It's no longer the house where people gather, where parties are thrown, and memories are made. Instead, it's a capsule that simply holds the necessities to survive, not live. I walk up the pathway that leads to the side door and question whether I'm no longer welcome as a side door guest. With my free hand, I grip the handrail and ring the doorbell. I'm certain that Lauren will retreat to the other side of the house and hide from me when she sees me on her doorbell camera. A moment passes before I press the bell again. I peek in the window and see a spotless house filled with flowers. On the counter, there is a skyline of vases and baskets embellished with what I imagine are cards that offer well wishes. In the middle of the flower display, there is a neat stack of unopened envelopes, all in pretty pastel tones. The pale pinks and yellows remind me that Easter is next weekend. Yet another holiday we were supposed to spend with our best friends. Even though our kids are now teenagers, they had been looking forward to the annual egg hunt the Rivers put on, because they are filled with bills that range from one dollar to fifty, thanks to Mr. McCue's contributions.

I turn around and go back down the steps, succumbing to the fact that nobody is going to answer the door. It's over.

And then I hear the twist of the knob, the sound of the Easter wreath knocking against the wood. I turn back and I see Lauren standing in the doorway with a river of tears cascading down her cheeks.

39

Before

MARCH 2020

Lauren

The forecast called for rain, so when I see the sun spilling in between our custom-made wooden blinds, I'm pleasantly surprised. A slow growl emerges from Ryan's lips. "Go back to sleep," I whisper.

He does as he's told and rolls over on his side. I want to be the first one up today. I have a lot to do to make sure this day goes perfectly. I slip into the bathrobe the girls got me for Christmas and I pad down the stairs barefoot. The surprising sun casts a glow on our kitchen floor and I stand in it and bask, hoping to bring some heat to the soles of my feet. Prepped the night before are the boxes filled with St. Patrick's Day paraphernalia; gold and green headbands with furry green antennas sprouting from the top, plastic beer mugs, and hundreds of chocolate gold coins to toss out at the spectators of the Flagport St. Patrick's Day parade.

It's McCue tradition to march in the parade, and as I open the plastic bags of coins, I think back to the leprechaun traps my girls have made over the years, the fun I used to have with filling the toilet with green food coloring and gold footprint stickers all over the windows and floors. Lily is seventeen now, one year away from applying to colleges and that fact sits heavy in my heart. Leprechaun traps and egg hunts, sleepy Christmas mornings, and first days of school will be replaced with a life where my kids live one life and Ryan and I another.

First things first. I take a glimpse in my reflection on the microwave and approve my taut skin, fresh from last night's mask.

"Good morning." I'm surprised to see Lily sitting at the kitchen island, behind the boxes of supplies, flipping through the Flagport Reporter. "What are you doing up already?"

"Nothing," she says. Curt responses have been the norm for her since she was sixteen.

I go to work filling bags for each family member and the Sullivans so we can pummel the crowd with coins. "Wanna help?"

"Why is Grandpa in the newspaper every week?" She ignores my question, using manicured fingertips to turn a page.

"You know your grandfather. He's heavily connected in this town." I watch the espresso machine grunt and then it extends into one long shhhhh as it releases the pressure and coffee gets spit into my cup.

"But seriously, he's even in the police blotter."

My heart drops and I'm filled with guilt. I avoid the police blotter at all costs, and I haven't looked at it for twenty-three years. It's filled with lies.

"Michael McCue called the line to get requests for the lunch he was purchasing for the department." She mocks the print on the page.

"Some of these are so ridiculous." Lily giggles. "Resident on One Devonshire Road reports a loud noise. Police responded and discovered it was a cat meowing in a nearby tree. Like seriously… that made the newspaper?"

"Everything has to be reported so the public can be in the know," I lie. Nothing is reported accurately in this town.

I change the subject. "Why don't you put on your St. Patrick's Day shirt I got you, so we can get a head start on photos."

"I'm not wearing it." She continues to look at the newspaper, flipping the pages casually.

"Excuse me?" I drop a pinch of cinnamon on the fresh foam that hits the top of my coffee cup.

"I gotta get ready to go to Taylor's house." She slides off the barstool and flips a curtain of hair off her face.

I almost miss the words when they slip from her lips, but then they sink in. I try to push past the anger that is swelling inside of me. I've dedicated every ounce of my life to making sure my daughters look perfect for our family photos, so I can admittedly share them on social media, and everyone can think I am crushing life. I'm a happily married woman with two beautifully perfect children, living in an affluent town. Everyone needs to think I am perfect, and I have it all under control, even if I don't believe it.

"No, you're not. Not until after we take a festive family photo and march in the parade."

"I'm going to Taylor's." She repeats her statement, as if she is being asked a second time in court for her side of the story.

"You most certainly are not. You're walking in the parade with your family."

"No. I'm. Not." She crosses her arms across her chest. "I'm done marching in your stupid parades, and I'm done dressing in ridiculous costumes and being manipulated like a puppet!"

Before I can respond, she spins and marches across the first floor. I follow her and stand at the base of the staircase shouting at her as she stomps up the stairs. "How dare you! You will do what I say!" And then I catch myself. I never obliged when my mother yelled at me.

By the time I take a deep breath and follow her up the stairs, she's already slammed the door and launched into a spiel about how she hates me. I stand with my nose inches from the white door, and set my palm on the knob, wrapping my fingers around it to steady them from shaking. I twist and push the door open and prepare for her to verbally whip me with more hateful words. But instead, she lies face down on her bed. Her shoulders rising and falling to the beat of her sobs.

I sit on the edge of her bed like I've done so many times in the past. Since she was a toddler, this is where we've had our evening chats moments before tuck-in time, but looking at her seventeen-year-old body now, I realize those chats are coming to an end. In less than a year she'll be applying to colleges, and soon she'll be away at one of the Boston universities sleeping in a bed half this size, with a potentially persuasive roommate. She doesn't know this yet, but I will make sure that she goes to school nearby, so I'm always minutes away if she needs me, and so I can swoop in at the drop of a dime if something goes wrong in her life.

I make circles on her back, feeling the sweat that has accumulated beneath her thin white shirt. It seems like just yesterday I was soothing her from a scraped knee. Lily has never had much heartbreak because I've always made sure she's gotten what she wants, and the irony is not lost on me. The one who provides her with everything is the one person she doesn't want to be around. Where did I go wrong?

She sits upright, and swats at her nose with the back of her hand, keeping her gaze trained on the round area rug that gives way to the hardwood floor. Her hair falls the same way mine does, in a side part that looks good if styled properly but can make her face look too round if it's not landing in just the right spot. I start to use a finger to make the part less severe.

"Mom! Stop!" She bucks her head back, nearly smacking me in the nose. She twists her body so we're now face to face. "Leave my hair alone!"

I try not to show the sadness that seeps inside me. She no longer needs me like she used to. Every day she's getting one step closer to leaving this house and one step closer to being an adult, where I will no longer be able to dictate her every move.

40

Before
MARCH 2020

Evie

I've lived in a million different places in my lifetime, but spring hits differently in Massachusetts. Maybe it's because of what feels like absurdly long winters, or maybe it's because the town of Flagport seems to come to life at the first sign of nice weather. This year, it's starting earlier than in the past. It's only March 17th and the temperature has already risen to the mid-sixties, record breaking to many. Technically, it's not even spring yet, but the air says otherwise, as does the energy in downtown Flagport.

As always on St. Patrick's Day, we are wearing green T-shirts with a McCue family logo on the front, a giant shamrock on the back. We aren't the only non-family members marching alongside the McCues. According to Lauren the group has expanded over the years. In front of us and behind us are other families that are somehow connected to the McCues, from the police department to the local scouts who Lauren's dad evidently contributed to greatly over the years. If I had money like Michael McCue, I'd give it back to my town too, I've told Matt on more than one occasion. It's admirable the way the McCue family shares their wealth and puts it back into the town where they live so generation after generation can benefit from it.

I'm certain that Matt, the kids, and I blend in, but Michael McCue stands out. His face, painted green by the students at the local art gallery, is quite the scene, especially because it's paired with a bright green suit that is covered in beer mugs and shamrocks. On his head is a green hat with a black buckle.

He steps to the outskirts of the moving parade and shakes hands along the way, giving out extra-large candy bars that he pulls from his pockets to young kids who high-five him in return. The man is a town legend, and he lives up to his reputation by making so many wonderful memories for the people in Flagport. I'm pretty certain that Michael McCue is responsible for all the entertainment this day brings, including Irish Step Dancers, a fully-paid-for ice cream stand, and a round of green beer at the local pub. "Is Lauren's dad seriously paying the tab at Tilly's Tavern?" Matt bumps my elbow and takes a swig from the matching flasks he and Ryan filled before we departed home. It's only noon and this party is well underway.

"I believe he did." I pause to toss a handful of beaded shamrock necklaces out to a few moms on the sidelines. They catch them and do a little shimmy as they put them on. "But, are you really surprised?"

"I shouldn't be, should I?" Matt sets one hand on Liam's shoulder to steer him forward, his wandering mind getting in the way of focusing on his steps.

"Nope, you shouldn't." We've lived in Flagport for eleven years and the events have gotten more extravagant over time. I'm not sure if Michael McCue is making even more money or if he is just having more fun spending it. The only types of events I was ever involved in as a kid, were ones that honored either a patriotic holiday or military retirements and promotions, a far cry from anything we've had the pleasure of experiencing in Flagport. Piper and Liam share a joke in front of us, and I turn to see how Jack is doing behind me where he was walking with Lily. I pause abruptly when I see Jack's zeroed in on something on the sidewalks. I step back so I'm walking side by side with him and ease in like I've learned how to do as a mom of teens. "Hey, bud, what are you looking at?"

Before he can respond, I see it. Lily tipping her head back and drinking a green beer in the center of a crowd of other teenagers. She drops her head forward again, looks around and tips it back, chugging until the mug is empty. My first reaction is to look up ahead to where Lauren was marching seconds before, and as if I'm the one doing something wrong, I'm filled with a sense of fear. I know Lauren well enough to know that she would never approve of her daughter drinking alcohol underage. The girl is only allowed to eat ten chocolate morsels when she has a sugar craving, she's never been allowed to drink soda, and while all the teenagers are hanging out at Starbucks after school drinking those fancy caffeinated concoctions, Lily is home doing homework or at track practice. To see her on the side of the road chugging beer is something that looks so foreign to me, I'm having trouble believing it. "Is that Lily?" I whisper to Jack, my inner teenager coming out, as if I'm slipping into Lily's shoes and fearing the repercussion of what her mother is going to do. As if I'm a teen all over again and getting caught drinking Boone's Farm with other military brats in a courtyard on base.

"She's in so much trouble," Jack says.

"Oh shit." As predicted, I see Lauren emerge from the parade. No longer marching in step with the others, she is now making a beeline right for the circle that Lily is standing in. Jack and I watch as if we're viewing an action film. Lauren grabs Lily's wrist and I watch as the now empty mug drops from her hand and falls on the ground rolling across the pavement and landing in a sea of other belongings from the day. *Lauren didn't see it.*

Lily gets pulled behind Lauren like a slow-moving dog on a leash until they are back in step with the parade, just a few feet in front of us. And that's when I decide that I'm going to pretend I didn't see Lily drinking beer, but at the same time I feel this little tug on my inside questioning whether Lily cares or not that her mother saw her. Has she reached the point of no return?

41

After
APRIL 2021

Lauren

I pull open the door so fast that the rush of air causes strands of hair to lift off my head and stick to my face where fresh tears are raining down my cheeks. It's the sight of Evie that pushes me over the edge. She turns back at the base of the steps, and I can tell she's preparing for me to yell at her.

But instead, I walk down the steps until we're eye level. I open my arms and fall into her. I hug her and for the first time since I got the news I feel as if I have a safe space to go, someone who will understand. She pulls me into a one-arm embrace and allows me to sob, letting every emotion fall out of me. I haven't even been able to do this with Ryan, because even though he's my husband, the other half who created Lily, I don't think he understands me the same way Evie does. If he ever knew about my past, he'd move on to another woman, maybe someone who also came from a family that is well off, but with less baggage. If Ryan found out about who I really was and all the lies I've told, I'm not sure if he would stick around but I'm certain I'd always have Evie.

I pull back and rest my hands on her elbows, circling my finger over the cast of her arm. "So, when can I sign this?" I joke for the first time in days.

"I thought you'd never ask." Evie's smile spreads across her face the way I love. It's big and wide, a powerful source of joy that naturally moves through me and lifts me up, just a little, in a way that makes me believe for a second that everything will be okay.

I motion for her to follow me inside. "I suppose it's time we talk." I was given another chance in life, a clean slate, even if it wasn't under the circumstances I wanted, and I think Evie at least deserves another chance.

She follows me inside. As if we are first-time friends all over again, I have to tell her to sit down at the island, gesturing to the bar stool, *her* bar stool, that she has sat in so many times over the years.

I hear Piper's footsteps thumping down the stairs and I watch as it registers on her face that Evie is in our home. She has heard enough back and forth between Ryan and me to know that our relationship with the Sullivans may not survive. She looks at me, half confused and half questioning. *Is it okay for me to talk to her, Mom?* I smile and nod and she races across the kitchen and into Evie's arms, the two reunited again. I often discount Piper's relationship with Evie, but they've grown just as close as Evie and Lily have over the years, maybe just in different ways.

I watch as Evie pushes Piper's hair out of her eyes, with the gentle touch that only a mother can emit. And then I watch as Piper's eyes land on Evie's cast, and all the memories flood back to her face. For a moment she forgot that her sister was in a coma. I can't tell if she still holds it against Evie, but she looks over at me and then says, "I'll go pack some stuff upstairs, okay, Mom?" She passes a tight-lipped smile toward Evie and then heads back upstairs.

"So." I look over at Evie.

Before another second can pass, Evie says, "They're in love."

"I know," I say. And then I tell her about everything I learned in

Lily's diary. As painful as it is to recite, I share all the hateful things that Lily wrote, directed at me, all the awful words she expressed between the pages of that leather-bound book. I'm so ashamed to tell another mother about how my child feels about me, but there is a part of me that feels cathartic in sharing my vulnerability. Now Evie knows there is another side to me, a side that is not perfect, and is filled with painful stories that I've told myself over the years. I continue telling her everything else I learned in Lily's diary. How Lily shared her love for Jack and how he was the only one who understood her. "It's all my fault," I continue. "I've been an awful mother, so in the way of everything, so controlling and obsessed with her going down a wrong path, making one mistake."

Evie studies me, she's witnessed my rules and demands swell over the years, but she's seen the best in me, and I've always felt that. "Don't you ever say that. You are the best mother. Look at all you've done for your daughters. Do you have any idea how lucky Lily is to have someone who is so present in her life." She pauses, rubbing a fallen yellow petal between the fingers that extend out of her cast. "None of us are perfect, Lauren. We all have our thing. For you it was making sure your girls had their ducks in a row. For me, it's been dealing with Liam and his poor behavior. Don't for a second think that every other mother in this town doesn't have some inner demons about how they parent their children. We all do. We're human."

Before I can continue, she says the five words that free a tiny part of my heart. "This is not your fault."

42

After

APRIL 2021

Evie

If the accident is anyone's fault, it's mine. I chose to react to Lily's text when she asked for a ride. Instead of checking in on Jack when he got home and inquiring about why Lily was left at the party with no ride, I grabbed the keys and got behind the wheel, my slippered feet struggling to get the proper foothold on the brake. I can't point the blame on my slippers, considering the driver that hit us was 100 percent at fault, but had I had a pair that fit my feet better, maybe my foot would've hit the brake faster and harder and we would've had a chance to stop before the girl, in her sleepy haze, ran the red light at the intersection, where we were stopped for a beat too long so Lily could get in the front seat.

But I don't tell Lauren that. That's a detail that doesn't matter. I also don't tell her the words that Lily slurred seconds before the car hit us. "I'm not going to college in Boston. I'm moving to California with Jack, and I'll work until I decide what I want to do with my life." Her words pushed together, the smell of strawberries and liquor hitting the air between us. It took me back to my own past when I got drunk on Boone's Farm, that awful malt liquor that teen girls mistake for wine. Much like I'm doing now for Lily, my own mother hid my teenage drunkenness from my father, knowing he would be appalled, and punish me with militant retribution. He never laid a hand on me, but his eyes had a way of setting beneath his brow with disappointment, his lips cut in a straight line on his angled jawline in a way that could make me feel like the smallest human in the world. In some ways, Lauren is like my father, how she handles disappointment when it comes to Lily, as if any mistake the girl could've potentially made was no different than errors made on a battlefield.

"I've been too hard on her, and she rebelled."

I try not to incite any more remorse in Lauren, so I steer clear from agreeing with her. "You love her, Lauren, that's all." I place my hand on top of hers. "We love our kids with everything we have, and no parent is perfect."

"You are." Lauren locks her eyes on mine. "Your boys go to you for things, they allow you to give them advice."

For the first time in days, I tip my head back and laugh. "Are you kidding me? First of all, boys are very different than girls."

She nods. Everyone has seen how poorly behaved my youngest son has been. Even at fifteen he still says off the wall things and I'm pretty sure he might still be considered a bad egg by some of his teachers. Lauren, as if reading my mind, laughs and rocks her head knowingly.

"But, I don't get it. Why would Lily not tell me that she's in love with Jack? After all these years of us trying to push them together kiddingly."

"Because she knew that you would try to stop her." Piper's voice punches the air. With dripping hair, she now stands just a few feet away, where the living room meets the kitchen.

She says the words that I want to say but I don't have the heart to. We all know that if Lily confessed her trip to California to her mother, Lauren would swoop in and try to control the entire scenario, or she'd try to stop it altogether.

I don't have to say it. Piper said the words for me, and I tighten my grip on Lauren's hands as her gentle tears transform into sobs.

She feels responsible for everything, and for the first time since we moved to Flagport, I witness a vulnerability in Lauren, as she unravels from the controlling grip she's had on her life, and I wonder, why does she feel the need to have it all together, to maintain a warden-like presence on Lily's life. I've read enough self-help books to know that we have a reason for our behavior, and it almost always stems from our upbringing and experiences.

"Really? Is that what she thought?" Lauren's words cut through her tears.

"Mom, there is something I have to tell you."

43

Before

JANUARY 2021

Evie

When I was younger, I remember looking forward to the winter months. If we happened to be stationed at a base that actually had a winter, I would pull out all my gear and spend hours in the snow, building forts, creating paths in the snow from one section of the yard to the other, and sledding with the slew of other military brats who would be out and about. Today, when I look out the window I see a few flurries falling from the sky, their destination not a one-way trip to the ground but one more indirect as they flutter about.

"Is it snowing?" Matt approaches me from behind where I'm standing, looking out to our front yard and the one massive hill that we are perched on. Even though our modest cape is set at the top of the street, it still feels as if every other house is hovering over us, looking through their floor-to-ceiling windows and across vast green lawns. When we first moved in, we were one of two small homes in our neighborhood, diminishing alongside the other near-mansions, but now, ever since the other small abode constructed a massive addition, we are officially the smallest.

"Not quite." I watch as one flurry manages to make it to the cement surface, melting upon arrival. I turn toward Matt, who is looking dapper in a pale-blue button-down shirt, and a navy-blue tie, what he likes to refer to as a power clash. He uses an index finger to smooth out the sweep of hair that falls across his forehead. "Does this look okay?" I step back from him and sweep my arms down my body, showcasing my outfit. A navy-blue dress that hugs my curves and falls to my knees, paired with nude heels that I may regret wearing if we actually do get a coating of snow on the ground.

"You look stunning." He pulls my head toward him and kisses my hairline, which I've just sprayed with hairspray to finish off my topknot. I walk toward my closet and remove my dress coat from the hanger and slip into the houndstooth wool fabric, only worn for occasions like tonight. "I'll go warm up the car." He pats my behind and saunters toward the staircase after he peeks in Liam's room and says goodbye.

I follow his path until I land in the entryway of Liam's room. "Hey, bud, you gonna be okay alone tonight?"

"Yep." Liam keeps his eyes trained on the game he's playing on his phone. I'm still regretting the decision to buy him a phone over a year ago. He's fourteen now but there are times when he seems like he is half the age, compared to how Jack behaved when he was this age.

I start to walk away but I'm stopped by a rare question emerging from his lips. "Why are you so dressed up?" he asks.

I'm surprised he even recognized that I'm wearing a dress at all. "Because we're going out to dinner with the Rivers. You know that, honey."

"But why do you have to get so dressed up? Why can't you just, you know...wear like, sweatpants or something?"

I toss my head back and snicker. "Because we are going to The Deck."

"So. Why can't you wear sweatpants at The Deck?" His question is not out of the norm. What is obvious to most people seems to be lost on Liam. This has been his MO since he was a little boy, and while I often get frustrated by his oddball questions, this time I find myself wondering the same thing. *Why can't I just be in sweatpants right now? Why must we wear such uncomfortable clothing just to go out to dinner with friends? Maybe Liam is actually asking the same questions that everyone is thinking.*

"You know, buddy, I really wish I could, but they have a dress code, and they won't let us go in and eat if we are dressed in sweatpants." I lean against his doorway and cross my arms, taking him in. It seems like just yesterday he was coming home from the second grade asking similar oddball questions. And now, he's in high school. I know Liam is what some may refer to as the black sheep of the family, a far cry from his popular and athletic older brother, but he will always be my baby, the one I worry about most. Since I recognized the differences between my two sons, I've grown used to the fact that Liam would always need more help in life. He'd always be the one who needed guidance and an extra layer of push to get him moving in the right direction.

He keeps his eyes on the phone using an index finger to move whatever game piece he is attempting to move on the screen, as he says, "Maybe go somewhere different then."

I push away from his comment knowing that a response won't get me anywhere. I've been a player in this back-and-forth game many times over the years and I know that Liam will never really see eye to eye with most he is conversing with. Doctors and therapists have told me that he will grow out of this, but I'm certain it is just who he is, and I've learned to adapt and sometimes I even feel like maybe he is speaking more truth than the majority of people. I undoubtedly would rather be in sweatpants eating a pizza on the couch with my friends, than sitting uncomfortably at a table minding my manners. "Be a good boy tonight." I leave him with words that sound like they are being presented to a three-year-old, and I carefully walk down the stairs in my heels and out the door.

The inside of the car is swirling with heat by the time I slide into the front seat. Unlike when I was a kid, I try to avoid going outside in the cold weather and I'm not exactly looking forward to this evening. I spent all day hunched over the computer learning a new landscaping design software so I can up my game in the springtime, and I'm exhausted. The cold months come along with a lack of opportunity for me to get my hands dirty and in turn an added layer of lethargy. Being outdoors and manipulating the earth for hours at a time is what gives me energy and breathes life into me. "Did Jack mention where he is going tonight?" I ask as we stop at an intersection.

Matt, who seems to have gotten better looking with age, has left his jacket in the back seat, and I watch as the veins in his forearms, sticking out from his shirt, ripple as he navigates the steering wheel. "Working at Montby's until nine then going over to a friend's. Don't ask me which friend because I don't remember. One of the C's I think," Matt says, referring to Jack's extensive social life. Connor, Cole and Conrad are three of the regulars he hangs out with and in my opinion, they are interchangeable, all with the same sweep of brown hair, and disguised in their Flagport High sporting gear. I still am unsure about who plays what sport with Jack, but his plethora of friendships outweighs the worry I have for Liam's lack of friends. Matt pauses. "Wait...he may have said something about a party?" He turns to me and squints.

"You think Liam will be okay alone?"

"Eves, he's fourteen, of course, he'll be okay alone," Matt says as he pulls into the parking lot of The Deck. "I was staying home alone when I was eleven, and for much longer than Liam will be tonight."

"I know, I know, I just worry about him." It seems to take everything out of me to push the door open. Above us, as the name implies, a massive white deck circles a round building made of rock that sits at the edge of the ocean. According to the locals, The Deck used to be a castle. Since then, it's been a handful of things. The restaurant has outlived all the other businesses, thanks to its well-known celebrity chef and elegant event space that serves as a hot spot for both tourists and locals. The sound of the waves hitting and retreating from the cylindrical wall joins the rustling wind and creates eerie background music as we walk up the winding staircase toward the entrance. A path of white lights twinkle along the edge of the walkway and guide us toward the entrance

Matt catches me by surprise and pauses before he opens the door. He cups my face in his hands and looks down at me. "Promise me you'll stop worrying about Liam tonight."

I grab his wrists, now covered by the cuffs of his jacket. "Yes, dear."

He pushes the door open, and a blur of smiling faces are staring at me and an orchestra of different voices yell, "Surprise!"

My heart escalates without warning and I'm suddenly hot beneath my coat, sweating where I had goosebumps just moments before. "What?" I turn to Matt who has a full grin stretching across his face.

"I know I know, but Lauren insisted," he says just as my vision steadies itself and there is no longer a blur. Front and center among at least one hundred people, Lauren is standing in a green dress holding up a sign that says "Happy 40th!" She tilts her head to the side and passes me a warm smile before she walks toward me and embraces me in a big hug.

"Oh my gosh!" I say, falling into her embrace. "Did you do this?" I look around the room, half the people have pushed away from the center and are forming their own conversation clusters and several others are still surrounding us holding up signs that I now realize are faces of me, reprinted from every age I've been since I was a baby.

"Matt helped." She tipped her head toward Matt, who is now in a man hug with Ryan.

"Are you serious?" I'm taken aback and caught completely off guard. So much so that I feel a tear escape my eye and run down my cheek. I look around and see half of Flagport there. All of the friends I've ever met, Mr. and Mrs. McCue. Even Megan made it home.

"You always said you wanted a surprise party."

"I did and you made that wish come true." I hug her again and when I release her grip, she grabs hold of my shoulders and turns me toward the bar.

━━━

MY FORTIETH BIRTHDAY party is everything I could've wanted. I spent the first half of the night mingling with guests and every time I passed by Lauren, I thanked her with squeezes of the arm and winks from across the room. If it weren't for her, we wouldn't have built up this Flagport community, I wouldn't have the landscaping business I do and this built-in family that I adore. I've been so busy talking and dancing, that two hours in I realize I haven't had anything to eat and the Manhattans are starting to catch up. In search of a breath of fresh air I pull on my coat and push through the back door that leads to a side deck area. It's closed for the winter months, but as the honorary guest of the party, a staff member named Enrico, allows me to slip out for a few minutes. I sip in the sea air, and while it's the middle of the winter, the smell of the salty sea makes me feel as if it's mid-July. We seldom go to the beach in the winter, but I now realize how refreshing it can be, how alert it is making me with just a few deep breaths. The background music bumps through the doors behind me and a dim light at a neighboring home awakens the waves below and I take in the white crush of the break as it hits the rocky wall.

And then, without warning, I hear another door close, but it's out of view. The sound of heightened whispers hits my right ear and I peek around the corner, where another platform of decking reaches outward. The silhouettes of two male bodies face one another, arms flailing. The only thing that gives away the identity of the man with his back to me is the white hair. Mr. McCue. I take one step back and press myself to the wall of the building, so I'm out of view. If it weren't for Mr. McCue's shoulders bumping up and down, and the hiss in his voice, I would've gone back inside and continued the night, but instead I listen and I know I'll never be able to erase the next words I hear. "We need to get her out of town now. I don't care what you have to do, just get it done, or I'll stop contributing money." There is a pause, then a mumble that I can't make out, followed by Mr. McCue's next words, "Why is this all coming up again now anyways…all these years later?"

44

Before
JANUARY 2021

January 2021

Lauren

I've been waiting for this moment for weeks. "Are you having fun?" I sidle up to Evie, who is perched at one of the high-tops embellished with teal tablecloths and sparkling gold confetti 40s.

"This is one of the best nights of my life." I've watched as Evie has danced to her favorite songs, mingled with the friends she's grown to adore, and laughed at the silly photos of her over the years in the slideshow I put together. But now, as she sits here nursing her Manhattan, I see a rigidness in her shoulders, a faraway stare that I've only seen a handful of times.

"Why did you do this?" She surprises me with the question.

"What do you mean?"

"I mean, this…all of this, Lauren" She waves a hand in front of her, nearly knocking down an empty glass.

For a moment I wonder if she is mad at me for putting her in the limelight, if surprises really aren't her thing. "I'm sorry—"

"Sorry?" She slaps a hand on the table. "Sorry! Why would you be sorry? This means the world to me, Lauren…nobody, nobody has done anything like this for me before." She doesn't have to say it. I know what she is referring to. Her parents simply put a roof over her head and food on the table, but I'm pretty certain they didn't treat her like she was anybody but their child. And that's when I realize that even though I'm hard on Lily, at least I hug her, at least I show her I care in ways that aren't just about survival.

I see the moisture come to the surface of her eyes and naturally my tendency to well up easily gets the best of me and I feel a swell in my throat, the throb behind my eyes that always comes before I cry. I reach across the table and grab her hand. "You mean a lot to me, Evie. I wouldn't think twice about doing something like this for you." I mean every word of it. Since I met her all those years ago, Evie has listened without judgment, she's offered advice when I've asked for it and she has made me laugh when she had no idea how much I needed it. It's for these reasons that I have to keep the secrets of my past locked safely inside. If she finds out the truth of my past and my family, I'm certain she is too good of a person to stick around with someone like me.

"Hey…what's the matter?" I recognize the look she has on her face now. It's her thinking face. Her brown eyes trained on the candle between us, her jaw set in a way that, if I didn't know any better, would come off as distracted and inattentive, but I know there are thoughts swirling in her head now. "Are you stressed about turning forty?"

Her brows scrunch together, and she waves a hand in front of her. "Tsss…please."

And then the boisterous voice of my father interrupts my interrogation of Evie. "Well, if it's not the most beautiful women in the room." My dad places a palm on each of our shoulders.

"Don't tell Mom that," I say, and I watch him look over the heads of the guests dancing on the floor and past the crowd of people lined at the door. His gaze is trained on the main entrance.

"I'm gonna call it an early night, okay?" He kisses me on the forehead and turns toward Evie. "Happy birthday, Evie…make it the best year ever." And then, he makes his way through the parting crowd and links arms with my mother before he pushes through the doors.

I watch Evie's eyes follow him. "That's odd, I feel like your dad is usually the last one standing at parties."

"He is," I say, equally confused by his early departure. I tried to avoid the tension on his face and the way his voice had that added layer of nervousness that I'd heard only a handful of times in the past.

And then, the song *This is How We Do it,* hits the air and I silently thank the DJ for his timing. Evie grabs my hand and leads me to the dance floor, and we sing to one another and engage in some nineties-style choreography, completely lost in our own world.

45

After

APRIL 2021

Piper

This is not how I had intended it to turn out. I've seen my mother cry over the years but never like this. In that way that makes her face contort so she looks kind of like a monster. She'd cried often, allowing tiny tears to escape her eyes when Lily learned how to ride a bike, when she got dressed for prom, even when she wore makeup for the first time. But those tears never made time for me. The irony is that the ugly tears, the ones that are forming a river that rapidly falls down her face right now, in front of me and Evie, are the ones that are technically caused by me. But not in a good way. Not in the way that is a sneak peek into the pride a mother feels for a child when they've accomplished something. Instead, it's her own tangle of remorse propelled by the crime I set in motion.

I overheard her talking to Evie about how Lily's accident was her fault because she's been so all-consuming with her oldest daughter. There's no denying that. I always assumed my mother was more attached to my older sister because she's a spitting image of her, whereas I'm not like either of my parents. I don't walk as fast as them and I certainly don't enjoy putting on shows for others or flaunting the McCue money. Don't get me wrong, I appreciate the finer things we've been given, but I've never felt like I belonged in this family. I've always found the Sullivans to be more relatable. Maybe I stem from my father's side, where money was something that you made for survival, not something you made to add the bells and whistles onto your home to flaunt what you could afford.

Even in this moment, as I stand with my hair dripping onto the kitchen floor, my mother is focusing her tears on Lily and how she raised her wrong. It's as if Lily was born with one of those red dots that cats love to follow. My mother is the cat, and her instinct to hunt is triggered when she sees the red light, keeping her attention always zeroed in on Lily, and without knowing, at all costs. I don't envy the attention Lily has received from my mother all these years, but I have felt envious about the bright light that she's always been placed in. Lily can do no wrong. Until, of course, she did do wrong, and I felt the need to make it known. My intentions were wholesome, as I thought it would benefit both my mother and my sister. My mother would know that Lily is not perfect, as is no human on this planet, and Lily would no longer be held to such ridiculously high standards. I thought I was helping. "It's my fault."

My statement attracts my mother's attention, and for the first time in my life, I feel like that red laser is directed on me. She's looking at me. Not with the pride that I want, instead, it's more of a confusion. "What are you talking about, honey?"

I step forward and feel a chill from the water that has now soaked through the back of my shirt. I move my gaze from Evie before I allow it to settle on my mother. She's hardly recognizable anymore, with her sallow cheeks, pale face and puffy eyes. Instead of telling her what I did, I show her. I slide my phone from my back pocket and swipe across the screen until I find the video. I set it on the island between them without saying anything. I leave it up to them to see the date and time at the top of the screen and do the math. *January 4, 2021. 8:30pm.*

They both look confused, so I press play. And then, the movie plays out. Jack and Lily are in Lily's room, beneath the covers, doing things that I'm definitely not proud of recording. I don't want to see it, but I had to record this to prove a point. *Lily's not perfect.* In fact, she's quite the liar and hypocrite, but I don't blame her for that. I blame my mother for that. Lily had no choice but to sneak around with Jack. My mother would've flipped if she found out this was going on, let alone under her roof.

I hear the gasp before I see my mother's hand go to her mouth. I'm grateful when she presses pause, freezing the picture on the ruffled comforter and the strewn-about undergarments on Lily's carpet. Red-laced thong, a matching bra, and Jack's boxer shorts. The sight makes me queasy thinking about them like that. After all, Jack is like a brother to me. "Where...where did you get this?" she asks the question as if I brought home a stray cat.

"Piper, what is this?" Evie asks, although, it wouldn't surprise me if she's been privy to this behind-the-scenes relationship the entire time.

I feel my throat swell, and I ready myself for the tears. I'm sick with regret over this. "I'm sorry." I shake my head. "I didn't mean for it to cause so many bad things."

My mother pushes herself off the stool and comes to me. I brace myself because I'm not sure if she's going to hit me or if she's going to hug me. After all, I'm the one who set Lily's accident in motion. She rests a palm on my shoulder and leans down. "I...I don't understand." She pauses to look at Evie for a moment, then back at me. She's questioning whether everyone but her knew about the secret relationship Lily and Jack were having. "Please, please tell me what is happening, Piper."

"The night you went to Evie's fortieth birthday party, Liam and I were downstairs watching a movie and Lily and Jack were upstairs. And I knew, I knew what they were doing."

My mom and Evie are only inches away from me, both perched on the edge of their stools at the island. "How did you know this?" Evie asks.

"Because they've been sneaking around for a long time now.

Meeting up in places where you guys couldn't see them…where they thought no one could find out."

"But this is the night of my party. Liam was home alone, and Jack was supposed to be out with Connor or Conrad…or whoever," Evie says.

"And I thought Jack had been dating Sydney for a while," Lauren adds.

I remain silent like a soldier in formation, and I let them figure it out.

"I know. Lily set them up, actually. But then when Lily saw them getting close—"

"She got jealous," Evie answers. My mother in all her sadness from the past several days, is slow to pick up on the scenario, her eyes dart, her mouth remains parted as the pieces fall into place.

I nod. "And—"

"And Jack has always been in love with Lily," Evie answers for me.

I nod again.

"But how did you get this video and why?" My mother's thoughts start lining up in order.

"I set my phone up in Lily's room the night of the party, knowing they would be up there."

"Piper, that's awful…why would you—" my mom starts.

"Because I wanted Lily to not be perfect for once! I was sick and tired of everyone thinking she was this perfect student, perfect friend, and athlete…and most of all…the perfect daughter!" I'm yelling now, all the anger and jealousy I've felt over the past several years, since I was old enough to know that I would never be as good as my older sister, is hitting the space between me, Evie, and my mother.

My mother's face crumbles, but this time it's not in the stressed-out, saddened state that she's been in since Lily's accident. This time it is one that is filled with shame and regret. She pulls me into her, and I smell the perfume she's been wearing since I was a little girl, before I knew I was second best. Then, she holds me back. "But why would Lily try to hide her relationship with Jack?"

"Because she didn't think you'd approve."

Her face floods with shame again and she looks at Evie, who I'm certain understood this all along, but has been such a supportive friend to my mother, that she never brought it up. She, just like me, witnessed the way no one was ever good enough for Lily.

Before I let it get any further, I say, "But there is more."

They both lean in again, eyebrows raised. I'm not sure our family can take any more shocking news, but it needs to hit the surface before I explode. "The video has been seen by almost everyone at school."

"What?" My mother and Evie say at the same time, their exasperation blended.

"I sent it to Sydney's sister, the night of the college acceptance party. And she sent it to everyone." I don't tell them that I knew Alley would send the video out to everyone, making it go Flagport-viral in three seconds. I don't have to. They know how technology works these days. "That's why Lily was so upset and that's why she got drunk and texted Evie."

"Piper." My mother's face is now a mix of disappointment and shame. This is the first time she's learning that my sister got drunk at that party. I knew she would. It wasn't the first time she got drunk. I knew that if I shared this video, she would do it again and maybe this time she'd get caught when she stumbled in the house. But, this time, she didn't have the chance to stumble in the house.

The sound of a ringing phone pulls our conversation apart. Every ring or text since Lily's accident has been jumped at, scrutinized and cause for concern, never knowing when communication on her progress or decline is going to come through. My mom holds a finger up, swipes at her phone and holds it to her ear as Evie grabs my hand in hers. We both watch my mother's face as it contorts once again, this time into a fit of tears. They come down fast and hard, like a river that has just been unblocked by a dam. Before she can explain, Evie grabs the keys from the counter and drives us to the hospital, with one arm on the steering wheel and her casted arm pinned to her side.

46

After

APRIL 2021

Lauren

When Dr. Keen tells me he has an update on Lily, I jump ahead to the worst-case scenario. *Brain damage.* I brace myself for his next words and I have to ask him to repeat them to make sure I'm hearing him correctly.

"We're not in the clear yet, but Lily has woken from the coma. She is moving and has surpassed all the physical exams we've given her so far. Her senses are in line. But, what is really going to tell us if she is in the clear is her memory."

Before Dr. Keen can explain any further, Evie is starting my SUV, with me in the passenger seat, in an emotional state and Piper in the back seat. "Wait…I can't drive like this!" Evie looks down at her cast. Both of us, still reeling from what Piper told us and the news from Dr. Keen, had forgotten about her cast.

"Matt…is Matt home?"

"No, he's taking Liam to practice. Jack is at the hospital already." Her response makes me think of the normal days, the days when all we had to think about was who was taking what kid to practices and parties, school and camps. It also makes me realize that Jack hasn't left the hospital once since Lily has been there.

"I'll drive," I say, pushing the door open.

"You can't drive, you're worse off than me. You won't be able to see through your tears."

"I'll drive," Piper says matter-of-factly from the back seat.

I turn to my youngest daughter, and for the first time I see her as a young woman, and not my baby. After all the years I've turned my cheek to her and moved my gaze toward Lily, Piper is the one who has grown up without me even knowing it.

Evie, paused in the driver's seat, looks at me, assessing what my response will be. "All right, Piper, you're driving us." Piper and Evie switch seats and I buckle up.

"You know Dad has been taking me driving, right?" Piper twists her neck toward me as she places her palms on the steering wheel.

I didn't know that. I put a hand on her thigh and allow my trust to move through me to her, and I watch my younger daughter's profile the entire way to the hospital. The way she maintains her focus on the road but lifts her eyes up when appropriate to check the rearview mirror. I watch as she looks over her shoulder when switching lanes and how she brakes before she even gets to the red light. I watch a confidence I never noticed before exude from my youngest daughter and I'm utterly proud.

By the time we make it past the reception area and to the family room, where Dr. Keen met us last time, Ryan, Matt and Liam are already there. Word spreads fast. The three of them look at the three of us with confusion. "We'll explain later," I say.

I'm sandwiched between Piper and Ryan, the three of us still standing and holding hands when Dr. Keen updates us on Lily. I listen more intently than I ever have before, as he tells us that Lily began stirring, her eyes started to flutter and when she woke, she looked around the room, in a haze of confusion. "This is normal behavior for someone waking up from a coma so don't be all that surprised if she doesn't recognize you at first, okay?" He waits until we give him a verbal agreement. This isn't Dr. Keen's first rodeo.

I turn to Evie and Matt. "Has anyone talked to Jack?"

"He left to go for a walk a little while ago," Ryan confirms.

"So, he really hasn't left the hospital?"

Dr. Keen nods. "If you're referring to the boy... say, this tall," Dr. Keen raises a hand over his head indicating Jack's height, "and built like an athlete with long brown hair."

"That's him," Evie says.

"I don't think he's left the hospital once since the accident. He may not have been in Lily's room the whole time, but he's been on the campus."

I look at Evie. She gives me an all-knowing look. She knew that Jack hasn't left, she knows exactly how much in love her son is with my daughter.

WE START to move toward the room, following closely behind Dr. Keen like a cloud, the six of us glued together. The sound of his running shoes squeaks when he turns and addresses us all. "You may want to go in two at a time, so she doesn't get overwhelmed." His gaze scans our group, waiting for us to break up. We stand, smashed together like the one giant family that we've become, and Ryan turns to me. "You go first, honey. With Piper."

I nod. Piper grips my hand, and we walk into the room. The beeps and swooshing of the machines are still there, the smell of flowers overtakes my senses and replaces the once antiseptic smell of this hospital. So many vases and cards, stuffed animals and well wishes line the narrow shelf inside the window. From where we stand in the entryway, it looks like Lily's eyes are still closed and I feel a sudden fear that she has turned a corner and went downhill from where she was during Dr. Keen's last update. Piper tugs on my hand, urging me to step forward. I'm afraid of what I'll see, afraid I won't be remembered. But maybe it would be a good thing if my daughter, the one I've put so much pressure on, didn't remember me. Maybe she would be better off. Piper, now at Lily's bedside, rests a palm on her sister's forearm. "Lily bear," she sings.

I move to the other side of the bed, and take in her face, turned toward the side Piper is standing on. The edges of her face are sharper than they were when I first saw her after the accident. Her lips, still cracked, are no longer attached to a feeding tube. And then I see her hand make a gripping motion and Piper puts hers inside it. Lily's chin lifts slightly and her eyes flutter open. I reach for her other hand, and set mine in her palm, waiting for it to grip me, to show me a sign of life, that she is the same girl I had dinner with just a handful of nights ago, fully intact. It doesn't move, but her mouth does. "Piper?" She looks at her sister before she turns her head to me, "Mama?"

And I cry tears that I thought I didn't have left. I cry so hard; my muscles begin to hurt. I cry tears of joy and push past the fear of what her recovery may entail. I cry because I've been given a second chance.

47

After

APRIL 2021

Evie

By the time Jack receives the dozens of text messages we send him about Lily's status, Ryan has had his chance to go in the room, and Lauren walks out and falls into my arms. Seconds later, the laminate floor squeaks with racing feet and Mr. and Mrs. McCue and Megan are standing in front of us. "Lauren, sweetheart? How's my sweet Lily?" Michael bellows as Mrs. McCue runs a hand down Lauren's free arm.

"Dad, she's okay. I think she's going to be okay." Lauren stands before her parents and updates them. And then I see Michael transform into the person he was the night of my fortieth birthday out on the deck. His hands shoot up and he points a finger in my direction.

"What is she doing here? She's the one who caused this! Lauren, honey, I already have the chief documenting everything for us. We have a strong case. She was paused at the intersection, for God knows how long, putting my granddaughter in a dangerous situation."

Michael's words sound absolutely ridiculous but that doesn't stop me from boiling with anger at the man. How dare he accuse me of intentionally causing harm to Lily.

Matt steps forward. "Hey listen, Lily is the one who contacted my wife to pick her up. Are you forgetting that Lily is eighteen? She's an adult and can make her own decisions."

Michael waves him off and continues his spiel, his voice getting louder and louder by the second. He's always been a man that likes to attract attention, but until recently I didn't realize it was this kind of attention.

"Stop! Just STOP!" The familiar voice hits my ears, and I turn toward it in shock. Liam steps forward, coming face to face with Michael McCue as if he is his wrestling opponent. "I am the one who started this."

Matt and I look at each other, both of us wrapped in the same thread of confusion. "Liam, what are you talking about?" Matt asks. "You don't have to get involved in this, buddy."

"Will you just listen to me for once?" His tone is that of an executive leading a room of board members, and we all stand at attention. "I knew that Piper was sending the video out to the school, and I knew that Lily would be upset."

We all continue to stand in silence, awaiting his next words.

"I went to the party to try and stop Alley from spreading the stupid video around but it was too late. I saw Lily. I knew she was drunk. Jack was with Connor because they were getting ready for an early baseball game the next day. They weren't invited to the party because…well, Jack didn't get accepted into any of the schools that were celebrating." He remained still like a statue as he spoke. "So, I texted you, Mom, from Lily's phone. Because I wanted to make sure she got home safe. I took her phone when she wasn't looking, hoping to delete the video, but it was too late for that, so I texted you, and told you to come pick her up. But then, she started running down the road and she was so fast." He shakes his head, defeated. "So, it's all my fault."

I thought about how fast she had been running even in her drunken state. "She was running," I said, agreeing with Liam's story and finishing it off. "And when I picked her up, she got in the back seat and started to feel sick. So, at the intersection, I stopped, probably for longer than I should have, and told her to hop into the front seat so she wouldn't be as sick."

"And you think this ridiculous story gets you a get-out-of-jail-free card?" Michael steps forward hovering over me now, spit flying out of his mouth.

And then, Lauren moves between me and her father and says, "I believe we've had a get-out-of-jail-free card for the past twenty-four years, Dad, so yeah…I do think that Evie deserves a free pass."

48

Before
AUGUST 1997

Lauren

For a yacht club that has such high annual dues, I'm surprised by how run down the gym is. I walk around the small space and take in the torn workout benches, the outdated machines that look more like torture devices than fitness equipment. I stand beside the windows and check out the view, the only area of the space that doesn't feel claustrophobic. If it weren't for these windows overlooking the Atlantic Ocean, this space would be just a low-budget gym, an afterthought for anyone who had an interest in fitness. It's eight-fifteen, so there is only a sliver of sun left but it's enough to pull out the color of the ocean, lifting the pigment out of the dark blue and jazzing up the scene with sparkling gentle waves.

My gaze is pulled down to the deck below where a circle of women from the event have escaped for a cigarette break. One of them is my aunt Jill. She always has at least one cigarette when she drinks, and tonight she's most certainly been drinking. I watch as the women talk animatedly, throwing hands forward into the circle and upward to the darkening sky to emphasize their points, getting louder as the conversation goes on. I look down at my watch. 8:18. He was supposed to be here three minutes ago. I step away from the window and drop onto one of the torn leather benches, as the metal bar above me rocks side to side in response. This room probably looks better than it actually is right now, since I've already had two lemon drop shots. Aunt Jill's daughter, Kristen, has become an expert at sneaking booze from the adults at the house parties, but tonight, she managed to sneak some from the bar below. This is always a packed event. August at the yacht club in general is busy, but nobody misses the annual sailing gala. So it's not surprising that she swiped a bottle of booze from the bar when the tender wasn't looking. It was either that or she was making out with the guy, also a go-to method for my boy-crazy cousin. Part of me feels like her tonight. Sneaking off to meet a boy. Drinking illegally. I start to laugh at myself, for this unlikely behavior, when I'm caught.

"What's so funny?" The creaky door opening, followed by Eric's voice brings my thoughts to a halt.

"Nothing." I lean back on the bench, crossing my legs so my flowery baby-doll dress doesn't reveal too much. Kristen prepped me before tonight and I'm using all the tidbits of boy advice she gave. Always present yourself relaxed and confident. The only problem is that I'm not Kristen and my Steve Madden black sandal threatens to fall off my foot, and lands on the floor a second later, it's chunky sole hitting the hardwood so loud it throws me off my game.

Eric walks toward me, balancing two more shots. "For you, madam." He presents me with it, and I tip my head back and take it with far more confidence than I have, the sugary booze hits the back of my throat, and I respond with an unattractive cough. If my parents knew I was up here taking shots with a guy, I'd be in so much trouble. Luckily, they are down there making the rounds, schmoozing with the best of them, and for once their attention is diverted from me and my sister and their obsession with making us appear perfect. Poor Megan is stuck down there hanging out at the kids table with the offspring of my dad's biggest clients. I did my time partaking in that fancy charade though. I deserve a break. Again, I laugh at myself.

"Are you laughing again?" Eric moves closer to me. I can smell the Nautica cologne on him, and it sends a ripple of excitement through me. It blends with the body spray Kristen aimed at me seconds before I headed to the gym for my secret meeting.

I turn toward him to respond, and his face is flush with mine, his lips land on my chin and I pull back and laugh again.

"Sorry, that went poorly. Let me try again." He uses a hand to guide my face toward his so he can reach his intended destination.

I've kissed boys before, but Eric Landers is not just any boy. His lips are magical. They part and his tongue greets mine, just as I had dreamt about since last year's gala. And just as I'm about to lean in further and grab his arm, the doorknob smacks into the wall, and a concert of giggles and hoots and hollers fills the musky gym.

Kristen is standing there clutching a mini backpack and framed by two boys and another girl, friends of hers from the senior class, all one year ahead of me.

"Seriously!" Eric says, as he puts an arm around my shoulders and pulls me closer. He's laughing now, and while I want to scream at Kristen for interrupting, I go along with it. I've been following her around since I could walk, and tonight is no different. Which is why I take the mini bottles of liquor she swiped from the bar and sip on them as I laugh along with everything the others are saying, agreeing when it's appropriate to agree and nodding in all the right conversational breaks.

By the time I stand up to follow them back downstairs, it's nearing ten o'clock and my body feels untethered to the ground, the steps blur together and I have to grasp the railing to keep my balance. By the time we reach the ballroom, where the party is dimming down, the space is one massive blur, marked by colorful moving bodies. The band is playing one final song, an island tune from what I can make out, and my little sister, Megan, tugs on my arm. "Lauren, it's time to go." I look down at her and see her one face expand to two. "Dad needs you to drive. He and Mom had a tad too much to drink." She laughs and rolls her eyes, then stops and catches the lopsided expression I feel forming on my face.

Meg digs her nails into my forearm so hard I can feel the skin breaking. Before I have a chance to pull myself out of her grip, she drags me to the ladies' room, slamming herself into the door and scanning the room, making a sport out of bending down and searching for feet beneath the stalls. No one else is in here. I drop onto the couch that serves as a resting area for female yacht club members, the sunflowers on my dress blending into the swirls of flowers on the cushions.

"What the heck is wrong with you?" Meg stands over me. "You're drunk. Are you drunk? Where—"

"Yes, I'm drunk!" I hiss. I lean to the side, my palm sinking into the cushion. "I'mmadrunk." The words come out mashed together. "I love you, sis. You're so pretty."

"Oh shit, Lo. You're supposed to drive us home."

"I know. Dad's gonna kill me." I hold an index finger to my lips. "But shhhhh, don't tell him, mmmkay?"

And then, just as she pulls me up off the couch, my lazy equilibrium causing me to almost fall on top of her, the door to the restroom smacks open and a voice follows. "Oh, there you girls are!" Aunt Jill exclaims. "Your dad is looking for you. You know how he gets when he wants to leave." The smell of cigarette smoke hits my nostrils as she darts by us and toward the row of sinks. She goes to work touching up her lipstick, a deep red tone that makes her black, off-the-shoulder dress stand out even more.

"Thanks, Auntie J." With arms still linked, we push through the door, and I hear her say something about how nice our sisterly bond is when the door slams shut. "Drink this." Meg pulls a water bottle out of her bag and hoists it at me. I chug it and feel the water move through me. "I'll be fine, kay? We're only like, a mile from home. We got this."

She looks at me uneasily. Meg, always the goodie goodie.

"There you girls are." My dad approaches and I smile wide.

"Hey, Daddy." I dim my smile so he doesn't get suspicious. He rocks back on his heels and looks back to acknowledge a few goodbye pats on the back from other guests who are filing out. Then, he pushes his hands in his pockets and rocks forward, the smell of alcohol fills the small space between us.

"Madam, can you escort us home?" He dangles the keys in front of me. A pull of hesitation tugs on me, but I ignore it. My parents will kill me if they find out I was sneaking booze.

"Of course, Daddy."

49

After

APRIL 2021

Evie

Twelve years ago, when we moved to 88 Sutton Lane, I was certain that we were moving to a town that was safe. From all the posts I'd read and social media sites I'd scoured, Flagport was not only safe, but it was a town that was filled with professionals, and those professionals raised younger professionals with even higher IQ's and so on. Generation after generation was spun from the Flagport cloth and sent out into the world as the finest in their fields. And while all Flaggers headed off to top colleges around the country and they may even live in other destinations for a handful of years, they always came back. Maybe this was the fact that served as my trust of the town.

I couldn't imagine moving back to one of the many towns or cities I lived in growing up, yet nearly all those who left Flagport, even if for a decade, came back to the town. It wasn't hard to get on the Flagport bandwagon. All you have to do is take a drive and see the homes that line the ocean's edge, the homes that always made me feel like I was living in a vacation town, and I'd never have to travel far away to feel like I needed a reprieve. This was my reprieve.

With its cobblestone sidewalks and coffee shops, its beach bars and old-town nostalgia. So close to Boston, but so separate and secluded at the same time, a destination for travelers and a place where homeowners never gave up their plot of land once they landed here. In all my naivety, I had assumed that people with money were always kind and people with professions were always honest, the cream of the crop in our society. Or that's what I thought, and that may have been what I continued to think if I had never picked Lily up from the side of the road that night.

But tonight, as I watch Lauren crumble into a million pieces, I learn that Flagport is nothing that I thought it was, but I'm still not certain it's enough to make me despise it forever.

I hand Lauren a box of tissues and sit on her bed beside her. Since we found out Lily is going to be okay, Piper is back to the normal routine of a fifteen-year-old, and Ryan is at the hospital. Lauren's tears spill down her face as if a faucet has just turned on behind her eyes. "Hey, honey, it's okay, everything is going to be okay now. Lily will be home in like, a week. And we'll figure everything out between them. Maybe Jack won't go to California, after all."

"It's not that." Her voice shakes when she says the words. She balls up a tissue and pats her cheeks and beneath her eyes until her tears are dry. She stops sniffing and crying and she looks at me with a look of determination as if she is preparing herself for a speech.

I look at her confused. "What? What do you mean?"

"There is something that I have to tell you. Something I've never told anyone before."

50

Before
AUGUST 1997

Lauren

I pinch my cheeks as I walk toward my dad's navy-blue BMW, hoping it will send a shock of sobriety through me. I sink into the driver's side seat, and I fumble trying to find the seat adjustor so I can alter the position so it fits my leg length. My father is a massive man, and the chair is so far back, I nearly hit the windshield when I over-aggressively push the lever and dig my heals into the floor so I'm closer to the pedals.

The smell of alcohol hits the air between me and my dad, who is in the passenger seat, adjusting his positioning as well. I'm grateful for the cough drop I found at the bottom of my purse and the fact that my dad's own boozy binge is the answer for the smell in the car. I've already sobered up a decent amount, so I think I'll be fine to get us home. I promise myself to never drink in a situation I may have to be the designated driver ever again. I may never drink again until I'm twenty-one. I should've known better. This isn't the first time my dad has asked me to drive us home from a family event because he's drank too much. He does it because he trusts me and if I break that trust, and he finds out I've been drinking, I'm petrified of the precautions. I rationalize that

I am doing us all a favor and I hold firm to the idea that I will get us all home safe.

After I hear the click of four buckles, I ease out of the yacht club's parking lot. It's the end of the night so luckily there are only a few cars still parked, but there are a few that I have to navigate around to get out and onto the main street. My dad turns up an oldies station on the radio and starts singing along to the song. A Beatles song. He tips his head back against the headrest and gets louder with the lyrics of the song Help. Just as he is confessing his desire for needing somebody, not just anybody, I turn onto Bellevue Street, the easiest route to the main street that will take us home.

I look over at my father and laugh, the euphoria of the alcohol still in my system and causing a carefree giddiness inside me. Bellevue is a hilly street, one with two massive bumps that cause stomach-dropping adrenaline to rush through if you take the hills fast enough. "Get the hills, honey!" My dad says as he looks ahead. He knows this street well and has spent many years as a teenager accelerating in just the right spots, to get the same rush that every other teenager still aims for today. I push on the pedal as we reach the sweet spot. Just before the top of the hill, where we'll inevitably catch some air if timed right.

"Slow down, Lo," Megan says from the back seat. But I don't listen. I keep my foot on the pedal and I wait for my stomach to drop. I wait to hear my father's boisterous laugh. But instead, I hear the sound of metal hitting metal, one loud crash. By the time my foot hits the brake, it's too late.

I look at Evie, whose brown eyes are two giant saucers. She looks as if she is watching an action film. "Oh my gosh." She pauses, and leans forward, hugging the pillow to her chest. "So, what happened?"

I'm surprised that my tears have held off this long, but they are overdue and come bubbling to the surface. "We crashed." And then I continue.

The BMW had no choice but to come to a screeching halt when it came face to face with a Honda going in the wrong direction on the one-way. My dad's car had successfully crashed into the Honda just as it was turning into a driveway. Because of the speed at which we were going, the BMW spun around and was now facing uphill in the opposite direction. Oddly enough, instead of looking around to see if everyone was okay, and to assess what had just happened, I remember thinking about how miraculous it had been that the Beatles were still playing. The car radio was still functioning while I was frozen in complete shock. In front of me, the front of the car was crumpled, the navy-blue hood that had always been smooth thanks to my father's dedication to getting it detailed regularly, was now wrinkled and dented, half the length it was just moments before.

And then I hear it. My sister shrieks from the backseat. She's screaming and howling in the back seat. I hear the back door open, followed by a thump. To the right of me, I hear the click of my father's door open. All I can think is that I killed my sister. My baby sister, but I remind myself that she is screaming. She can't be screaming if she is dead. My father bashes his elbow into his door until he gets it open because he's pinned between the air bag and the seat. I still can't move. With my sister on the ground outside of the car and my father pushing through the door, I can't move. Where am I? Is this a nightmare? And then I remember my mother. I twist my neck, and that's when I feel a surge of pain run down my left shoulder. I move my body and my mother's head falls forward. The seatbelt did its job and stopped her from getting thrown forward but she is unmoving, still. "Mom! Mom!" I push past the pain in my shoulder and climb into the back seat. I shake my mother left to right. I unbuckle her seatbelt and watch as she flops onto her side. "Mom! Dad, we need to help Mom!" Although later I felt the pain in my throat from all the screaming I was doing, at the time I felt like there was no sound coming from my lungs. I leave my mother and go out the side to get my dad, where he is hovering over my sister. I watch as Megan pushes herself up onto her elbows. She's crying but she's alive. "Your face," I point to her forehead where a river of blood is cascading down her skin. And that's when I feel heat move down my shoulder. I reach for my neck and glide my hand downward and that's when I see all the blood. The glass from window breaking sliced through the back of my shoulder. I tap at the cut with my index finger and feel the gash. It doesn't hurt like I imagined it would.

From the other side of the car, I hear my father screaming my mother's name. "Colleen, Colleen! Wake up!" And then I hear my mother's sobs. There is a scramble of assessing one another and unintelligible exchanges that I don't remember. Bruised and bloodied, my family stands at the top of the hill where we'd gotten joy from rollercoasting over so many times in the past, and we see the other car. I didn't know at the time, but it was a Honda Accord. A four-door with a booster seat in the back.

The four of us stumble down the hill and that is when I realize I'm completely sober. All that drunken giddiness has disappeared, replaced with bullets of fear that seem to hit me with every step closer to the car we get.

I look at Evie, and take in her expression, knowing this may be the last time she will sit in the same room as me. What she hears next may cause her to run away from me, never turning back.

By then the sirens were whirling and getting closer and I remember all I could think about, as I stepped closer to that car was how hot I was. And how I tried to sip the air and take in breaths to no avail. It was as if someone had me in the tightest bearhug ever and they wouldn't let me go. My dad looked into the door of the Honda and that's when I saw the woman's face. She didn't have the gash like I had across my forehead, but the left side of her body had to have been hit hard because the door was smashed in and her body was flopped toward the right side, her head lolling over and a curtain of brown hair concealing her face.

"Don't touch her, Dad! You're not supposed to touch an injured person!" Megan's voice punched the air, making demands. She'd always been the smarter of the two of us. Much more knowledgeable about important things where I'd been more consumed with my social life and my popularity rating at school.

The booster seat was upside down on the same side of the car the woman's body was leaning toward. And as I stepped to the other side of the car, I braced myself for what I would see. But, there was no child. It was the only thing I was grateful for that day, but at the same time I realized the booster seat had been empty, I realized that the woman, now pale and completely lifeless, was some-body's mother.

We had been about one mile from the police station, so it didn't take long for them to arrive on the scene. Paramedics came seconds later and went to work pulling the body out of the car while the police cordoned off the area, and asked questions. By the time my adrenaline started to dim, I looked around and realized lights had been flicked on in the homes that lined the street, several front doors had been flung open as neighbors had congregated on front lawns to assess the situation. The hill that had been known as a safety issue for years but was never really addressed no matter how many speed bumps were placed, or camera threats were made.

My sister and I, still shaking, stood huddled together on the front lawn of one of the neighbors who brought out a blanket and some waters for us. While our father talked to the police. The chief, at the time, was on the scene and I remember seeing my father throwing his hands up in the air. I was afraid he would get in trouble, so I walked over and said, "Daddy, it's all my fault, it's my fault." And before I could tell him I had been drinking and I would've never pressed the gas so hard otherwise, he turned to me, his lips one hard line, his eyes darting between me and the chief. He stepped aside toward me. "Lauren, I need you to stay quiet and I never, ever want to hear you bring this night up again. Let me handle this.

"Sorry about that, Chief, my daughter is pretty worked up and emotional from all this as you can imagine."

"Of course." The chief nodded. He too had daughters my age.

"Listen, I hate to even bring this up now, considering the circumstances, but the Honda, well, it was coming up the hill the wrong way, and that's when it crashed into us. It's just awful." My dad dragged a hand down his face, and I bit my tongue and watched as he continued his lies. "She came from nowhere really."

Just then another police officer who had been assessing the scene stood beside the chief and my father, waiting for them to finish conversing. "Sir, I have an ID," he finally said. "Jessica Milburn, she's from 111 Canter Street in Bridgeton."

And then I watched my father as he transformed into a horrible monster. "Ahhh, that explains it, Chief," he said as he massaged his right leg. "She's not from here, she doesn't understand the streets. And her negligence could've killed my family."

The chief shook his head side to side, and clapped my dad on the shoulder, then addressed my mother. "I'm so sorry, Mrs. McCue, that you had to go through this."

My father stayed behind and an ambulance came to pick up my mother, Megan and me. And I've never driven down that street again.

51

After

APRIL 2021

Evie

By the time Lauren finishes telling me the entirety of her story, I'm frozen. I can tell she is assessing me. She's attempting to figure out what I'm thinking. But, this really has nothing to do with her, it's about the family she was raised in. And the first question that springs from my thoughts comes to the surface. "So, this is why Megan is in New York?"

Lauren nods. "She's a smart kid. And she's always been someone who is very particular about who she spends time with. Her principles are strong."

"Which is why she doesn't want to be around your father."

"My father is an awful person." Lauren massages the edge of her pillowcase with two fingers. "And maybe I'm just as awful for never saying anything or simply for sticking around."

"Does Ryan know any of this?" I ask.

"No. He got so attached to my father right from the start. I didn't have the heart to tell him." She scrunches her face up. "Ryan, well as soon as I met him, I saw him as my way out of Flagport. I was looking for a way out, but those ideas vanished when he met my dad and started working for him. And then I thought that maybe life could go back to normal in Flagport, you know. We had the perfect setup. They were working together. My dad wasn't telling any lies as long as things were okay. And things were okay. They've been okay since I met Ryan at the diner, and they were even more okay when you guys moved in. They were okay until the night of the accident. And then, the truth had to come out. All of it. My obsession with Lily, my negligence toward Piper, who my father was. I'd been holding onto so many lies since I was seventeen."

I felt another question rise to the surface. "Why were you in the diner the night you met Ryan anyways? From what you say, you weren't a booksmart kind of student, so why were you there reading, of all things?"

"I never went to college." She shook her head side to side as if she was trying to shake out the lies. "After the accident, I was a mess, as you can imagine. But, Mr. and Mrs. McCue, being the upstanding citizens that they were, couldn't have that. They couldn't have me walking around sulking all the time in front of the towns-people and their friends. They couldn't let me cause a shift in their perfect reputation. So, they sent me away to Pembroke Academy. And they had to send Megan along with me because, well that would just look weird if one of their daughters was away at private school and the other wasn't. Megan was furious about it and that is what set her on the path to bitterness toward my parents. It's a well-deserved bitterness, obviously. Megan was always smarter than the rest of us, more capable of independence and unlike me, she never needed anyone else. She didn't need others to validate her and she has maintained a pulse on who she is. I was happy to be in another town for several hours every day, in a place where no one really knew my parents or my family name. They may seem like a big deal in Flagport, but Michael McCue is just another rich real estate guy outside the borders of this town. And after I graduated high school, I still wasn't back to myself. The pain of causing that accident and killing an innocent woman is not something that leaves you. So, I took the money my parents gave me, and I lived in an apartment not far from Kline College, not all that far from here. The diner… well, that was my little act. I wanted to feel like a normal student, so I would go to the campus diner almost every night and pretend I was just an average college student. I would sit there and pretend I was reading but I'd really be watching the other students interact. It sounds sick, but I so badly wanted to be them. I wanted to be normal. And then Ryan walked in one night, and well, as they say, the rest is history."

I nearly fell backwards on the bed. All this time I thought Lauren had met Ryan while they were both attending school, but there were so many little clues over the years that said otherwise, especially the way Megan responded when I asked her if she went to the same school. "And Ryan doesn't know."

She waves a hand in front of her. "Now that right there, that's what I call a white lie. And he got so much out of it because he had been wanting to break into real estate, and my dad was his gold coin. The thing is…my father really is a good guy…as long as you're on his side of things."

"I figured that out the hard way." I think about how Mr. McCue acted like he was a second father to me until he needed someone to blame for his granddaughter's accident. "But, instead of blaming me, why didn't he just go after the girl who hit us?" I inquire.

"Because my father will do anything in his power to look powerful. He knew that you guys weren't from here and he felt threatened…maybe he was scared that you would tell people that Lily isn't the upstanding citizen we all thought she was. Heaven forbid, if his daughter and granddaughter make a mistake."

"Do as I say not as I do." I say the words that my mother repeated to me on occasion. The words that led me to do exactly what she did. And then I tell Lauren about what I overheard her dad talking about on the deck at my birthday party.

I'm no different than Lauren in some ways. I too block out the things I've done in my past. "So, what now?"

Lauren lets out a long exhale and slaps her palms on her thighs. "Well, I have a lot of making up to do to both of my daughters."

We both push up off her California king-size bed and walk toward her door. "Think you'll stay in Flagport?" She stops and turns, settling her gaze on me.

"That depends."

I form a question mark in my brow. "If you remain my friend. Because without you, I have no reason to stay in this town."

"You couldn't get rid of me if your father tried." I pull her into a one-arm hug and my cast smacks into her arm. .

"Ouch," she says, and I step back.

"Oh no, did I squeeze too hard?"

"It's my shoulder." She massages the space between her neck and rear delt. "A constant reminder of what I did twenty-four years ago. My shoulder got impacted in the accident and it's never been the same. It tends to act up when I'm stressed."

As we walk into her kitchen, we hear the sound of four doors slamming shut. Lauren turns to me, a silent cue to follow her to the front window. "It must be my house," I say when we don't see anyone in her driveway. Our two homes are so close that I've often mistaken a car door slam at her house with mine. She follows me as I lead us through the pathway that drops into the street between our two homes, and I stop and look at the stones we've made over the years, as I say, "Looks like we're due for a stone for 2021," over my shoulder. In my driveway, Matt, Ryan, Liam, and Piper emerge from the car swept up in a conversation. They don't see us until we howl at them from the pathway. And then the four of them turn.

Lauren yells, "Guys, come here…I have an idea!"

I watch her voice land on their faces, and they are thinking the same thing I am. *Lauren and her ideas.* We all act as if we have to brace ourselves for her idea, but the truth is, I think it's safe to say every single one of us appreciates her ideas, her parties, and the over-the-top moments that make her who she is. I watch as she races toward her garage and comes back seconds later.

Now, all of us are circled around Lauren as she presents us with something she is hiding behind her back. A blank slate of moldable clay, this one far bigger than the others we've created. "It's for all of us." She looks around the circle as we all shake our heads.

"Where did you get that?" Piper asks.

"I've had it. I've just been waiting for the right moment." She looks around. "Who's first?" When nobody volunteers, she looks at Liam and says, "How bout you, Liam, since you were so good about looking out for Lily the other night." She winks at him and then smiles at me, and we all stand around as he presses his hand into the mold. I notice how much bigger his hands have gotten and for the first time, I realize that I think my younger son is actually growing up.

After we all tattoo the mold with our palms, I say, "Wait, what about Jack and Lily?"

"We'll bring it to the hospital. I don't think you're gonna get Jack to leave Lily's side any time soon." She winks at me and asks, "Feel like going to see our kids with me?"

I nod and follow her to her car, and we drive back to see Lily. This time, we talk about things the way we used to. "Do you think Piper has a crush on Liam?" she asks.

And we both laugh.

52

After

AUGUST 2021

Lily

"All right, that's it." I put all my weight on the trunk of Jack's car.

"You sure you got everything?" Matt asks as he pulls Jack into a hug and my dad pulls me into his side.

Evie steps forward pulling me into a hug. "Take care of him, okay?" she whispers in my ear.

I hold her at arm's length, letting my fingertips run over the scar on her left arm. I don't remember anything from the accident, but the scar on her arm shows me that she was injured. Not just physically, but I know that she still holds onto some guilt that she was the one who picked me up that night. Sometimes I wonder what would've happened if Liam hadn't used my phone to text his mom. Would my mom have found out and put an even tighter leash on me? Would I have gotten hit by a car while I was running on the side of the road in the dark. The questions have circled in my mind for the last four months, but I don't let them wreak havoc on my life. Because sometimes things happen. Bad things. Like how my mother drove drunk and killed a woman, a mother no less. Sometimes there is no rhyme or reason to the chaos that circles our lives. Sometimes it's simple luck. As my grandfather would tell me, "you will always have good luck as long as you're a McCue." I'm certain he's spreading his good luck around now since he moved and decided to travel the world with my grandmother. I never in a million years thought they would leave Flagport, but people change.

Speaking of, I look at my mom, who is standing furthest away from me. I open my arms up and motion for her to come in. And I give her the biggest hug I've ever given her, hoping her perfume will stick to me and I'll be able to smell it the entire drive to California. Maybe I won't wash this t-shirt so I can always hold it up to my nose and know that my mother is with me.

If anyone has changed these last few months, it's her. Since my grandparents left, I've seen a freedom in her disposition, as if for the first time ever, she's been free to be herself. And that tight leash that she's had on me all these years, well, that is gone. As mad as I am at Piper for inadvertently sharing that video with the school, I'm grateful that my little sister will be able to spend her next few years of high school under the same roof as a mom who accepts her for who she is, without that suffocating grip that she had on me.

I hold my mom at arm's length and take in the looks we share. Our physical likeness has only seemed to get stronger over the years, while our identities have managed to pull apart so there is a clear line between her and me. "I love you," I say.

"I know you do." After a moment she says it back, but I know there is no need for the words. She loved me so much all these years that she didn't want me to end up like her. Some might say that is a warped way of showing love, but I now know that she was only doing what she knew how.

53

After

AUGUST 2021

Evie

I raise my good arm in the air and wave as we watch Jack and Lily drive off and I can't help but think of their love story.

"Gosh, when you think of it, it's kind of been easy for those two, huh?" I say as Ryan, Matt, Piper, Liam, Lauren and I walk back to our driveways.

"How so?" Matt asks.

"Well, their one true love always lived right next door to them all these years."

"Yeah, but that doesn't mean they didn't have to go out there and try out all different kinds of relationships on for size." Ryan asks, "Remember that goth dude Lily dated for a week?"

"Until I put a stop to it." Lauren laughs. "See, my crazy was good for some things."

"You've got a point," I say. "Sometimes you really do need to step in and take control of certain situations." I wink at Lauren, knowing that she will pick up on exactly what I'm referring to. This time it doesn't have anything to do with Lily. Instead, it has to do with her parents. I hadn't been imagining it when I saw Michael McCue getting upset that night at The Deck. When I brought this up to Lauren after she confessed her father's shady past to me, she went digging. It turns out, Savannah Kennedy, the little girl whose house Katie Milburn was being picked up from that tragic night on April 13, 1997, had kept telling her mother a different story over the years. Even at thirty years old she believed that what she saw was the truth. That the blue BMW was going down the street so fast and she was certain, when she looked out the window that night, that the silver car was turning in the driveway and the blue car was going fast, real fast.

Savannah Kennedy's mother Robin had chalked her daughter's ideas up to a creative imagination, until she brought it up again while they were visiting relatives in Flagport, having moved away a long time ago. That's all Lauren and I needed to get her father to move out of town. Mr. McCue had been talking about "getting rid" of Savannah Kennedy, afraid her memory would tarnish his reputation. There was no way we were going to allow another person to die and the only way to be certain to do that was to threaten Michael McCue. If he stayed, Lauren would tell the police the truth, even if she had to confess that she was drunk. She would tell them the lies her father told to the police that night. The lies that were believed simply because he was Michael McCue. If he stayed, his reputation would get dragged through the dirt, and being the most important thing in his life, he simply couldn't have that.

The End

FOR MORE BOOKS by Kate Anslinger, please visit Amazon.

To receive updates on new releases and giveaways, please signup for my newsletter at: www.kateanslinger.com

Next up in The Town Series, The Secrets We Keep. Now available on Amazon.

HOW FAR WOULD *you go to uncover the truth?*

When Sarah Walsh packs up her teenage daughter to move to Flagport, Massachusetts on a whim, no one really questions it. After all, the career soldier spent twenty years in the Army where moving was a way of life for her and her daughter Laney.

When she meets Ryan Rivers, a real estate mogul and the father of Laney's new best friend, Sarah counts her blessings that she landed in such a tight knit community with strong family values. She is quickly welcomed by Ryan's wife, Lauren, and her best friend Evie Sullivan, and immersed into a town that boasts of low crime, stunning views, and a family-friendly feel.

But before she finishes unpacking, secrets start to reveal themselves and she discovers that trust doesn't always go hand in hand with charm, and what you see is not always what you get.

Just as more answers start to surface about each person she

encounters, the tables are turned and the questions are directed at Sarah.

Why did she come to the small beach town of Flagport in the first place?

Who did she leave behind?

What is she running from?

Can she uncover the truth before the town's darkness consumes her and her daughter?

In this absolutely twisting domestic thriller, nothing is as it seems, and trust is a dangerous game. As Sarah digs deeper into the town's secrets, she finds that the answers she seeks might be the very things that destroy her. Will she solve the puzzle in time, or will Flagport's shadows claim another victim?

The Gift

MCKENNA MYSTERY SERIES BOOK 1

Chapter One

Grace McKenna was only three years old when the first vision catapulted her into what her mother assumed was a really bad tantrum. They had been walking down Main Street in Wentworth, a small Massachusetts town that boasted the best holiday shopping. It was almost Christmas, and Grace had been mesmerized by the colossal Christmas tree on display at the center of the bustling ice skating rink.

"Wait right there, Grace. Don't move," her mother said, as she turned toward the clerk at one of the stands selling homemade Christmas ornaments. Her mother kept one eye on her and one eye on the clerk as her hand navigated through her tattered faux leather fringe purse to retrieve her last five-dollar bill to purchase the glittery ornament. Money was low as it always had been, but Ellen McKenna did her best with what she had and was determined to make Christmas special for her daughter. The small, artificial Charlie Brown tree that they had at home had been swiped from a dumpster after the holidays last year, and Ellen used what few ornaments had been handed down to her. She couldn't leave the rest of the tree bare, so she hung silver measuring spoons from the scrawny branches, showing her daughter that they didn't need to spend a fortune to add some shine and sparkle to their lives.

"Mama! Look!" Grace yelled, pointing to a little girl who was twirling effortlessly in the center of the skating rink in a short pale-blue skirt, shimmery tights and a sparkly turtleneck sweater.

"I'll be right there, sweetie," Ellen said as she watched the clerk wrap the ice skater figurine ornament, complete with tissue paper and a sparkly red bow. Grace fell in love with watching the skaters glide across the ice, their ribbons trailing from their heads like the dolls she thought they were. Her eyes followed the skater in the blue skirt as she used a toned leg to push off the icy surface and accelerate across the rink and into the arms of a boy who skated with as much finesse as she did. She positioned herself in front of him, their arms linking as they soared across the ice arm in arm, creating a dance to the background music of Sinatra's voice bellowing "I'll be home for Christmas."

"Do you want to be an ice skater someday?" A man's voice pulled Grace from the trance. Startled, she dug her hands deeper into the pockets of her red hand-me-down pea coat. One of the big black buttons on the pocket dangled by a thread, partly from her habit of twirling them when she was nervous and partly from the wear and tear of a winter coat worn by several children before her.

As a little girl, Grace was painfully shy. Had her mom been within a few feet, she would've darted to her and maneuvered her way between her legs, using them as a security blanket in which she could wrap herself to get away from the stranger. Instead, she slowly looked up at the man, the owner of the deep scruffy voice that interrupted her concentration on the dancing skaters. She parted her lips to speak; the few sentences that she could put together at her young age mashed together and clogged her thoughts. Her wide-set green eyes, innocent until that moment, widened and latched onto his as if being pulled into a tunnel. Their eyes locked like two forces of opposite energies, hers pure and green, and his bloodshot, brown, and filled with corruption.

Maybe her first vision was the worst simply because it was the first, and it transformed the clarity of her innocence into a murky mess, having wiped her clean of any natural thoughts she had yet to form. Or maybe it really was the worst. It started with the body of a fair-skinned woman being dragged across muddied earth, the kind that is usually the result of a rainy spring day. Bursts of the woman's placid face flashed in and out like a blinking light. Grace was only three years old, but she was old enough to have the innate ability to know wrong from right; something about these images left a sick feeling in her stomach. A flash of red hair splayed across the woman's emaciated face, chunks of crusty mud cemented into the corners of her mouth and deep into the hollows of her eyes. Dried blood left a line of color down the woman's ashen body, starting at the neck and dipping between her breasts, ending at a jutting hipbone. A flash of the woman's face, displaying a pair of terrified eyes just seconds before a knife ran the length of her neck, leaving a neat slice for a pool of blood to spill out and onto her sharp collar bone. The images didn't come in order, but rather in short bursts of disarray.

The vision made Grace emit a high-pitched scream.

"Grace!" Ellen looked up from her interaction with the clerk and ran over. The freshly wrapped ornament fell to the ground, landing on a bed of fake cotton snow that enveloped the outside of the skating rink. Completely unaware of the man, she ran right past him, nearly jabbing his burly body with an elbow. By the time Ellen reached Grace, the little girl was lying on the ground flailing her limbs in protest, as if someone was holding her down against her will.

"Grace! Grace, honey, what's the matter?" Ellen's voice escalated.

As a crowd started to gather around the scene, the man meandered away, hidden by the puffy winter coats and hats of the audience.

The visions kept coming, flashes of crime that infiltrated Grace's mind. The red-haired woman's naked body being pulled and dropped into a pool of murky water. Her red hair fanning out above the smooth black pool, making her look like a mystical mermaid.

Her eyes were closed, a look of peace masking a face that had just witnessed her own murder. And then a flash of her sinking.

"Grace! Please, honey, what happened? Did something happen?" Ellen looked up at the audience, seeking witnesses who saw the start of her daughter's breakdown. "I just looked away for a second!" she shouted, feeling the need to defend herself. "Grace! Baby, what happened?" She cradled Grace's little body in her arms, pulling the peacoat closed where it had been torn open from the jerking movements of her daughter's arms and legs.

"The man." Grace pointed a delicate finger toward the crowd, as heads swiveled in search of a mystery man. When no one came forward as a witness, the crowd opened up and dispersed, going back to their Christmas shopping.

"Maybe you should pay more attention to your child," a heavyset woman said as she waddled by. Her eyes were so small, they looked like two raisins pushed into her head.

"Dude, that was weird," said a teenage boy to his friend. "Maybe she's like that chick in *Poltergeist*. She looked possessed."

"That man is bad, mommy," Grace said between bouts of shaky sniffles.

"What man, honey? Which man is bad?" Ellen asked, shaking off the comment of another passerby who accused Grace of seeing ghosts.

"He's gone. I don't see him anymore." Grace craned her neck, looking beyond the elegant skaters who hadn't missed a step in their routine. They soared across the ice like figurines in the center of a snow globe, far from the world Grace had just witnessed.

"Baby, are you sure you saw a man? What did he look like?" Ellen asked, trying her hardest to push out any doubt that had surfaced. Grace had a tendency to be a creative little girl, often having tea parties with invisible friends, but she'd never gone to extremes like this, especially in such a public place. She was painfully shy and did anything she could to divert attention from herself. "Honey, was the man one of your invisible friends?"

"No, mommy. The man is bad. He hurt the girl." Grace's voice was still slightly heightened by her adrenaline.

"Honey, let's go home." Ellen had reached her limit. Now there was a girl, too. Surely Grace was making this one up. She turned, remembering the ornament she had dropped, but there was no trace of the shiny red package.

After the incident at the ice skating rink, Ellen put every earned penny toward psychologists, behavioral specialists and psychics on a mission to find out what her daughter was seeing and if her behavior was normal. Nearly every shrink said that Grace was lonely and using her imagination to build worlds inside her head. The behavior specialists claimed that Grace's "visions" were normal and it just meant that she was searching for more attention. "This behavior is quite common in single-parent homes," one specialist told her. The psychics went to the opposite extreme, saying that Grace had powers from the other side and for ten more dollars they could tell her what her daughter should do next to protect herself from the visions and evil that were headed her way. Ellen became fed up that no one was taking her seriously; she was determined to keep at it, believing the girl and standing by her when everyone else thought she was a freak.

While not a religious person, Ellen had a childhood friend who went on to become a priest at a church in Boston. As a last resort, Ellen brought five-year-old Grace to Father Burke, begging him to see her and give her an explanation. His response had been the most simple and straightforward: "Grace has been chosen as the recipient of a special gift. She was created by God to see visions of sinners. There are people of all backgrounds who have used meditation and hypnotic tools to receive the gift that Grace has naturally been given." Father Burke said the words calmly, as if he were talking to a friend about the weather. He was the first person to treat them with respect.

He told Ellen that Grace's visions were called "pictures," and that based on his experience, these pictures would contain one scene and usually appear in a flash without prior notice. "It happens very quickly," he said, "and the images will remain just long enough for Grace to notice them before they vanish." Ellen nodded. "When God gives you a gift, you are to use it and share it with the world—

to help others. So, my advice to you is to take these visions and piece them together to bring down the sinners. I know it's not the easiest thing to do, but I'm sure Grace will find a way."

Father Burke passed away from a heart attack only two years after their initial meeting. With Grace too young to understand, Ellen saved his words of advice and gently nudged Grace throughout her life, pushing her daughter to get involved in the world of law enforcement where she could use her gift to help people.

If you liked this book...

I would be so grateful if you left a review on Amazon so other readers can discover me. As always, thank you for taking a chance on me and choosing my book out of the millions out there. Xoxo.

Acknowledgments

As always, I have so many people to thank. First and foremost, I'd like to give a shoutout to my readers. From the ones who have been following me since I released my first book, to the ones who are just discovering me today. Readers like you have given me the opportunity to keep writing books and creating worlds I hope you love as much as I do.

Thank you to my husband and girls for allowing me to put on the sound cancelling headphones and get lost in my characters' worlds as chaos surrounds me. I'd be lost without you.

www.ingramcontent.com/pod-product-compliance
Lightning Source LLC
Chambersburg PA
CBHW020130120726
47903CB00007B/2196